"Time travel, ancient legends, and seductive romance are seamlessly interwoven into one captivating package."
  –*Publishers Weekly* on Midnight's Master

"Dark, sexy, magical. When I want to indulge in a sizzling fantasy adventure, I read Donna Grant."
  –Allison Brennan, *New York Times* bestseller

5 Stars! Top Pick! "An absolute must read! From beginning to end, it's an incredible ride."
  –*Night Owl Reviews*

"It's good vs. evil Druid in the next installment of Grant's Dark Warrior series. The stakes get higher as discerning one's true loyalties become harder. Grant's compelling characters and continued presence of previous protagonists are key reasons why these books are so gripping. Another exciting and thrilling chapter!"
  –*RT Book Reviews* on Midnight's Lover

"Donna Grant has given the paranormal genre a burst of fresh air..."
  –*San Francisco Book Review*

DON'T MISS THESE OTHER SPELLBINDING
NOVELS

BY NYT & USA TODAY BESTSELLING AUTHOR
DONNA GRANT

Contemporary Paranormal

DRAGON KINGS

(Spin off series from *DARK KINGS SERIES*)

Dragon Revealed (novella)

REAPER SERIES

Dark Alpha's Claim

Dark Alpha's Embrace

Dark Alpha's Demand

Dark Alpha's Lover

Tall Dark Deadly Alpha Bundle

Dark Alpha's Night

Dark Alpha's Awakening

Dark Alpha's Redemption

Dark Alpha's Temptation

Dark Alpha's Caress

Inferno

DARK WARRIORS

Midnight's Master

Midnight's Lover

Midnight's Seduction

Midnight's Warrior

Midnight's Kiss

Midnight's Captive

Midnight's Temptation

Midnight's Promise

Midnight's Surrender (novella)

Dark Warrior Box Set

CHIASSON SERIES

Wild Fever

Wild Dream

Wild Need

Wild Flame

Wild Rapture

LARUE SERIES

Moon Kissed

Moon Thrall

Moon Struck

Moon Bound

SISTERS OF MAGIC

Shadow Magic

Echoes of Magic

Dangerous Magic

Sisters of Magic Boxed Set

THE ROYAL CHRONICLES NOVELLA SERIES

Prince of Desire

Prince of Seduction

Prince of Love

Prince of Passion

Royal Chronicles Box Set

Mystic Trinity (connected)

MILITARY ROMANCE / ROMANTIC SUSPENSE

SONS OF TEXAS

The Hero

The Protector

The Legend

The Defender

The Guardian

Check out Donna Grant's Online Store,

www.donnagrant.com/shop, for autographed books, character themed goodies, and more!

EVERSPELL

THE KINDRED

DONNA GRANT

EVERSPELL
© 2020 by DL Grant, LLC
Cover Design © 2020 by Charity Hendry

ISBN 13: 9781942017646
Available in ebook and print editions

www.DonnaGrant.com
www.MotherofDragonsBooks.com

Western Scotland

Her quarry wasn't far now—though Runa enjoyed the hunt. Long ago, she'd been taught to become a master of patience. Only when her target was close did her heart begin to pump excitedly. There was nothing more satisfying than taking out evil.

Stars blinked above her in the inky sky. Large, gray clouds slowly made their way across the heavens, their silhouettes highlighted by the crescent moon. The night was her favorite time. She could pretend the world was hers alone during those dark recesses of the night when most slumbered.

The one thing Runa *didn't* like was people. They were liars, thieves, and deceivers. Their hypocrisy knew no bounds, and no matter how many times she gave them the benefit of the doubt, they continued proving why she was better on her own. Morea had told her that she belonged with the humans, but Runa knew better.

Her short time with them had only reinforced her decision.

She blew out a breath as she thought about the woman who had raised her. Morea had passed away several years ago, but Runa still missed her with the same ache. The woman had been Runa's family—the only family she had. Or...the only one that mattered.

Runa pushed aside the tinge of melancholy that always came when she thought of Morea being gone. She couldn't let her thoughts get in the way of her hunt. Especially not this one. It was too important.

There, in the distance, she picked up the sounds of her quarry. She heard the rapid, harsh breaths, proving that they had been running for some time. Runa smiled when her prey came over the small rise, making themselves visible. When she was younger, she had rushed out to meet her targets in her eagerness to finish the job. Now, she waited for them to come to her.

It was almost too easy, really. She had a knack for knowing the path they would take. Then, all she had to do was lay in wait for them. Morea had told Runa that something passed down from her birth parents had given her that ability. She didn't care how or where she got it. The fact that she had it was enough for her.

But once she realized that she had such an ability, hunting lost some of its appeal. She had enjoyed the chase. Liked tracking her quarry and then finally catching them. There was no getting around trailing them. That was now her favorite part of the job.

Her target was getting closer. Runa cautioned herself to wait, to remember the patience Morea had taught her. Only when her prey was nearly upon her did Runa step into their path. Her eyes locked with black ones that widened in surprise —that brief instant when her target wondered if they could get away.

"You can't," she stated.

A small frown creased the Gira's bark-like skin. Even the tree nymph's hair looked like limbs, reaching toward the sky. The young Gira stared at Runa, fear and apprehension filling her visage.

Runa blew out a breath as she pulled her short swords from their scabbards that crisscrossed her back. She then placed the flat side of the blades against her shoulders. The nymphs tended to stay in groups, and because the Gira blended in so well with the trees, few forests didn't have their fair share of them.

"You know who I am?" Runa asked.

The nymph nodded slowly, never taking her gaze from Runa.

"The Gira have put a price on your head for dishonoring your clan."

At this, the nymph snorted. "I'm not the one who dishonored anything."

"I'm not here to pass judgment. I'm here to carry out the sentence. Besides, you wouldn't be running if you hadn't done…something."

The nymph rolled her eyes. "You think you're so high and mighty. You, Runa, know nothing. So much has been kept from you. You were sent to kill me for dishonoring my clan. What do you think your precious Morea did? If it hadn't been for the old queen, Asrail, Morea would've been killed."

"I know the story you speak of. Morea and Asrail were close friends for years. When Morea found me and decided to raise me, Asrail didn't stand in her way."

The Gira's smile was slow before she began laughing. She tilted her head to the side and regarded Runa. "Asrail is your grandmother. You've been kept alive because she and Morea made sure that neither you nor your sister could be found by the rest of us. But that's all about to change. Asrail has been caught, and your sister has been found."

Runa felt as if she had been kicked. *Sister?* Surely, everything this Gira said couldn't possibly be true. Could it? But she remembered being very young and asking Morea why they weren't with other Gira. Morea had told her it was because she preferred to live apart from the others.

Runa never had a reason to question that. Not even when she began to see for herself that the Gira rarely went out on their own. They nearly always remained in packs. Their strength was in their numbers and the many whispers that drew unsuspecting humans straight to them.

"You're lying," Runa told the nymph.

The Gira shook her head, the smile now gone. "I'm not. I'm running from my clan because they want to kill Asrail. After they use her to draw out your sister, that is."

Runa didn't want to believe any of it, but something within her said there was truth in the Gira's words. She didn't want to think about why Morea hadn't told her about Asrail or her sister. There had to be a good reason.

It would be easy for Runa to finish her mission and forget anything the nymph had told her. But she wasn't going to. Now that the words had been spoken, Runa would always remember them. And if she wanted to discover the truth, she needed to seek out her sister and Asrail to get it.

"Where are they holding Asrail?"

The Gira stared at Runa for a moment before she replied, "North."

Not once had Runa ever let someone she hunted go. She wasn't sure what would happen if she didn't finish the job now. But none of that mattered at the moment. Her mind was too full of the fact that her grandmother was alive, and the knowledge that she had a sister. Neither of which she had known.

"What are you going to do with me?" the nymph asked.

Runa pulled herself from her thoughts. "I was paid to do a job."

"I'm not the only one who doesn't agree with what Sybbyl is doing, but I'm the only one who spoke up," the Gira said.

"Who is Sybbyl?"

The nymph jerked back as if struck. "How do you not know of the Coven leader?"

"The Coven is led by three elders," Runa corrected.

"Not any longer. Sybbyl took the Staff of the Eternal and killed them."

Runa began to wonder if she was dreaming. She felt as if the world were turning a different way than she was. "What is the Staff of the Eternal?"

"You really don't know anything, do you?" the Gira asked in disbelief.

Runa gave her a flat look and lowered her arms so the blades of her short swords pointed downward.

"All right," the nymph said while lifting her hands, palms up. "The staff contains a bone of the First Witch. The Coven elders have been trying to locate and possess them ever since the Coven was formed. The Blood Skull was only found recently, but not by the witches. A Witch Hunter and a lord located it. The Blood Skull chose the lord to be its Warden and protect it."

Runa digested that bit of information. She knew of the Hunters. She had even spotted one a few times, but she never saw them go up against a witch. "The Coven lost out on the skull, which I assume belonged to the First Witch?"

"Exactly. It was a race between the Hunters and the Coven to get the next bone. One of the Hunters got close, but an elder actually got hold of it first. Her mistake was letting

Sybbyl get her hands on it. Then, Sybbyl killed the others and took over."

"I gather this bone she managed to get her hands on made her powerful?"

The Gira chuckled. "You could say that. There was no other way she could've killed the elders. The more bones she has, the more powerful she becomes."

"What does Sybbyl want?"

The Gira shifted uneasily. "She wants to rule."

"The witches?"

"Everyone. She wants to make sure witches are in power while those without magic live in fear."

Runa glanced away. After all the years of people killing those they thought were witches, she could see Sybbyl's side of things. Maybe it was time for witches to live out in the open. But the thought of the Coven in charge sent a chill of foreboding down Runa's spine.

"How many bones are there?"

The nymph shrugged. "I don't know, but Sybbyl has twice been denied a bone. Well, one wasn't a bone exactly. It was a witch named Helena, who is the Heart of the First Witch."

"A descendant? You're telling me a witch of the Coven wouldn't give herself to Sybbyl?"

"That's the thing. Helena wasn't part of the Coven. She stood and fought them, along with a Varroki warrior."

Now that got Runa's attention. Morea had told her stories of the Varroki, but she'd thought they were just made-up stories since she'd never encountered one herself. "The Varroki are real?"

"Very," the Gira said with a shudder. "And extremely powerful. Sybbyl was on her way to take out the Varroki after she wiped out the Hunters."

Runa frowned. "The Hunters are gone?"

"I was with the Gira and Sybbyl when we attacked the abbey and wiped out any and all who lived there. Sybbyl didn't care if they were witches or not. She said that anyone who stood against the Coven deserved death."

The more Runa heard about this Sybbyl, the more she didn't like her. Though, Runa had never really made any kind of stand in the human world. But how much longer could that continue if everything the nymph said was true?

"Go on," Runa urged.

The Gira swallowed and glanced around. "On the way to find the Varroki, Sybbyl ordered one of her followers, Avis, to track down your sister."

"How do you know this woman is my sister?"

"Because she has Gira blood. Something Synne—your sister—didn't realize until Asrail told her."

Jealousy that Synne had spoken with Asrail rose up within Runa. She cautioned herself against such emotions. She wasn't sure if anything this Gira told her was true. While she wanted to believe it, she knew she had to tread carefully.

"You seem to know a lot about my family," Runa said.

The nymph briefly lowered her gaze to the snow-covered ground. "Your grandmother told everyone what she had done after Sybbyl captured her."

Runa quirked a brow in question. "Tell me."

"Asrail saved Synne when your parents were attacked by the Gira. Asrail then brought Synne close to the abbey where the Hunters lived so that she could grow up without the fear of being discovered by the Gira. The leader of the Hunters, Edra, took Synne in and raised her. Your sister had no recollection of Asrail or you until recently."

Runa tightened her fingers around the hilts of her swords. "I'm supposed to believe you?"

"I'm telling you what I know. I was there to witness most of it. Some of it I heard from others."

"If Synne was raised as a Hunter, how did she escape the slaughter?"

The Gira shrugged. "I don't know. What I do know is that after Asrail saved Synne and you disappeared, she was removed as queen of the Gira."

"What of my sister?"

"She met a Highlander named Lachlan, who had a finger bone of the First Witch in the pommel of his sword. Together, the two of them went north to find the Varroki."

Runa frowned when the Gira paused. "Is that all?"

"With the help of a young witch named Elin that Asrail befriended, Synne met Asrail on her trek north. That's when Sybbyl trapped Asrail."

Runa wasn't sure what to make of Asrail. She had been queen, but had given that up to save her grandchildren. Then she'd lived alone for years before befriending a witch? That wasn't something a nymph did. Or maybe Runa was the one who didn't know what the Gira did or didn't do. "And the rest? Did Synne make it to the Varroki?"

"She did. As did the Highlander and Elin. Unfortunately, so did Avis, who happens to be Elin's sister."

Runa really didn't like what she was hearing. "Was my sister harmed?"

"Synne and the Highlander fell in love, which was unfortunate because Avis made her watch as she killed Lachlan and took his sword. What Avis doesn't know is that the Highlander survived."

Runa didn't care. The need to avenge her sister was strong. It felt strange to have such intense feelings about someone she didn't even know. But they were there, nonetheless. "Was Elin part of all of this?"

"No one has seen Elin since, so I can't answer that."

"What do the Gira have planned now?"

"They have pledged themselves to Sybbyl because she has the staff. The plan is to use Asrail to draw Synne out, find Avis, and get the sword. Then kill the Varroki."

"What about the other bones?"

"If there are other bones, Sybbyl will go after them."

"It isn't easy for a Gira to live alone."

"Asrail did it. So did Morea. Others have, too."

Runa shrugged a shoulder. "You don't really have an option. You either live alone, or you die with them."

"Are you…?" The Gira blinked, hope filling her eyes. "Are you going to let me go?"

Runa knew it was the wrong decision, yet she found herself saying, "I am."

"So, you believe me?"

"I don't know what to believe, but something is telling me that I need to find out the truth." Runa slid her blades back into their sheaths. "I'm going to check out your story. If you've told me lies, I'll come for you. There won't be anywhere you can hide."

"They aren't lies."

"Good luck, then. I hope I don't see you again."

The Gira bowed her head. "Half-human or not, you still have royal blood."

"A lot of good that has done Asrail."

"It might do you and Synne some good."

Runa grunted and stepped around the Gira.

She had more hunting to do.

2

F *ind her.*
 Brom's eyes snapped open. He pushed the blanket away and sat up. The woman's face was etched into his memory. He released a shaky breath. Many incredible things had happened to him over the years since he'd discovered what he was, but nothing like the dream.

He swung his legs over the side of the bed and stood. Brom ran a hand down his face and dressed before he walked outside. Hues of purple and pink streaked across the sky as dawn approached. He walked to the stream and let the soothing sounds of the water running over rocks calm his racing heart. Only then did he allow himself to think back to the dream.

The woman was…striking. She had an oval face, large eyes, and plump lips. With her clear, blue eyes, golden hair, and pale skin, she appeared ethereal. Until he saw the double swords she carried. He didn't know who the woman was or why he needed to find her.

Brom let his gaze move over the area. He had ventured away before, but he hadn't stayed gone long. Nothing held him to this place anymore. Hadn't for some time. He wasn't sure why he remained, other than the fact that it was home. Now, it appeared as if he was going to leave.

And he wasn't sure if he would come back.

To be honest, he wasn't certain of anything but that he needed to find the woman. He didn't know where she was, didn't know why he needed to find her. Nor did he know her name. Or what he would do once he located her. Brom debated going up the mountain to his cave to see if he could discover something more, but a feeling within prodded him not to waste time.

He squatted next to the stream and splashed the frigid water on his face. Then he straightened and returned to the cottage. It didn't take him long to gather the items he would need for his journey. With his cloak clasped around him, he hefted the bag over his head to wear across his body before walking out the door.

Brom waited until he was at the top of the hill before he looked back. The last time he had set out on a journey, he had been just a lad. His mother had stood outside the door of the cottage that spring day and gave him a wave and a smile. Still, he had seen her eyes glistening with unshed tears.

Eventually, he had returned. This time, he had a feeling that wouldn't be the case. The cottage nestled in its small glen next to the stream had been a glorious place to grow up. They rarely had visitors, but he hadn't cared. He had the wilds of Scotland to roam, animals to play with, and the freedom with which to do it all.

Those days had been simple. But they were long gone.

Brom drew in a deep breath. "Farewell," he murmured before he continued walking.

He hadn't chosen a direction. Instead, he let the magic within guide him. His pace was steady, and his strides long.

He gave the nearest village a wide berth since he didn't want to see anyone. He had to go into town on occasion, and each time, at least one person asked him how it was that he could live alone. No one understood that he preferred his company to that of others.

At noon, he paused to rest near a tree and ate a quick bite. The sky was filled with clouds, warning him that more snow was likely on the way. He didn't mind the cold. There was something soothing about being surrounded by all the glittering whiteness. However, his favorite was watching the snow fall or see flurries that danced upon the air as if they were fairies.

His thoughts took him once more to the woman from his dream. The voice he'd heard in his head was female, but he didn't think it belonged to the one he searched for. There was so much unknown about the entire situation. Most others would've ignored the things prompting him and forgotten all about the dream.

But he wasn't most people. He was half-Varroki. It was a part of himself he'd learned to keep secret. He had thought to seek out the Varroki and learn his magic, but he didn't regret not finding them. The path that he had taken was the one he was supposed to be on. And while he might not have formal training, he had garnered enough knowledge to ensure that no one messed with him.

After he ate, he packed away his food and waterskin, then climbed to his feet. When he set out again, instead of continuing east, he turned slightly right and walked more south. The farther he traveled, the more he realized that something was wrong. It was as if the balance of the Earth had shifted.

He couldn't pinpoint what was wrong, but something was definitely off. The next time he spotted a village, he decided to take a closer look. Instead of people milling about or standing around conversing, the streets were deserted—except for some chickens, a couple of goats, and a cat.

Brom stood at the outskirts of the town and let his gaze move from building to building. Smoke billowed out of chimneys, so he knew people were there. And it wasn't the cold that kept them indoors. Scots embraced the winter months. No, something else had them huddling inside their homes.

Brom didn't venture farther into the village. He walked to the next one, and the next, and the next. All of them were the same as the first. Finally, he stopped at the fourth town. It was nearing dusk anyway. He'd thought to sleep outdoors, but the way to learn what was going on somewhere was to visit a pub and rent a room for the night.

A dog barked in the distance, and a cat ran across his path while chasing a mouse. The somberness of the village would have given anyone reservations about staying. Brom made his way to the pub and entered. The moment he stepped inside, every eye in the room turned to him as all the patrons fell silent.

He ignored them, shutting the door and leaving the cold behind him. Brom noted that the pub was nearly completely full with a roaring fire in the hearth. It wasn't filled with music and laughter, but instead whispers and fearful looks. He walked to the bar and nodded at the man behind it.

"Not many travelers nowadays," the man said in greeting.

"I've noticed. Do you have a room available for the night?"

"Take your pick," he said with a shrug.

Brom spotted an empty table in the back corner. "I'll have an ale and whatever you have to eat."

The man nodded and turned away. Brom walked to the table and removed his bag to set it on the floor before he unclasped his cloak and hung it on a nearby hook on the wall to dry. Once he was seated, he let his gaze slowly run over everyone. Most of those inside were older and leaned forward so others couldn't hear their whispered words.

A woman set down his ale. Before Brom could reply, she was gone. He lifted the cup to his lips and drank heartily. The ale warmed him as much as the heat of the room. Fortunately, he didn't have long to wait for the stew placed in front of him.

"Why is everyone talking in whispers?" he asked the barmaid as he jerked his chin to the others.

She swallowed nervously. "Do you not recognize fear?"

"I do, but what could keep everyone inside? Is it wolves?"

"If only," she said beneath her breath.

Now, he was intrigued. "If it isn't an animal, then it must be a person."

The maid glanced over her shoulder to the owner of the pub. "You better hope you don't run into her."

Her. Unease ran through him. "What woman is this that I should be afraid of?"

"Keep your voice down," she admonished as she anxiously looked about to see if anyone had overheard.

"They're too busy talking to hear me."

Her thin lips flattened as she looked back at him. "I shouldn't talk about it."

Brom held up two coins. "Will this help?"

She didn't hesitate to try and snatch them from his fingers.

He tsked as he pulled them away before she could get them. "First, you talk. Then, you get the coins."

The barmaid clearly wasn't happy, but she moved closer anyway. Then, in a low voice, she said, "A woman came through here about a week ago. She killed two men without even touching them. They just fell dead at her feet. She made the rest of us get on our knees before her."

Brom knew it was a witch the barmaid referenced. However, most didn't realize that magic was part of their world. When they saw it or found out about it, their reaction was to kill whoever wielded it. He could've told the maid exactly what was going on and probably helped the village. But he wasn't going to. Not when the odds were that they would react by trying to harm *him*, leaving him no choice but to defend himself. It would only make things worse for the village and for him. So, he kept his mouth shut.

The barmaid raised her brow, waiting for the money. Brom handed it to her and pulled the bowl toward him. While eating, he took the opportunity to continue sizing up the individuals in the pub. Witches were a fact of life. They had been persecuted, which was why they usually kept to themselves. Except for those in the Coven. He knew the Varroki had warriors that searched for Coven members who had killed those without magic. He was also aware of a group of humans called Hunters, who also fought—and killed—witches who had harmed others.

While Coven members didn't care about hiding, they didn't generally come out and show themselves either. Then again, so much had changed after the three elders had been dispatched, and Sybbyl took over. The Coven was strong, always had been, even since the days after the First Witch. But something more had changed. Something Brom wasn't aware of.

That didn't sit well with him at all. Brom should've taken the time to learn what was going on in the world around him before setting out. If he wasn't careful, he could find himself in a tricky situation. Though, as long as no one discovered that he had Varroki blood, he should be good.

He finished eating, then sat back and leisurely drank his ale. Try as he might, he couldn't pick up snippets of any conversations around him. Finally, he gave up and placed a coin on the table as he grabbed his things and made his way upstairs to one of the rooms.

Once inside, Brom bolted the door and started a fire in the hearth. When it was blazing, he sat before it and closed his eyes. Bit by bit, his mind disconnected from the present and sought out the Varroki. He picked up voices but wasn't able to discern words. It took several tries before he was able to make out anything.

"...*we can't just wait around*," a woman stated angrily.

Brom was surprised at the English accent.

"*We can no' rush out either, lass*," replied a deep Scottish voice.

Then, Malene, a woman Brom had heard before, said, "*Synne, we're well aware that Sybbyl has Asrail. They're using her to get to you*."

"*Because Sybbyl thinks we have the sword*," said the first woman.

Armir, the man who was usually with Malene, said, "*If Asrail had her wish, she would rather us find Avis and Lachlan's sword*."

"*You doona believe the witch is taking my weapon to Sybbyl? You think she's going to keep the bone within the pommel to use on her own?*" asked the first man.

Malene released a breath and said, "*I don't. I believe Avis plans to use the bone for herself. Like Sybbyl, she wants power. The two of them are going to clash*."

"*And my grandmother will be right in the middle*," Synne said.

Armir made a sound in the back of his throat. "*Sybbyl wants to destroy the Varroki, and she wants to find another bone. She'll do whatever is necessary to accomplish both goals*."

"*Like I said, we need to find Elin*," Synne said. "*She made me believe she was a friend. Then she released Avis from her prison. If we want the truth, we need Elin."*

The more Brom heard, the more intrigued he became. He wanted to know who Synne and the man were. More importantly, it sounded as if they'd had a bone of the First Witch—and lost it. Was he after Avis, the witch they'd said had stolen the sword? Or was he after Sybbyl? He wished he had a name to go with the face from his dream.

No matter how he tried to keep listening, the voices faded. For whatever reason, that's all the magic allowed him to hear at the moment. A lot more had happened with the Coven and the Varroki since the last time he had listened in. He knew of the Blood Skull, the Staff of the Eternal, and the Heart of the First Witch, but he hadn't known that another bone had been found.

There was only one more. And no one would ever discover where it was.

Brom opened his eyes and stared into the fire. Things weren't going according to plan for Sybbyl. He really hoped the woman he was after wasn't the new Coven leader. He wasn't afraid to face her, but he knew from listening to the Varroki that she was incredibly powerful. Helena and Jarin had spoken in-depth about their battle with her.

Synne, Sybbyl, Malene, Elin, Avis. Any of them could be the female he was meant to find. Or, it could be none of them. Brom couldn't focus on that right now. He would continue learning names and see who these people were in the grand scheme of things. It was the only way he could safely navigate this sea of magic and betrayal.

He wished he could speak to the Varroki. He might be able to get a lot more information if he did. But he had tried that numerous times. Brom wasn't sure why he could hear them, and they couldn't hear him. And no matter how he tried, he couldn't see them either. Whatever connected him to the Varroki was done only through his hearing.

Brom rose and went to the bed to lay down. He rested his eyes, but he didn't sleep. He went over everything he'd learned that day since waking up, seeing the woman's face, and having every instinct within tell him he had to find her.

He was dressed and out the door before the sun rose. When he walked out of the building, a light dusting of snow had fallen, while more flurries swirled around him. He blew out a breath, watching it puff in front of his face. He looked first one way and then the other before he set out in the same direction as the previous day.

Brom was half a league from the city, making his way through a dense forest when something caused him to halt. He looked around but saw nothing—not even tracks in the snow other than his.

Yet he *knew* someone was near.

He turned in a full circle, searching for whoever it was. When he came back around, a woman stood before him with two short swords pointed at his throat. Clear blue eyes gazed at him from a visage of exquisite beauty. A face he knew all too well.

"Who are you?" she demanded in an accent he'd never heard before.

3

When the man didn't respond, Runa quirked a brow and gently pushed the tips of her swords against his skin. She didn't prick him, but it was a warning all the same. "Who are you?" she repeated.

What worried her was that, for just an instant, there seemed to be a flash of recognition in the man's hazel eyes. As if he knew her. That wasn't possible since she had never seen him before in her life.

"My name is Brom," he said.

She heard the deep timbre of his voice as well as the brogue that pegged him as Scottish. Runa found herself unable to look away from his eyes. There was something magnetic about them. Just as there was something different about the man himself.

This wasn't the first time she'd had her swords at a man's throat. Usually, they sneered at her, not believing that she could wield them. Or, whoever it was quivered in fear. She had never had someone stand solemnly, their face devoid of expression.

"And you are?" he asked. "Seems only fair that you give me your name since I gave you mine."

"I've got blades pointed at your throat."

His lips turned up slightly at the corners. "Your swords are short. Which means, you've got to get closer."

Something tapped against her inner thigh. Runa frowned as she looked down to find a curved dagger in his hand, the blade set against her leg. No one had ever managed to do that to her before, and she didn't like it. Now she knew why he hadn't seemed bothered by her weapons at his throat. With just one flick of his wrist, he could have her on the ground bleeding out.

"Your name?" he pressed.

She stepped back and lowered her blades. "Runa."

"Runa," he said, drawing out the syllables.

Suddenly, she wanted him gone. She took another step back, needed to separate herself from him. Even if she couldn't stop looking at his face. His light brown hair brushed his shoulders, the top part tied back with a strip of leather. Thick brows slashed over unusual eyes that were steady and penetrating. The color was a mixture of gold, green, and blue, as if they couldn't decide which color to be.

As remarkable as his irises were, that wasn't what kept drawing her gaze. His face was all hard angles, as if it had been chiseled from granite. The short beard he wore couldn't hide his impressive jawline. But it was his full lips that seemed so at odds with the rest of his face. They were...sensual.

She'd never in her life used that word to describe anyone or anything before. But it fit him.

While she couldn't see much since his cloak covered his body, there was no denying his broad shoulders. He didn't act like a warrior, but she had a hunch that there was much about this man. Things that others underestimated. There was clearly more to him than he revealed, and she knew from experience that anyone who purposefully hid things about themselves did so for a powerful reason.

Brom might intrigue her, but she had no time for such things. She sheathed her swords and started to walk past him. Then she looked over her shoulder deeper into the forest where she knew the Gira were. "You should give these woods a wide berth," she told him before continuing on.

"Why?"

Runa stopped and blew out a breath. Why hadn't she just left well enough alone? Why did she have to warn him? Without turning around, she said, "There are dangers you can't imagine waiting for you."

"And how do you know of them?"

At this rate, she'd never leave. "Because I do." She headed out, telling herself that no matter what he said, she wasn't going to stop.

With each step she took, she expected to hear him call out to her. When he didn't, she found herself frowning. It should make her happy that he hadn't pressed her. And she shouldn't care if he was stupid enough to ignore her warning and proceed deeper into the forest. She shouldn't care at all if the Gira got him.

"Bloody hell," she murmured and then stopped.

Her gaze rose to the sky, but the sun was quickly swallowed by thick, gray clouds. Snowflakes landed on her lashes, making her blink. She should keep walking. She didn't know Brom.

But he knew you.

That's what'd got her. She wasn't sure *how* he knew her, but it was clear that he did, and she wanted to find out how. It wasn't like the Coven to send a man after her, but then again, with Sybbyl ruling the group now, nothing was the same.

Runa turned and found Brom standing where she had left him. "What are you doing?"

"Watching you."

She took two steps toward him. "Why?"

"Why no'? It's no' every day I encounter a woman who no' only brandishes swords but also wears trousers. Even more curious is that other than the tracks you just made, there are no other footprints but mine."

Runa wasn't used to anyone being aware of such things. Normally, if someone noticed the lack of tracks, it didn't matter because she was about to end his or her life. But she hadn't been sent after Brom. Perhaps he was hunting her.

She walked closer.

He shrugged and continued talking. "From what I understand, this is no' a safe time for a woman to be traveling alone."

"I don't think it's safe for *anyone* to be traveling. You included."

Once more, his lips curved into a half-grin. "Perhaps. You doona seem afraid of much."

"Because I'm not. Why do you care?" She took two more steps toward him. Her gaze moved to his hands. She couldn't see his dagger anymore, but she knew it was there.

He glanced over his shoulder to the forest. "You warned me. I'm simply doing the same."

"You've done your duty. You can continue on."

"That I can."

Yet, he didn't move. Runa took the last two steps that put her back where she had begun. "Who are you?"

"I told you."

"Maybe I should've asked a better question. Like, how do you know me?"

"If I knew you, would I have asked for your name?"

Her gaze narrowed on him. "Answering a question with a question isn't answering."

Hazel eyes lowered to the snow-covered ground for a heartbeat before his head issued a single nod. "Nay, it's no'."

"You don't intend to tell me, do you?"

When he didn't utter another syllable, Runa spun on her heel and left him. For all she knew, he was a distraction that would keep her from discovering the truth. If the Gira who'd told her of her grandmother and sister being in danger was right, then Runa had to cover as much ground as she had the previous day. If only she knew where to go other than north.

The farther she went, the colder it got. The trek would've been easier if she had a horse, but she found that she moved quicker, especially in the forest, without one. Now, however, she wished for one of the animals. She could cover twice as much distance on horseback. But that wasn't an option, at least not at the moment.

Runa left the safety of the woods. She tried to walk in a straight line, but she soon found that the snow was just too deep. She had no choice but to get back on the road. The open lane, however, made her easy to spot. She didn't like being so exposed. But the farther north she went, the less that became an issue. There was simply no one around.

A prickling sensation along her neck had her pausing to look behind her. She half expected to see Brom, but there was no sign of him or anyone else. Nor did she sense any Gira, which made her frown, since something or someone had caused the reaction within her.

She turned back around and kept walking. All the while, she tried to come up with a plan. She had no idea where Synne was, and since the likelihood of her finding the Varroki was slim, her best bet was to locate Sybbyl and the Coven.

That would be the easiest thing since the Gira would be near Sybbyl.

Runa crested a hill and spotted a small grove of trees in the glen below. She smiled and jogged to them. When she reached them, she flattened her palms against the bark and closed her eyes as she attempted to discern where the Gira were.

It didn't take her long to discover where they were located. The largest gathering of Gira she had ever heard of before was about ten leagues from her current location. She hadn't spoken to the nymphs in the forest last night, mainly because she wasn't in the mood. They hadn't come to her either, and she had been glad of it.

Most times, the Gira steered clear of her. She was an anomaly in their world, something they didn't want to admit to or recognize. That had once hurt her, but not anymore. She had found her place despite the nymphs wishing to kill her. Now, they feared her.

She had assumed that was why the nymphs in the forest the night before had given her a wide berth. But what if she'd been wrong? What if they kept away because they were hiding? The young Gira she'd tracked and spoken with had run for her life because she had stood up to Sybbyl. She'd told Runa that she had been the only one, but Runa suspected that other nymphs had made their exit quietly, as well, hoping not to draw attention. If that were the case, it wouldn't be long before their absence was noticed.

The Gira generally went after their own, but there were instances when they preferred to pay someone to do the dirty work. Since Runa had been able to move freely between the humans and the Gira, she took the opportunities given to her —and the coin they provided.

Morea hadn't approved. Runa had tried to make her foster mother understand that she didn't hunt for pleasure. It was a job. Simple as that. Besides, the Gira had killed numerous humans over the years. At least, that was Runa's argument—one that had always ended with Morea turning away.

Runa opened her eyes and dropped her hands from the trees. The nymphs' magic was powerful. In many cases, more powerful than any witch's. Runa would even garner to say it was stronger than the Varroki's. The problem was, the Gira were selfish. They gave only the magic they were forced to give to the group. The rest, they kept for themselves.

Morea, and it seemed Asrail, as well, were two exceptions to the rule—in everything. They had sacrificed their standing, and even their lives, to give both Runa and her sister a chance. She just wished that Morea had told her about Synne. She didn't understand why her foster mother had kept that secret from her, and there was no way to get the answer now.

Her thoughts turned back to the Gira. She wondered if Sybbyl knew how potent the nymphs' magic was. Add that to Sybbyl's magic, which the Staff of the Eternal boosted, and the Coven leader could well take over the world.

Runa pulled the hood of her cloak up to cover her face as she thought about the Hunters that had been killed. Synne had been raised with them, but her sister had escaped the massacre. There was a chance that other Hunters were also out there somewhere. There wasn't nearly enough of them, however. Not with the sheer number of Gira.

Then there was the Varroki. Runa could only hope that Synne wasn't being treated differently because she was half-Gira.

The snow began to fall harder. Runa looked northeast, where she knew the pack of Gira were. She would only be able to get so close before they sensed her. It was doubtful that she could get close enough to see Sybbyl or even her grandmother, Asrail. While the Gira tended to stay away from her because she hunted them when an offer came through, that didn't mean they would allow her near. Most likely, the moment they realized that she was there, they would descend upon her. She wouldn't help anyone if the Gira killed her.

She couldn't go to her sister since she didn't know where the Varroki were.

She couldn't go to the Coven for her grandmother since the Gira would alert Sybbyl.

She couldn't find a Hunter for help because she had no idea where to locate one—or if there were any left.

Runa looked back the way she had come and debated trying to find the Gira who had hidden in the forest to see if they would join her, but she already knew the answer. They were running away. Otherwise, they would've alerted the others that she was here.

An owl hooted above her. She raised her head to see a small white owl high in the branches of a tree. It blinked its big, yellow eyes at her before swiveling its head. Runa watched it for a few minutes before the bird flew away. When she lowered her gaze, a woman stood off to the side, watching her with deep blue eyes.

"I wondered if you would find your way here," she said with a smile as she drew back the hood of her cloak to reveal wavy, pale blond hair.

Runa narrowed her eyes on the petite woman. "Is that right?"

"It is, Runa." The woman's smile widened. "I see I've surprised you. Good. I think you need more surprises. I'm Asa."

"How do you know me?"

Asa nodded toward the owl that flew toward her. The moment Asa lifted her arm, the bird perched upon it. "Frida told me."

That's when Runa knew. "You're a witch."

"I am. I lived at the abbey with the other witches and Hunters, including your sister, Synne. I've been searching for you ever since."

Runa flexed her fingers, ready to grab her blades. "Why have you been looking for me?"

"The same reason you're here."

4

Brom watched Runa and the witch from a distance. He had opted not to tell Runa that he had been looking for her before they met. She was already wary, and she likely wouldn't have believed him. Just the brief interaction they'd shared had told him so much about her.

She was capable of taking care of herself. There also didn't seem to be much that frightened her. She had stood her ground against him, unwavering in her knowledge that she could take him down. Though, she *had* underestimated him and allowed him to get the drop on her by way of his dagger.

Still, Runa obviously had skills. She held her short swords as if she used them every day—which she most likely did. Her comfort level with the blades told him that she wouldn't hesitate to use them if needed.

Then there was her stature. She held herself with grace and confidence. Her breeches did nothing to distract from the fact that she was a woman. Quite the opposite, really. He found himself wishing her cloak was gone so he could see all of her legs as well as her backside. But he hadn't gotten that view.

Yet.

It was difficult to determine how long her blond hair was since it was twisted into so many plaits that he didn't know where one ended and another began. Her eyes, however, were the gateway to not only her soul but also her mind. When she'd looked at him, he could see her mulling over different responses to whatever he might say. She wasn't just any woman. There was something distinctly different about her. What that might be, he couldn't pinpoint quite yet. He still wondered how she had moved in the snow without leaving any footprints. It wasn't done with magic, because he'd looked for that. So, how had she done it? He would have to get her to tell him. Right after he got close enough and convinced her to trust him.

Brom chuckled to himself. That wasn't going to happen. Not that he blamed her. He didn't trust anyone either, so he knew this wasn't going to be an easy task. He hadn't imagined finding her so soon. Now that he had, he still wasn't sure what to do.

Help her? Hinder her?

Stop her?

The possibilities were endless. That was the main reason he hadn't told her that he recognized her face. She'd asked if he knew her, and he'd said no. Because he didn't. She hadn't asked the right question. Of course, he was splitting hairs. But until he knew exactly what he was doing, he would be cautious.

If he were lucky, he might find out more tonight as he slept. Then again, he wouldn't actually allow himself to go that deep into sleep since he wasn't sure who his friends or enemies were. At least now, he knew that Runa wasn't Synne or Malene. He had put one face to a name.

He cocked his head to the side and tried to get a better look at the woman currently speaking with Runa. Brom kept his distance from witches for a great many reasons. Foremost was that he didn't want to give them any indication that he was a warlock and therefore gain the Coven's attention.

Brom jerked when the witch's gaze briefly landed on him. He knew without a doubt that she looked directly at him. Even from a distance, there was no denying it. She knew that he was there. Would she tell Runa? As the seconds ticked by and Runa didn't turn around to look for him or even appear as if she knew he was around, he began to wonder what the witch was up to.

He got even more curious when he saw a white owl land on the witch's outstretched arm. She stroked the bird with a familiarity that said the two had known each other for some time. He knew some witches could speak to animals. This woman may be such a witch. That could explain how she knew that he was there. The owl had told her.

Suddenly, the bird of prey stretched out its wings and took to the air—and flew right to him. It landed on a tree, blinking its big eyes. He flattened his lips then turned his attention back to Runa and the witch. They stood in a glen, and he was still at the top of the hill. It gave him a slight advantage, but not much since there were few places for him to hide. He was off to the side, far from the path that Runa had traveled. It had made his progress much slower since he had to traverse through the deep snow, but he had maintained his pace to keep up with her.

Brom looked at the owl as it hooted softly at him. The way it stared at him made him feel as if the bird were sizing him up. Most likely, it was doing exactly that for its mistress. If he had that ability, he would absolutely use it to his advantage. He couldn't even be upset with the witch. She had no way of knowing whether he was friend or foe.

It wasn't yet noon, but the gray skies and snow made it feel as if it were much later. Brom could use the weather to his advantage and creep closer to Runa, but he didn't. He didn't trust her or the witch, and he would watch his back until he got a better feel for them. Not that he expected to ever trust them. It wasn't in his nature.

Secrecy had surrounded him since before his birth. Afterward, even more so. He lived alone because he preferred it, but also because no one could ever know who he was. The only way that would change is if he happened to find the Varroki, and he knew that was a remote possibility. They were sequestered for a reason. Because of that, he remained hidden.

"Yet, here I am," he mumbled.

Brom shook his head. He was on a wild goose chase, that much was clear. He might have found his target, but that was all he'd done. He had learned nothing more than he knew that morning.

You know her name.

"Runa."

He liked the way it rolled off his tongue. It made him think of the ancient Celts, of the time of the Norse. When magic was embraced, and witches were revered. She would've fit right in with either the Celts or the Norse. Runa had a warrior's soul.

The question was: which side did she fight for?

Brom couldn't ask her that earlier because she might have pieced together that he was a warlock. It was better for him to pretend ignorance, at least for the moment. The problem was that he'd liked her instantly. There had been a connection that he couldn't ignore.

That could be because he was attracted to her. His body's response to seeing her face-to-face had been...thrilling. Such an effect on his body could have resulted in his mind being clouded. Desires of the flesh had a way of hindering a person's normal thought processes and actions. While he very much wanted to give in to the hunger, he held himself in check.

Suddenly, he frowned, remembering how she had cautioned him about the forest when they had met. Brom wasn't sure if she had been warning him against bandits or the Gira. He'd run enough nymphs off and away from the area around his home to know that they were lethal creatures, especially to the unsuspecting.

Brom winced as a sharp pain went through his head right before he heard voices.

"...Jarin and the others are waiting," Armir said.

Malene sighed. "I'm not afraid of war."

"No one said you were."

"You question why I don't send our people out to meet Sybbyl."

"You are Lady of the Varroki for a reason," Armir told her. "Look where you have led us. We will follow you anywhere. I will follow you anywhere."

Malene was quiet for a moment. "I'm waiting on something."

"What did you see?"

"Nothing," she told him.

Armir's voice held a note of insistence when he asked, "What happened?"

"There's an unknown participant."

Brom grabbed his head as it began to pound. He turned onto his side as he struggled past the pain to hear the voices again, but they were gone. Several minutes passed before the agony finally ebbed.

He blinked up at the sky as he drew in deep breaths. Nothing like that had ever happened before. Normally, he had to concentrate for a while before he got into a deep enough trance to hear the Varroki. He sighed and sat up, shaking the snow from him. He wasn't sure how he felt about what had just happened.

On the one hand, he liked that he'd gotten another glimpse of things with the Varroki. But on the other, for it to come out of the blue like that meant that it could be a detriment to him if it happened at a time when he was facing his enemies. They could overtake him easily given the distraction.

Brom wasn't sure what had alerted him to the fact that he was no longer alone. He glanced up to the limb where the owl sat before he turned his head to find the witch Runa had spoken with. She gave him a welcoming smile that he didn't return.

"Don't worry," she told him in an accent he couldn't quite place. "Your secret is safe with me."

He quirked a brow as he looked into her dark blue eyes. "My secret?"

"You're a warlock."

"I doona know what you mean."

She laughed and wrapped her beige cloak tighter around her. "By your face, whatever just happened was a first. Perhaps I can help with that."

"Why should I tell you anything?"

Her gaze slid away for a moment. "You're right. You don't know me."

Brom looked over his shoulder, searching for Runa, but he couldn't see her. He looked back at the witch to find her watching him silently. He suspected that whatever he said next would determine whether he discovered where Runa had gone. He shouldn't care. After all, he'd found her once, he could do it again.

"I came to this land when I was a young girl," she told him, a note of sadness in her voice. "I came because my path led me here. Because this is my destiny. I knew even then that I would spend my life fighting against the Coven."

He gazed at her for a long moment. Brom chose not to reply to see if she would say more.

The witch drew in a deep breath and moved a strand of blond hair from her face. Brom saw the markings of a tattoo on her hand and fingers.

"I found a home with Edra. The moment I heard that she had fought the Coven and won, I knew I needed to be with her. Edra and her husband, Radnar, set up a sanctuary for witches hiding from the Coven. Soon, it became a haven for anyone needing a home. Each of us had skills we used. Mine was that I could communicate with animals. Frida has been my companion for many years," she said and motioned to the owl.

Brom glanced at the bird and could've sworn the damn thing smiled.

"I also read people," she said, gaining his attention once more. "I'm able to draw the things I see, and I gift it by marking it on a person's body."

He frowned as he got to his feet. There was something about her words that pulled at a distant memory.

"I wondered if you would remember," she said in a soft voice.

Brom shook his head as he met her eyes. "Remember what?"

"We met once. Long, long ago. In a dream."

"That's impossible," he scoffed.

She gave him a flat look. "Brom, how do you think you're here?"

He thought about the voice from his dream. It had been a female's, he knew that much. But he'd thought it was from someone older. The more he tried to recall it, the deeper his frown became.

"You have the ability to listen to the Varroki. With a special spell, I can speak with certain people as they sleep. It's how I met you when you were very young, when I had just come to this land. It's how I told you to look for Runa the other night."

Brom wanted to deny all of it, but the more she talked, the clearer his memory became of that long-ago dream. He searched it, trying to remember her name. The information was elusive, just out of his grasp each time he thought he'd found it. Then, finally, he had it. "Asa."

A smile lit up her face. "There you are."

"Why did you want me to find Runa when you found her?"

Her gaze dropped to the snow. "I thought I was here to battle the Coven. However, my path is taking me elsewhere. It's up to you to help Runa."

"Help her with what?"

Asa swallowed and lifted her eyes to his. "I've seen your path. I've seen *her* path. They converge. For a time."

"What does that mean?"

"You are the answer."

"The answer to what?" he demanded.

Asa's smile was sad, her eyes filled with sorrow. "There are two paths. Everyone has two paths. We each have to choose the one to walk upon."

"You want me to stop her."

"I honestly don't have an answer for you. All I know is that you need to be here."

He nodded slowly. "Did you tell her any of this?"

"Of course, not," Asa said with a chuckle. "She wouldn't believe me."

"Then talk to her in dreams as you did with me."

Asa's lips twisted. "I can't. I can tell you where the Varroki are."

He stilled. "You know of them?"

"I do. The closer you are to them, the stronger your magic will become."

"Is that how it works with all Varroki?"

She smiled as she shook her head. "Just you. You're unique in many ways."

"Where are they?"

Asa took a deep breath and slowly released it. "I can tell you where the Varroki are. Or, I can tell you where Runa is. You must choose."

5

Nothing turned out like it was supposed to. Runa still wasn't sure what to make of her encounter with the witch. Everything Asa had told her left her feeling more lost than ever before. The more Runa learned, the more it seemed as if she were pulling herself out of quicksand that continued to suck her down quicker and deeper. At this rate, she'd be swallowed in a matter of hours, not days.

Runa hadn't hesitated to leave the witch behind. Not because she had a bad feeling about Asa. In fact, she liked the witch. No, it was more because the longer she was around Asa, the more she sensed she would learn things she was better off not knowing. And that went against her general rule, which was that knowledge is power.

However, two separate people had told her similar stories about Asrail and Synne. Runa was glad because it meant she didn't have to hunt down the Gira from a few days ago again.

"You're going to be pulled in two different directions. You'll have to choose a side."

Asa's cryptic words rang in her head like a bell. She had asked the witch to give her more, but Asa had simply smiled.

Runa couldn't imagine what she would have to pick a side for. She was merely trying to find her sister and save her grandmother.

Each time she thought of Asrail, pain, sharp and searing, cut through her. Why hadn't her grandmother come to visit her? Why had she stayed away and instead chosen to seek out Synne? What was it about her sister that made her better than Runa? And what of her sister? Why hadn't Synne sought Runa out? Some might argue that Synne had been running from the Coven, but she still could've tried to look for her sibling.

The more Runa's thoughts churned, the angrier she got. She might have been saved from the Gira as a child, but she had also been discarded by her family as if she meant nothing. She remembered nothing of her parents or her sister—or the day her parents were killed and Morea secreted her away.

She halted and took in a steadying breath. Her mind had to be clear if she wanted to sneak up on the Gira and the Coven. The past didn't matter. She needed to concentrate on what was happening now.

Runa shoved everything out of her mind. She had discerned the Giras' location. They were situated deep in the Cairngorm Mountains. The Rothiemurchus Forest was vast, holding ancient pines and countless places to hide. Runa knew of two Witch's Groves there. No doubt that's exactly where Sybbyl was holed up with the Coven while the Gira hid amongst the trees.

If the weather held, it was still two days' walk for Runa to get to the forest. She eyed the sky and the clouds, unable to see where the sun was. Another storm would most likely hit, prolonging her journey.

With a sigh, she continued walking. To her surprise, her mind drifted back to Brom. She wasn't sure why she kept thinking about the man. Sure, he had surprised her, and he was incredibly handsome, but they had shared few words. What was it about him that kept bringing him to mind?

But she knew.

It had been the way he looked at her. As if he couldn't tear his gaze away if he tried.

Coupled with the fact that he hadn't dismissed her as some frivolous female or someone in need of saving, it made him even more intriguing. Though she usually went out of her way to avoid others, she had wanted to stay and continue talking with him. To discover who he was and find out why it seemed he'd recognized her face.

But that wasn't the only reason she wanted to be around him more. There had been something between them. She had felt the unquestionable attraction, the enticement of pleasure that swirled around them like the wild flurries of a snowfall. And, oh, how she wanted to give in to it. She just knew his sensual mouth would feel amazing against her lips. Certainly, that intense look of his would translate to heated kisses.

It became difficult to swallow when she thought about his large hands on her body. Runa came to a halt as her stomach fluttered in excitement, and her sex clenched in need. She didn't turn away from the emotions, but neither did she embrace them. She let them float through her until they were gone.

The last time she had given in to her desires, it had been monumentally catastrophic. She was of two worlds, and yet she didn't fit into either. Most of the time, it didn't bother her. Then there were times, like this, when she found someone she wanted to spend time with.

Not that it mattered. She would never see Brom again. He had been going in a different direction. Knowing he was gone forever made her sad, which irritated her. She didn't even know him. How could she be forlorn that he was gone?

"Get ahold of yourself," Runa stated.

She blinked and looked around, belatedly realizing that she had been walking for some time lost in her thoughts—again. She never did that, and yet, that was twice in one day. If she didn't want to get killed, she couldn't let herself do that again.

It wasn't just the distance she hadn't noticed. She also hadn't felt the drop in temperature, or the fact that it had begun to snow once more. The flakes came down fast and thick, making it difficult to see. She needed to find shelter quickly.

Runa turned in a slow circle. Her tracks were nearly covered by the newly fallen powder. She had been climbing upward, following the gradual rise of the land. Seeing nothing near, she hurried as fast as she could in the thick snow to the top of the hill. When she reached it, she looked out at the mountains before her, now merely dark shadows against an even darker sky.

She might have Gira blood running through her veins, but Runa could still die in the cold. Shivering, she started to the left and the edge of the forest. She paused and looked around when she thought she heard something, but no matter how hard she looked, she couldn't see anyone. Runa kept walking. She had to keep her head down to stop the flakes from hitting her face. The hood of her cloak was up, and she had to hold onto the sides to keep it in place. Her hands hurt from the bite of the wind, but she kept her feet moving because once she found shelter, she could get a fire going and warm up.

When she finally made it to the forest, she breathed a sigh of relief. The trees blocked some of the wind while their sturdy branches gathered more snow atop them. The trees creaked as her feet crunched in the snow. In her haste, she wasn't careful where she put her feet and slipped, sliding down the mountain's slope. As she twisted to try and stop her fall, her knee slammed against a rock hidden in the snow.

Runa cried out and grasped her knee as she fell to the side. Her cheek stung from the impact against the ground. She gritted her teeth and pushed herself into a sitting position to look at her leg. Pain radiated through her, and the last thing she wanted to do was move her limb. But she didn't have a choice. She had to in order to see how injured she was. All she could hope for was that her kneecap wasn't busted.

She bent forward and used her hands to feel around her knee. Nothing felt broken, but that didn't mean anything. She slowly shifted her leg. At first, everything was going fine, then a sharp, stabbing pain shot through her. She bit back the startled yelp that rose, but not before a sound made it past her lips.

"Bloody hell," she murmured.

This was the last thing she needed. She had no other choice but to get to her feet and find shelter. She couldn't stay outdoors or on the ground. No matter how much it hurt, she had to get moving.

"It appears as if you could use some aid."

Her head jerked around at the sound of the deep voice. Even before her gaze landed on his face, she knew it was Brom. Runa wasn't sure how she felt about the joy that leapt inside her at the sight of him. He didn't wait for her to reply as he made his way to her and squatted down beside her.

He inspected her knee, then lifted his hazel eyes to hers. "Can you walk?"

Runa nodded, unable to find words.

"Come, then. Let me help," Brom stated as he wrapped an arm around her.

She was so stunned by his touch that she wasn't prepared when he straightened, taking her with him. One moment, she was in the snow. The next, she stood next to a tall Scot who held her as if nothing could make him loosen his grip.

"All right?" he asked.

Runa nodded once more as the heat of him wrapped around her, melting away the cold. She liked the feeling of his strong arm around her and how his hand cupped her waist. His hold was firm without crushing. Unable to help herself, she turned her head toward his and found him looking at her. His expression was unreadable, and she hoped hers was, as well. Though she had a feeling it wasn't.

"Can you put any weight on it?" he asked, shouting over the wind that had suddenly grown louder.

Runa looked around as unease filled her. Her eyes snapped back to Brom to find his eyes narrowed as he too scanned the area. She didn't feel any Gira near, but there could be witches about. Then she spotted something ahead that looked like a cave. She tapped Brom's arm and pointed to show him. He nodded to let her know that he had seen it, as well.

She tentatively put her weight on her leg and hissed in pain. In response, Brom pulled more of her weight against him. Runa was able to lean on him and walk with him. It wasn't dignified or easy, but at least she was on her feet. She kept looking around because she wasn't going to let an enemy blindside them.

Brom didn't stop or slow, even when the snow became so deep they had difficulty wading through it. Their pace was steady, but even with that, they made little progress through the storm. If it was this bad within the forest, Runa couldn't imagine what it was like outside of it.

The wind howled, sounding ghostly as it rushed through the trees. She fisted her hand in Brom's cloak to keep her grip. Her fingers were numb, which made it difficult to know if she was holding onto him or not. Despite the frigid temperature, sweat ran down her face. She glanced at Brom to find him sweating, as well. The beads froze to their faces almost instantly.

Runa hated that she had injured herself. If she hadn't, neither of them would have gotten caught in this weather. But she couldn't change what had happened. She put a little more weight on the leg without any pain. Then she made the mistake of thinking she could do it again. She bit her lip to keep from crying out, but Brom must have felt her jerk against him.

"What is it?" he asked close to her ear.

She kept her face turned away from him so he wouldn't see how much pain she was in. With the wind at its deafening roar, she didn't even attempt to speak. Instead, she shook her head.

Brom mumbled something beneath his breath. The next thing Runa knew, he lifted her into his arms. She was so surprised that she couldn't find the words. No one had ever carried her in such a manner. And she wasn't sure if she liked being handled in such a way or not.

But it wouldn't have mattered if it did bother her. She needed Brom's help.

She might not like being manhandled, but she had to admit—at least, to herself—that she liked being in his arms.

6

Brom had managed to catch up to Runa quicker than he
thought. Just as he did, the storm descended upon them.
He shouted to her, but she hadn't heard him. Then, she had
slipped. Seeing her roll down the slope had left him shocked.
He started running toward her even before she came to a halt.
When she did stop, he winced at her startled cry of pain that
she quickly cut off.

He was even more surprised when she didn't rebuke him
for offering aid. The fact that she had accepted his help told
him how bad the injury was. He would've preferred to take a
look at it there, but a sense of dread ran down his spine.
Something was near. He didn't know if it was an animal or a
person, but he knew it meant danger for them. Runa must
have sensed it, as well, because they were soon off.

If he thought trying to get through the deep snow on a
mountain to what he hoped was a cave was tough, it was
nothing compared to having her lithe body against his. He
knew the feel of her soft curves, her warmth that seeped
through his clothes and into his flesh.

He shouldn't be thinking about what Runa looked like

without her clothes, or how he wanted to run his hands up and down her body, learning every inch of her. They were in a blizzard, she was wounded, something dangerous was near them. He needed to keep his head clear. The problem was, he couldn't when it came to Runa.

Ever since he had woken with her face in his dreams, she had occupied his thoughts. Once he met her and felt the instant, irresistible yearning, he'd thought of nothing *but* her. His body craved her, hungered for her as if he were starving, and she was sustenance. It was ridiculous, wasn't it? Surely, one person couldn't make another feel this way.

He'd just about convinced himself of that when he heard Runa gasp in pain. Without a second thought, he'd lifted her up into his arms to carry her. Instead of demanding to be put down, she'd wrapped her arms around him and looked behind them. He knew without a doubt that she would watch his back.

Brom's pace was slowed when he had to feel his way with his feet up the slope to avoid the rocks and boulders buried in the snow. He nearly lost his balance once but managed to catch himself before they both tumbled back down the mountain.

"It'll be easier if I walk," Runa said in a loud voice.

It was the first time she had spoken since he'd found her. He looked into her eyes and grinned. "I've got you."

"I'm not a petite woman."

She certainly wasn't, and that's what he found so damn appealing. Well, that and so much more. She was tall, toned, and striking. A combination that knocked him off his feet.

"Brom," she started.

He shook his head to cut her off. The wind was so loud, they had to yell. He smiled again and gripped her tighter, telling her without words that he had her. She didn't say more.

He focused on putting one foot in front of the other. His muscles throughout his body strained. He kept his gaze locked on the cave's entrance as it grew closer and closer until, finally, they reached it.

Brom gently set Runa on her feet. He waited until she was propped against the side of the cave before he loosened his hold on her. His gaze swept the area. There were no tracks—human or animal—near the entrance or the slight outcropping of the mountain. But that didn't mean there wasn't something inside.

Once more, a shiver raced down his spine. He looked over his shoulder back the way they had come and then at Runa. She too peered into the distance. Her gaze swung to him, and their eyes clashed. She reached behind her and withdrew her blades. To his surprise, she offered one to him. He shook his head and then faced the entrance.

Brom walked toward the yawning darkness of the entry. He kept to the side in case something rushed at him. The cave quieted the howling wind by several decibels. He stood still, letting his eyes adjust to the darkness. Two steps later, a growl stopped him in his tracks. It wasn't the deep rumble of a wolf, but that didn't mean whatever animal had made the sound wasn't dangerous.

Then he heard the unmistakable hiss of a wildcat. They might be on the small side, but they were still fiercely territorial. Brom sighed as he listened to the blizzard. There were really only three options open to them. He turned on his heel and hurried back outside to Runa, helping her inside.

Only once she was within the cave did he say, "We'll be sharing this space."

"With what?" she asked as her body grew taut against him.

At that moment, the wildcat issued another hiss and growl.

"The feline on the other side of the cave," he told her. "We're going to remain over here. There's plenty of room for all of us."

"Or you could make it leave."

He looked at her. "The cat found this place first. I'm no' going to make it leave, and we're no' going to leave. So, we share."

"You're right," she said as she flattened her lips.

Brom got her situated as far back from the entrance as he could. Then he removed his bag and dug inside for the peat that he had gathered earlier. He used it to build a fire. Once the flames were high enough to light the cave, he could see the wildcat huddled against the far wall with its ears flattened, staring at them. He decided the best course of action was to ignore the animal completely. He didn't want to frighten it out into the weather or make it feel as if it were cornered.

"He's pretty," Runa said.

Brom looked at the cat again. Its distinctive black and brown stripes stood out starkly against its sandy-colored fur. It had a thick, banded tale, perfectly tipped in black. His yellow eyes were locked on him and Runa.

"That he is," Brom replied.

Runa rubbed her hands together and held them toward the fire while Brom made sure there was enough peat to get them through the night at least.

"We need to look at your knee," he told her.

Runa nodded without looking at him. "Are you going to tell me what you're doing here?"

"I wondered when you would get around to asking me that." In fact, he'd expected the question much sooner.

Her head swung to him as she raised a brow. "Well?"

Brom stood and removed his cloak, spreading it out so it could dry. Then he held his hand out for Runa's. She sighed loudly and removed the sheaths for her swords before she unclasped her outer garment and handed it to him. He shook it out and put it near his. Then he faced her.

"What would you say if I told you I had a dream about you last night?"

She didn't so much as bat an eye. "What was the dream?"

"Just your face with a woman's voice telling me to find you."

"Hmm," she said. "That's why you appeared to recognize me when we first met."

He bowed his head in a nod. "Aye."

"Since you didn't tell me about this earlier, I gather you weren't sure what to do."

Brom smiled despite himself. "Something like that. You looked to be in a hurry, and I could no' think of anything plausible to get you to stay or allow me to remain with you."

"There was nothing you could've said."

"Which is why I followed you."

She eyed him as she put her hands in her lap. "Am I to guess that you know what to do now that you've found me again?"

He laughed, shaking his head. "Actually, I doona know any more than I did this morning."

"You could've been looking for me for years. Perhaps you just had a strange dream."

"I come from a world where there isna such a thing."

She didn't reply, just held his gaze.

He waited, hoping she would say something. Brom had no idea who she was, and Asa hadn't given him much information to go on. Unfortunately, it didn't appear as if Runa were going to elaborate either.

"You have the stance of a warrior, yet you carry no sword," Runa said.

He drew in a breath and shrugged. "As you learned this morning, I'm not without protection."

"Usually, a man such as yourself carries a weapon large enough that others can see."

"I'm not generally around other people."

She cocked her head to the side, interest sparking in her gaze. "Why?"

"I...doona like people. Most are rude, arrogant, and self-absorbed. There are only a few exceptions." He nodded in her direction.

A smile pulled at her lips. "I think you just complimented me."

"You sound surprised."

"I am. Especially since I tend to stay away from others, as well. For the same reasons you mentioned."

They shared a grin. Brom could carry on a conversation with anyone, but few people made him actually *want* to talk. And the fact that he had told Runa the truth spoke of how much he enjoyed conversing with her.

She laughed softly. "I don't think I've ever come across someone who likes their solitude as much as I do."

"You're no' Scottish, but you're no' English either. I can no' quite place your accent."

Her smile died as she looked away. "I'm from all over."

"You doona have to tell me. I like your voice. I was just curious where you're from."

She licked her lips and looked up at him. "What kind of man has a dream about a woman he doesn't know and then leaves his home to look for her? What kind of person tracks down that woman without knowing what he's supposed to do?"

"The kind who follows his instincts. I was supposed to find you."

"I could be leading you to your death for all you know."

He shrugged, twisting his lips. "You verra well might be. It doesna matter. I'm doing what I'm supposed to be doing."

"Brom, you seem like a nice man—and coming from me, that's saying a lot. I go out of my way to avoid people at all costs. I…don't fit in anywhere, and I've accepted that. Embraced it, even. Things are…complicated. Trust me when I say I'm the last person you should be around."

"Perhaps it's because things are so complicated that our paths were meant to cross."

"You wouldn't say that if you knew everything."

He crossed his arms over his chest and eyed her. "Then tell me."

She lowered her gaze to the fire. "You say that as if I trust you. I don't."

As much as he hated to admit it, she was right. It wasn't as if he were opening up and telling her all about himself, either. He couldn't admonish her for the lack of trust when he couldn't give her the same courtesy. He'd chosen Runa over the Varroki. Even now, he didn't regret that decision. It didn't matter that Asa had spoken to him in his dream, telling him about Runa. The witch had sent him to find Runa for a reason. Asa might not have told him what that reason was, but he knew it had to be a good one.

He blew out a frustrated sigh. In one breath, he talked about not being able to trust, and yet he had trusted the dream without knowing details. Learning the voice was Asa's should have made him wary, but it didn't. He wasn't sure why —and he suspected he never would.

"Let me check your knee," he said as he dropped his arms to his sides.

Runa held up a hand. "Turn around."

Brom hesitated for a heartbeat before he did as she

requested. As he stood there, he could hear her moving. Then, the unmistakable sound of pants being removed had his balls tightening and blood rushing to his cock. He closed his eyes, imagining what Runa was doing. His body heated, desire pounding through him. He wanted to turn around and get a glimpse of her bare skin, but he somehow maintained control.

"All right."

He swallowed, wishing he could palm his aching erection to get some relief. Brom drew in a steadying breath and pivoted. Thankfully, Runa's eyes were lowered so she didn't see his obvious arousal. He quickly moved to her and squatted in an effort to hide it from her. He hadn't expected to get so turned on by only listening to her remove her clothes. Then again, something about the woman made him want to give in to his basest instincts.

Brom's gaze lowered, landing on Runa's bare legs. He was fast losing control. He'd just been imagining touching her, and now the thought made him want to run back out into the blizzard. Because if he touched her, he knew he wouldn't be able to stop.

He fisted his hands as hunger unlike anything he'd felt before rose up in him. It demanded that he take Runa, kiss her, claim her as his. It ordered him to meld their bodies, to fill her with his seed.

It commanded him because she was meant to be his.

And he was meant to be hers.

7

R una had always gone after whatever she wanted. Nothing held her back. And it wasn't going to this time either. The direction she was headed in was one of danger and risk. The odds were stacked against her. She may not make it out with her life. She accepted that possibility because this was about her family.

Some might have turned their backs on Synne and Asrail —and with good reason. But Runa couldn't do that. It was within her abilities to help them, and that was exactly what she was going to do.

Meeting Brom had been unexpected and entirely amazing. She had the opportunity to share something with a gorgeous man who made her stomach flutter and her heart race. There was no way she would allow that opportunity to pass her by when it was within her grasp. The idea of removing her clothes with him nearby was very appealing. How could it not be when she was so attracted to him?

She left her tunic and vest on but removed her boots and pants. Then she waited for him to look at her. When he hesitated, she glanced at her legs. Sadly, she missed his reaction when he turned around. Her eyes were now on his face, watching, waiting for some sign that he wanted her. She was putting herself out there, and as scary as that was, she knew it was the right thing to do.

Whatever she felt for Brom was something unique and exceptional. Nothing and no one could make her change her mind about sharing a night with him. She didn't know what it would bring her, but it didn't matter. All she knew was that when he was with her, everything felt…*right*.

She had been around magic her entire life. She knew when something was real and when it wasn't. This…*feeling*…was definitely real. There had never been another time in her life when she had known for sure what path to take.

"Does it still hurt?" Brom asked in a rough voice.

Runa was shaking, and it had nothing to do with the cold and everything to do with yearning for the man beside her, needing him to put his hand on her once more. "It's manageable," she said in a breathy voice.

He nodded, swallowing hard. "The skin is already coloring. You're going to have a nasty bruise that will make walking even more difficult."

She didn't want to think about tomorrow or how her injury might alter her plans. She only wanted to think of Brom and how he made her feel.

His gaze slowly moved up and down her legs before he eventually looked at her. The desire she saw in his eyes made her heart skip a beat. It was as if invisible hands pulled them closer, an unknown force that melded their souls.

"I don't know what tomorrow will bring," she whispered. "But I know what I want tonight."

His nostrils flared as his eyes dropped to her lips. Runa wasn't a virgin, but she also wasn't experienced enough to know how to entice a man. She reached out a hand and placed it atop his. Brom closed his eyes. He didn't pull away, so she took that as an invitation. Her fingers skimmed over his hand, then ran up his arm and across his shoulder to his neck, finally settling on his cheek. The moment her palm cupped his face, Brom released a shaky breath.

When his lids reopened, his eyes blazed like gold. He moved so fast that it caught her by surprise. One moment, he was squatting beside her. The next, he was over her, one arm around her, pressing her against his hard body as he braced his other hand on the floor of the cave, holding them both up.

No words were spoken. It was simply there in their gazes, in the heat of their bodies. In the passion that wouldn't be denied.

Her chest heaved as his head lowered to hers. When her eyes closed and his lips met hers, she forgot about the cold, ignored her knee, disregarded her mission. In that instant, there was only the two of them. Time stood still for a heartbeat as something electrifying and thrilling rushed through her, enflaming her already raging desire to an inferno of need that only Brom could extinguish.

His lips moved over hers, nipping and nibbling as their kisses grew hotter, deeper. When his tongue slipped between her lips, she felt a tremor go through him. His hold tightened as he gently lowered her to the ground. A storm raged outside, but it couldn't outshine the passion between them that burned brighter than the sun.

When Brom lifted his head, she opened her eyes to find him staring down at her with a mixture of surprise and hunger. She knew exactly how he felt. Runa cupped her hands on either side of his face, then moved them around to the back of his neck so she could pull him down for another kiss.

In response, he ground his arousal against her, causing her to moan. She yanked at his tunic, trying to get it off him so she could run her hands over his body. He tore his lips from hers to rise up on his knees and yank off his shirt, tossing it aside to return to her. But she stopped him before he could kiss her again because she was finally getting to see him.

She placed her hands on his chest and gasped at the muscles beneath. The heat of him was scalding, the sinew firm and powerful. Her fingers traced his chest, moving around his nipples then down his stomach lined with muscles, all the way to his waist. She saw the outline of his arousal through his breeches.

Her eyes lifted to see him watching her, his breathing was erratic, and blatant hunger shone in his visage. She held his gaze as she opened his pants to free his cock. At the sight of him, her mouth grew dry, and her sex clenched. She wrapped her fingers around his rod, feeling the steel through the velvet of his skin as she slid her hand up and down his length.

A groan tore free from him. She looked up to see his teeth clenched, a muscle moving in his jaw as he squeezed his eyes shut. A feeling of empowerment filled her at the sight of him, knowing that what she was doing brought him pleasure. She wanted to continue stroking him, watching him, but all too soon, he got to his feet and stepped away.

Runa feared that he had changed his mind until she realized that he was removing the rest of his clothes. She started to do the same, but in a blink, he was before her, his hands over hers. He smiled and gave a shake of his head. When she started to speak, he put a finger over her lips to silence her.

It had been a long time since anyone had tried to tell her what to do. She liked that he did, however. She raised a brow and motioned for him to stand once more. When he complied, she saw the sly grin on his lips.

She sat up, taking in the man before her. Just like the first time she'd seen him, Runa recognized the warrior that he was

—even without a visible weapon. Her lips parted as she took in his broad shoulders that tapered to trim hips then down to his muscular legs. There wasn't an ounce of fat anywhere on his body. He was all hard muscle that her palms itched to learn. His cock jumped when her eyes landed on it, causing her to smile.

Runa reached for his arousal once more, but Brom shifted out of range and shook his head. He dropped to his knees and ran the backs of his knuckles down her cheek. The caress was featherlight and went straight to her heart. The way he touched her, the way he looked at her…no one had ever done that before. She knew, deep down, that no one would ever again.

He held her gaze as he smoothed his hands from her shoulders down her arms to her hips. He gathered the hem of her tunic in his hands and slowly began drawing it upwards. The first contact of his finger against her stomach made her catch her breath, but she didn't stop him. She raised her arms, helping him remove the shirt. Then he sat back and looked at her as she had gazed at him.

Beautiful didn't begin to describe her. Brom was stunned at the creature before him. Runa wasn't just lovely, she was stunning. He'd fantasized about what she looked like without her clothing, but nothing had prepared him for this. She took his breath away.

The muscles in her arms and shoulders were defined, proving that she regularly used her swords. Add that to her wonderful curves and pert breasts, flared hips, and impossibly long legs, and he'd never wanted a woman more. He was almost afraid to touch her, fearful that she was just a figment of his imagination. Worried that as soon as he reached for her, she would disappear and he'd wake back at his cottage.

Runa reached up and began to unplait her hair. He watched, mesmerized as more and more of the golden locks came undone and fell around her in soft waves. When she was finished, her hair fell down to her hips, cementing the ethereal thought he'd had when he first encountered her.

Runa's lips curved as she smiled at him before she slowly lay back on the floor of the cave, using their discarded clothing as a blanket. Brom leaned forward on his hands and crawled over her until he held himself over her body. Her arms wound around his neck as her blue eyes sparkled with the same need he felt within him.

Unable to deny either of them any longer, he kissed her, gradually lowering himself atop her, careful not to jar her injured knee. Just as before, it only took one touch of their mouths for the kiss to erupt. Their hands were suddenly all over each other, each trying to get closer to the other. He'd never felt such yearning before, never experienced such hunger.

And he couldn't wait to bury himself deep within her wet heat.

She couldn't get enough of him. Runa wanted to touch Brom everywhere. Something about their bare flesh touching triggered something within her. She almost didn't recognize the wanton that she was, but it was all because of Brom. He brought it out in her, this undeniable need, and irrefutable craving...*for him*.

When he found her breast and rolled an already hardened nipple between his fingers, she cried out and tore her mouth from his. Her back arched as pleasure shot straight to her sex. She needed to have him inside her immediately.

Runa desperately tried to reach for him, but her movements halted when he bent and wrapped his lips around her other nipple. All thought ceased. She was incapable of nothing more than experiencing the untold pleasure that swirled through her body.

But if she thought Brom would stop there, she was wrong. His lips traveled downward until he settled between her legs. She watched him, her breathing ragged as he hovered his lips above her. Then he winked before slowly moving his tongue over her sex and then stopping at her clit.

With one move, he captured her, taking her body prisoner as he leisurely kissed between her legs. Each time she felt an orgasm approaching, he shifted slightly and changed his pace until she built back up, again and again. And again.

With sweat covering her flesh, she cried out his name, needing him to give her release. But he didn't heed her. He continued teasing until she was mindless with need, her body his to mold as he wanted. Only then did he give her the final push when she was on the edge of release. She fell, floating upon clouds of ecstasy as her body convulsed with pleasure she hadn't known was possible. The climax went on for what felt like ages. Just when she was beginning to come down, he filled her.

Runa cried out from the feeling of him sliding into her. She'd wanted this from the first moment she saw him. Finally, he was where he was supposed to be. It took everything she had to open her eyes and look at him leaning over her, his hands braced on either side of her face. She placed her palm on his chest and wrapped her legs around him. She felt a slight pull from her knee, but the pain was overshadowed by the pleasure.

Seeing her climax, hearing her screams had only fueled Brom's raging desire. He'd barely held back from plunging inside her when she bucked against him with her orgasm. Then he hadn't been able to think of anything but being inside her.

Once his cock slid inside, something within him that had always made him feel as though he were lost disappeared. It was as if he had found the thing he'd always been looking for. As if he had come home.

He began rocking his hips slowly, enjoying the feel of her. When she locked her legs around his waist, all he could think about was finding his release. His thrusts grew harder, longer as he drove into her again and again, their moans filling the cave.

The climax came upon him quickly. He pumped his hips furiously, driving into her hard and fast until it claimed him.

8

Rothiemurchus Forest

Sybbyl had never known such fury. She stood on a small knoll and stared out over the faces of the witches who had come when she called, as well as the Gira who had joined her. She usually found peace and solace in a Witch's Grove, but nothing could bring that now other than Avis's death.

She kept her cloak closed so no one could see the wounds on her neck and wrist that had yet to heal. Her battle with Helena had taken much out of her. She'd expected it to be replaced by the Staff of the Eternal—and it had been, to an extent. However, no spell was able to heal her.

The black crown atop her head denoted her as queen, but not just to the Coven or the Gira. She was queen of the world. It wouldn't be long before everyone knew that. Avis, the idiot, had actually thought she could compete with her. It was laughable, really. Avis had potential, but her magic couldn't compare to Sybbyl's, not even with the sword Avis had stolen.

"We've been deceived," she said to the crowd who stood in

silence before her, waiting for her to speak. "One of ours has disobeyed a direct order and gone out on her own."

Sybbyl had done the same thing. It was why she was leading the Coven now. But Avis wasn't that smart. Or powerful. All this did was prolong the time it would take for Sybbyl to wipe out the Varroki and take over the world.

And she was tired of waiting.

"Avis, who I initially took under my wing to instruct, has betrayed us. I sent her after a Hunter. It just so happens that Hunter met up with a man who had a bone of the First Witch."

A gasp went through the group. The Coven had been looking for those bones since Trea, the First Witch, died. Trea had known how powerful she was and suspected that others might wish to use her magic. She'd had her most trustworthy followers burn her body, then distributed the bones amongst them and scattered them far and wide. It had taken centuries, but finally, the bones were being found.

Sybbyl might not have the Blood Skull or the Heart of the First Witch right now, but it was only a matter of time before they fell into her hands. She could take over the world with just her magic and the staff, but she wanted more. Because she knew the only ones who had a chance of defeating her were the Varroki. If she could wipe them out before they could come at her, then the world was hers for the taking.

"Avis was supposed to bring me the bone," Sybbyl continued. "Instead, she has vanished."

Laughter sounded in her head. She knew it was coming from the staff. The bone had been talking to her for some time, reading her thoughts, and even trying to lie to her. Sybbyl ignored the laughter, even as it grew louder and louder.

"You think you have it all planned out, but you don't."

She wanted to tell the voice to shut up, but Sybbyl

managed to keep her comments to herself. Her gaze swept from left to right across the crowd of faces. "We've lived in the shadows for too long, hiding what we are and what we can do. We're the ones with magic, and yet we allow others who have none to dictate what we can and can't do. They burn us, hang us, and torture us. Because they fear us!"

A cry of agreement went up.

Sybbyl smiled. "All my life, I've known we should be in power. We're the ones who should be in control. The Hunters tried to contain us, but they're finished now. There are a few stragglers, but they can't harm us. Look around the land. See how those without magic hide in fear. They do that because of *me*," she stated, pointing to her chest. "I showed them what was coming. I gave them a taste of the terror we've lived with for far too long."

Another cheer sounded, this one louder and longer than the last.

"We've nearly reached our goal, my friends. The world is waiting for us to take it. There are only two things we need to do first. We find Avis and get the second bone. Then, we go after the Varroki."

As the cries of agreement filled the air, Sybbyl turned her head and looked at where Asrail hung suspended from a tree by her arms. The former queen of the Gira didn't hide her contempt as she glared at Sybbyl. She respected the nymph for that. Some would've done anything to gain Sybbyl's favor, but not Asrail. She had been resolute in her opposition.

"I'm not the only one who wants justice," Sybbyl said when there was silence once more. She motioned to the Gira. "They were betrayed by their queen long ago. It's only now that Asrail has been found. The nymph hid her granddaughter from those of her own kind who decided to end the child's life. Synne, the Hunter Avis went after, is half-nymph."

Sybbyl met Asrail's gaze. "You've only delayed what was meant to happen many years ago, Asrail. Your granddaughter would've been too young to know what was happening then. Now, she'll suffer as an adult."

Asrail barked out a laugh. "If you think Synne will come, you're delusional. I mean nothing to her. She only just met me."

The Gira hissed in anger.

Sybbyl lifted a hand to quiet them. She didn't have any control over them, but because she led the Coven and had taken a bone of the First Witch, they had pledged themselves to her. She wasn't stupid enough to believe they wouldn't change their minds in the next heartbeat, so she was careful about how she treated them. It was one of the reasons she had taken Asrail.

"You went to great lengths to save her," Sybbyl said. "You gave up your throne, watched your son and his human wife be slaughtered. But you saved Synne. I know for a fact the Hunter will come for you. And we'll be waiting for her."

"It would be suicide for her to come. Synne is needed. I've lived my years. She knows this." Asrail looked away as if ending the conversation.

But Sybbyl was the one in control. "Oh, I'm going to make sure she comes."

She gave a nod to the Gira, who surrounded Asrail. They weren't gentle as they pulled the former queen down and dragged her away. As far as Sybbyl knew, there hadn't been another queen of the Gira since Asrail. She assumed one would've come forward to speak to her. Then again, the nymphs acted as one. Perhaps the queen was already amongst them. Not that it mattered. They could do whatever they wanted, as long as they helped her win against the Varroki.

There had been many, many clans of Gira. They had eventually come together to form one large tribe. She had witnessed the Gira kill nymphs who tried to leave. They, like the Coven, didn't take no for an answer and didn't handle defectors. It's why the Gira were so strong and moved as one.

After the nymphs left to do whatever they had planned for Asrail, Sybbyl turned back to the witches. "I want four groups looking for Avis's sister, Elin. The witch actually believes she can hide from us. Her magic is strong. We could use her. As for Avis, I suspect she'll try to return. No one stop her. Let her come to me."

More laughter filled her head. How Sybbyl hated the voice.

"Want to be rid of me? Then give the staff away. It's that easy."

Sybbyl had dreamed of ruling her entire life. She wasn't going to throw that way because of some voice in her head.

9

If only they could pretend they were the only two people in the world. Runa knew it was a dream she could never make a reality, but it was nice to imagine. She lay with Brom, their limbs intertwined as the fire popped. Her cheek rested on his chest as he played with her hair. She was so content that she didn't even feel the pain in her knee anymore.

The silence between them wasn't awkward. It was comfortable, each lost in his or her thoughts. Even the wildcat had curled up and gone to sleep. Now that the flush of sex was gone, Runa once more felt the cold from the blizzard.

"The storm doesna appear to have died down at all," Brom said.

She shook her head. "I think it'll go all night."

"That's a lot of snow."

Runa twisted her lips. "It won't be easy to travel, that's for sure."

"Then wait a day or two. Your knee could probably use it anyway."

"I can't."

A beat of silence passed before Brom said, "You're on a schedule."

"Something like that."

"I see."

She waited for him to ask her about what, but he didn't. That's when she realized that he wouldn't. He wouldn't ask because he didn't want to share anything about himself, and if he wasn't willing to share, then neither would she. And he was right. Besides, he wouldn't react well if she told him everything. No one had the few times she'd actually told others.

"I doona know what brought me to you or why, but I'm supposed to be here. I doona think you can argue that point." He blew out a breath. "I want to help you, but I doona think you're going to let me."

She rose up on her elbow to look at him. "You're right. I won't. This isn't your fight. It's mine."

"It isna coincidence that your face came to me in a dream. It isna coincidence that I found you so quickly. And it isna coincidence that our attraction is so fierce. Like it or no', lass, we're meant to be together."

"As good as that sounds, I know from experience that it isn't. We're attracted to each other, and I'm going to take full advantage of that because I like how you make me feel. I like being with you like this. But in the morning, we'll go our separate ways."

"I can follow you."

She sighed and glanced away. "And I can make sure you don't." She took a breath.

"There are things about me you don't know."

He quirked a brow. "There are things about me *you* doona know."

"Brom, please. I'm doing you a favor. You don't want to be anywhere near me where I'm going."

"Because I doona carry a sword."

She lay back on his chest and shook her head. "That has nothing to do with it. What I'm going to face is…something only I can do."

"I understand."

"You do?" she asked in surprise. She'd expected him to argue more.

He gave a single nod. "Aye."

Runa should feel happy that they didn't spend their time arguing, but she couldn't help but be disappointed that Brom hadn't tried harder. She'd never had such conflicting emotions before, and she didn't like it. What she'd told Brom was the truth. He couldn't help her against the Gira or the Coven. Not only did he not have a sword, but he also didn't have magic. She would be leading him to certain death.

They why did she want to cry at leaving him behind? She'd been gloriously happy just moments ago. Now, she wanted to wail at the unfairness of it all. Runa stared at the flames of the fire. Brom continued to hold her and play with her hand. He threaded the fingers of his other hand through her hair, relaxing her. She had never known she might like someone to play with her hair. Now, she wanted Brom to do it for the rest of her life—it felt so good.

She wasn't sure when it happened, but she finally fell asleep. When she woke, she was still on Brom's chest with his arms around her, but she no longer heard the howl of the snowstorm. She blinked, shocked to find the fire still burned. Runa was surprised that she had slept through Brom tending to it. Normally, she was a very light sleeper. Then again, she'd been injured the day before, then had sex with an amazing man. It was enough to tire anyone out.

"It's no' quite dawn," he whispered as he kissed her forehead.

Runa smiled and snuggled closer to him. "The storm has passed."

"I'll get dressed and take a look at everything in a moment. Right now, I'm enjoying you against me."

"I'm enjoying that, as well," she told him as she shifted to look at him.

They shared a smile. What they had found in the cave was...well, magical, for lack of a better word. The moment they left, they would lose that connection. If only she could take a day and spend it with Brom just as they were.

"You're frowning," he said as he touched her face reverently. "What is it?"

Instead of telling him the truth, which would bring about the talk from the night before, she said, "I'm glad you found me."

"I'd like to think that wouldna cause you to frown," he said with a grin.

She chuckled and ducked her head, holding him tighter. "I wish my life was different."

"You have control of your life. You get to decide what you can and can no' do. Where you will and willna go."

"You make it sound so simple."

"Because it is," he replied.

She drew in a breath and slowly released it as she sat up to look at him. "You've done more for me in a few hours than anyone has my entire life. The way you look at me, hold me, touch me. It's absolutely incredible. I never dreamed I would find anyone like you."

He sat up, leaning his weight on one hand. "I can say the same about you. I know something special when I find it, lass, and we have it."

"I know. That's what makes leaving so difficult."

"My offer to go with you still stands."

She smiled, tears filling her eyes. The last time she had cried was when Morea died. How Runa hated tears. "I wish with all my heart you could come with me."

He smiled and pulled her close for a soft kiss. Then he pressed his forehead to hers. "I'll always be with you."

With that, he rose and began to dress. Runa wanted to stop time so none of this would happen. She turned to reach for her clothes and felt something wet hit her leg. That's when she realized that she was indeed crying. She hastily wiped the tears away and began to dress. It wasn't until she thought about her breeches that she looked at her knee. The kneecap and surrounding area were different shades of blue, black, and purple. She carefully touched it and then hissed as pain exploded. She jerked her hand away. If touching it caused that much pain, there was no way she could walk on it. She looked up to find Brom watching her.

He jerked his chin to her knee. "I was afraid of that. Walking in this snow on the mountain will be extremely painful. And you would be doing more damage than good. Wherever you're going, I gather you doona wish to be injured."

"Nay, I don't," she said.

He looked outside the cave then back at her. "Even if I carry you, I fear I'll still do damage to the knee. You need rest."

"That's time I don't have."

"It's your decision." He finished pulling on his boots. "I'm going to see if I can find us some food."

That's when she realized that they hadn't eaten last night. Her stomach chose that moment to grumble.

Brom chuckled. "I'll be back as soon as I can. Stay off that knee until I get back."

He pulled a blanket out of his bag and tossed it to her.

With a wink, he was gone, leaving her entirely to her thoughts. She wrapped herself in the blanket and looked at her knee. After a few moments, she tried to move it. Pain shot through her leg, causing her gasp and bend over.

Even if she wanted to head out, there was no way she could. Not in the mountains in the middle of winter. The problem was, she wouldn't heal in one day. She needed weeks, if not months to fully recover. And her family didn't have that kind of time.

10

The clear sky was beautiful after several days of no sun, but Brom couldn't enjoy it as he usually would because his thoughts were on Runa. If he'd learned anything about her in their short time together, it was that she didn't like being told what to do.

She wanted to leave regardless of her injury. He knew when he returned to the cave that she would be gone. It was why he'd left. No matter what she said, he would follow her. Letting her get a head start made that easy.

He sank into the freshly fallen snow as he made his way through the forest. With the storm gone, he saw more signs of animals. It didn't take him long to track down a game bird. On his way back to the cave, he checked the area for signs of anyone, but there was nothing but animal prints.

Brom steeled himself as he neared the cave. He told himself that Runa didn't leave because she didn't want to be with him. She left because she had something she needed to do. He would take the time to eat before he started tracking her. It would be easy in the snow. And she'd never know it.

Though, he would have a hard time keeping his distance from her after having her in his arms.

Being with her made him feel as if he'd found the other half of himself. As if their souls had been severed at birth and were now one again. It didn't matter why Asa had come to him in his dreams to tell him to look for Runa. Now that he had found her and had been with her, he never wanted to be away from her again.

He stopped outside of the cave and drew in a deep breath. Then he turned the corner to enter. The sight of Runa tending to the fire made him want to rush to her and scoop her up into his arms so he could kiss her.

She looked up at him and smiled. The rush of emotion that went through him made him weak in the knees. He didn't want to think about that or the fact that she could cause such a reaction in him. He was simply overjoyed that she was still there.

"I tried putting on clothes, but it hurt too badly," she said as she huddled under the blanket. "I'm glad you left me this."

He tossed the bird onto the ground and took out his remaining peat. He'd used magic last night to keep the fire going while she slept, but he couldn't continue that because she'd notice. Even though a part of him had wanted her to ask if he had used magic. He couldn't explain it, but the need to keep his secret from her wasn't as great as before.

"That should be enough to cook the grouse," she said.

When she began reaching for the bird, he shook his head. "I'll get to it after I return from finding some wood."

"Whatever you find will be wet."

He nodded in agreement as he strode out. With whispered words, he said a spell to keep the fire going. Brom knew it would be difficult to find dry wood, but what other choice did he have? He had to dig beneath the snow, but he finally gathered an armload of wood. Except that it was wet—just as he knew it would be.

On the way back to the cave, he debated whether to use magic to dry it. He decided that would be too obvious, so he opted to leave it as it was to dry out in the cave. When he walked inside, he found she'd removed the feathers from the bird. One look at Runa's pale face, and he knew she'd gotten up to take the feathers away.

"How bad is the pain?" he asked as he hurried to her.

She shook her head. "I'm fine."

"I didna ask that. I asked about the pain." He held her gaze until she relented.

With a small smile, she said, "I won't be going anywhere today. And maybe not tomorrow."

Brom wanted to rejoice at the news, but the distress that flashed in her eyes wiped it away. He could help her with his magic. It would only take a little while before she was healed and on her way. To do that would mean telling her who he was, though—as well as letting her go.

"I was in such a hurry," she said and tugged the blanket closer. "I should've paid more attention."

He said nothing as he took the bird and one of the sticks he'd gathered to set over the flame. A sound drew his attention. When he looked to the side, he found the wildcat watching them.

"He's been eyeing the bird since you brought it in," Runa said with a laugh.

Brom tore off a piece of the bird and tossed it near the cat. The feline didn't rush toward it. Instead, his yellow eyes stayed on Brom until he turned away. Then, out of the corner of his eye, Brom saw the cat slowly slink toward the meat. When he was close enough, he snatched it with his teeth and hurried back to his corner.

"The weather has cleared," Brom told her.

She looked out the entrance, nodding. "I can see the sky. It's been days since I've seen the sun. Any more storms?"

"It's Scotland, they show up when you least expect them."

"What is it? You're acting different."

He sat across from her with the fire between them. Brom leaned to the side with a hand supporting him. "You're playing it off well, but I can tell you're disappointed that you can no' set out to do whatever it is you're on your way to do."

Her gaze slid away for several seconds before she looked at him. "I never knew my family. A friend of my grandmother's raised me. I only learned a few days ago that my grandmother is still alive. And I have a sister."

"You're going to meet them?"

"They're mixed up in some…danger," she said.

Now it made sense. Her urgency, telling him that he would get hurt. "How near are you to finding them?"

"Close. At least, my grandmother."

How could Brom not help her now? He knew very little about Runa, and no matter how he'd asked, Asa refused to tell him anything. He didn't know if Runa knew about magic or the Coven or the Varroki. If she did know and he told her, she might use it against him or tell others who would then hunt him. Or…she could be so repulsed by him that she'd try to use her swords on him again.

In the end, it really didn't matter. He'd been sent after her, and he'd come to care about her. Deeply. He'd never be able to live with himself if he *didn't* help her—no matter the outcome.

"If your leg was healed, would you leave?" he asked.

She studied him for a heartbeat before she nodded. "Not because I want to leave you, but because I must do this for my family."

Brom rose and walked around the fire to sit beside her.

When he reached to pull aside the blanket, she put a hand on his arm.

"What are you doing?" she asked.

"Healing you."

Her brows drew together. "I don't understand."

Brom sighed, his heart heavy. He swallowed and looked at the ground. "I doona trust anyone. Ever. It's one of the key reasons I live alone. I'm different than others. I can...do things." He lifted his hand and thought the spell. The magic shot from his hand to the fire as the flames roared upward for an instant. Only then did he look at her. "I have magic, Runa. It will heal you. If you'll allow me."

"You're a warlock?" she asked in a soft voice.

So, she *did* know about magic. Brom wasn't sure how to feel about that. "I am."

"The only known warlocks are the Varroki."

Brom nodded once.

Her blue eyes widened, her mouth parting as if she wanted to say something. She must have thought better of it because she licked her lips. "You're wise to keep that secret. Some would use it against you."

"Will you? You obviously know of magic to speak so freely about the Varroki and warlocks."

"I won't tell anyone your secret, but things are dangerous right now."

He briefly raised his brows. "I know."

"If I allow you to heal me, I still don't want you to come with me."

"We'd do better to stick together and watch each other's backs."

A sad smile touched her lips. "I would agree at any other time. But not this one."

"I can take care of myself."

"Brom," she said and put her hand atop his. "The very last place you should be is with me when I leave here, especially if you want your secret to remain hidden."

He wasn't convinced that he couldn't help her, but he let it go. For just a moment, he almost asked if she was going up against the Coven, but he didn't think she would do that. She didn't have magic. If she did, she would've healed herself.

Brom moved aside the blanket and gently cupped his hands over her bare knee. He closed his eyes and began whispering the healing spell. He felt the magic shift from him into Runa. Over and over, he said the spell, until he sensed that her injury had been mended fully. Then he lowered his hands and looked at her. To his surprise, her eyes were filled with tears.

"I...felt it," she told him in a soft voice. "Your magic. I felt it. It was...amazing. Mesmerizing. Euphoric."

He blinked, taken aback by her words for a moment. He'd never heard of anyone being able to feel magic like that before. When a tear fell and rolled down her cheek, he reached up and caught it with the edge of his finger before he brought it to his lips and tasted it with his tongue.

They stared at each other, neither speaking. Runa leaned forward and pressed her lips to his. He wrapped his arms around her and pulled her against him so their bodies were flush. While he didn't regret healing her or telling her his secret, he knew she was about to leave. And even knowing that he would follow her didn't stop the ache that grew in his chest.

She lifted her head and caressed her fingers down his beard. "Thank you."

"You're going to want to eat before you leave. You need your strength."

Brom set her away before he made love to her all day. It's what he wanted, what he craved. But no matter how much he wanted to keep her here with him, he couldn't. He knew all about the pull of family.

As he saw to the roasting bird, Runa dressed. He watched her, captivated by everything she did. She tested her knee, then flashed him a bright smile when she was able to bend it and put weight on it, seemingly without any pain. He couldn't help but grin. When she finished dressing, he noticed that the various shades of brown of her attire only highlighted her golden hair even more.

She sat across from him and took out a comb from her bag. After brushing the length until all the tangles were gone, she began braiding the strands. He couldn't look away, watching as her fingers moved quickly and effortlessly to shift the hair this way and that, plait after plait after plait. When she finished, she had one braid running down the middle of her head from her forehead back with two smaller ones next to it. She brought the three braids together to make one large plait that she let hang down her back.

"I could watch you do that all day."

She chuckled and shook out her arms. "It's exhausting, but it keeps it out of my face."

"I love it. The color, the length, the way it feels running through my fingers."

Her expression grew serious when she said, "And I loved you touching it."

Letting her go would be the single hardest thing he'd ever done. Trailing her or not, he knew there was a good chance that this might be their last hours together.

11

The food was eaten all too soon, and there was no other reason for Runa to remain. Her family was in danger, but a part of her was reluctant to—nay, insistent that she not —leave Brom. The fact that he'd revealed he was a warlock only confirmed that he should stay as far from her as possible.

They stood at the cave's entrance, facing each other, but she couldn't leave. This place had come to mean something incredibly special, and it tore her to pieces to walk away from it. No matter the reason.

"When I'm done, I'll look for you," she told him.

Brom gave her a crooked grin. "I'll hold you to that."

She didn't bother to add *if I survive*. That would only ruin the moment.

"You'll be fine," he said as he took her hands. "Watch your back."

Runa nodded as her throat clogged with emotion. She almost blurted out that she was half-Gira but changed her mind at the last minute. It was just a reason to stay, she realized. The story was a long one, and it would mean spending more time with Brom. It was what she wanted, but if she got to her grandmother or sister too late, she would never forgive herself.

If she survived this run-in with the Coven and the Gira, she would search until the end of time for Brom and tell him everything. But that wasn't going to be today.

She looked at the wildcat, still watching them from his side of the cave. "Good luck," she told him. Then she looked at Brom. "Stay safe."

"You, too."

"Don't follow me. Please. I couldn't bear it if anything happened to you."

His forehead creased. "What are you walking into?"

"Something that doesn't involve you."

"I'm beginning to feel that perhaps it should. Tell me I'm wrong to think there's a chance you willna come back from this."

She didn't want to lie to him, so Runa decided not to reply at all.

Brom turned away and released a string of curses. Then he stopped and turned back to her. "Why would you go into something like that alone?"

"Because this is my fight."

"You feel what's between us. We'll be stronger together."

She smiled, wishing with all her heart that he was right. "Last night was the best of my life. I'll find you again. You have my word. In this life or the next, we'll be together again."

Before he could argue, she walked to him and rose up to place her mouth on his. His hands grasped her face and held her to him as his lips lingered on hers. She pulled away and turned on her heel to walk out as her eyes prickled. With every step, she felt her heart breaking.

She dashed the tears away. No matter how hard she tried, she couldn't stop crying. With her feet crunching on the snow, she kept her gaze focused ahead. She was also aware that Brom would follow her. He'd given up the fight not to go with her too easily. And since he'd come after her once already, she knew he'd do it again.

But Runa had a plan. One he'd never suspect.

A part of her was excited by the prospect of seeing him again, but she knew it would only worsen the ache that already filled her.

She kept walking, no matter how much she cried or her heart urged her to turn back. Her conscience argued that she didn't know her grandmother or sister. That they wouldn't care if she came to help them or not. Runa didn't listen. It was merely a reason—any reason—for her to go back to Brom.

With him, she could have a good life. A quiet existence. They could disappear somewhere together and spend their days making love and growing old—if she never told him what she was. If he never learned that she had Gira blood running through her veins.

How many years would they have before the Gira stumbled upon them? How long would they have if Sybbyl and the Coven won and took over the world? No, she had no choice but to keep going with her mission. Asrail had sacrificed everything to save Synne. Morea had also given up all that she had to secret Runa away.

Runa might not remember her parents or that fateful day, she might not even know Asrail, but that didn't mean she would turn away from doing the right thing. And if Synne were anything like her, then she would do whatever she could to help Asrail, as well. Which was why it was doubly important that Runa get there as quickly as possible. She hoped that her dalliance with Brom hadn't stopped her from being able to help.

She couldn't even be angry at Brom for not healing her the

night before. He might have shared his secret, but she had kept hers. All of them. She didn't want to tell him and face his revulsion. Because there was a very real possibility that he would be repulsed. Especially once she showed him....

Runa halted her thoughts there. She didn't want to go down that road. She didn't know how Brom would react because she'd been too much of a coward to tell him. And she was scared because she knew how others had responded when they learned the truth. Her night with Brom had been epic and amazing and magical, and she refused to ruin that. Or even taint the memory with how she imagined Brom might react.

She gritted her teeth and climbed up an especially difficult section of the mountain. There was likely an easier way, but she didn't want to take the time to find it. She wanted to go straight as the crow flew. She had no pain in her knee, showing how powerful Brom's magic was. Then again, a warlock's power was usually strong since there were so few of them.

Witches, however, were everywhere. Runa had always thought it odd that there were no warlocks outside of the Varroki. What was it that made them so special? Why did other magic not move into the males as it did the females? There had to be something that made the difference. Whatever it was, Brom had it.

And for a brief moment in time, he'd been Runa's. She hadn't lied to him. In this life or the next, they *would* be together again.

When emotion began to choke her once more, she pushed aside all thoughts of Brom and their night. Of magic and secrets. Instead, she started plotting how to get through the Gira to find her grandmother. There were few options left to her, but there had to be something the Gira wanted in return for freeing Asrail. Whatever it was, Runa would find it.

As for Synne, if Runa had to tackle her sister to stop her, she would do it. Synne had been raised a Hunter. She knew how to track and kill witches just as Runa did. What Runa didn't know was if Synne had the same...skills...as Runa did as a result of being part Gira.

Runa's fingers were stiff with the cold by the time she reached the top of the mountain. She stood amongst the tall pines and looked out over the Cairngorms. They were a spectacle to behold. She had been here only a handful of times before, but it had always mesmerized her. From the steep crags, to the tall trees and the mist-shrouded peaks, she understood why the Gira loved this area.

The forests were vast, giving them ample opportunity to find humans stupid enough to follow their whispers. The immensity of the woods also gave the Gira more hiding places. Which made it perfect for Runa. The only problem was that the Gira could detect her human blood, which made her a target.

She had kept them away for years now, but only because she'd agreed to work for them. The fact that she was here for Asrail would mean the Gira wouldn't give her any quarter. They would attack her the first chance they got. The nymphs were predictable. They had used the same tactics for centuries now, and they believed that no one could beat them. Runa would prove them wrong.

She knew all their secrets, all their schemes, because she had been raised by a Gira. It was for that reason alone that Runa had thought she could find a place among the nymphs. They had quickly divested her of that notion. In return, she'd started taking payment to hunt them. And it hadn't taken her long to build a reputation of someone who always found her mark.

They didn't know how she did it. No one but Morea did. And since she was gone, no one else ever would.

Runa lifted her gaze to the sky to see clouds beginning to roll in. Breath billowed past her lips, creating a cloud. She missed Brom's warmth, and she knew it would be some time before she was warm again. This was the price she paid for helping her family.

She wished she had Morea with her. It would have been nice to have someone watching her back. Her thoughts drifted to Brom, but she shut them down again. He was a distraction she couldn't afford. From here on out, she needed to make sure every step, every move, every word was done just right. Otherwise, she would pay with her life.

Runa drew in a deep breath and looked down the mountain to where the forest grew even thicker. This was her last chance to turn back. Once she started the descent, there would be no changing her mind.

She might like the notion of magic. She might even like the idea of witches being able to walk freely without persecution. But she wouldn't stand by and watch Sybbyl and the Coven take over the world. It wasn't a perfect scenario, but there wasn't such a thing. There was only good and bad and the balance between both.

Sybbyl had altered that balance dramatically, and the Gira had helped. Someone had to take a stand. The Hunters had done that and been squashed by Sybbyl in the process. The only ones left were the Varroki. Runa knew little about them other than that they had warlocks and lived in a secret location that couldn't be found unless they wanted you to find it.

The Varroki might well be able to save the day—eventually —but she wasn't going to wait around for someone else to do what she could. Too many sat back and let others do the hard work. That wasn't Runa.

She had been raised by a dedicated, strong Gira, who had loved her. Runa's parents had thrown caution to the wind for their love. They'd had a few years together and two daughters, but in the end, the nymphs had caught up with them and cut short their happy life. Runa and Synne should have been killed, as well. But somehow, they had survived.

Now, the Gira were going to pay for what they did to her parents, and whatever they had done to Asrail.

Runa started down the mountain, a plan forming.

12

Blackglade

Armir walked up the tower's winding steps as the bitter wind of winter blew from the sea and iced everything in its path. He pulled his fur-lined cloak tighter around him as he reached Malene's door. The Lady of the Varroki had once been a frightened young girl who had resisted her destiny.

Now, she was a woman who embraced all that she was and had become the leader long prophesied for the Varroki. She might be petite, but the power running through her veins was tremendous. He didn't think she had a clue how much she had —not yet, anyway. Soon, Malene would be tested.

He knocked on the door and then opened it. A look inside showed the chambers empty. He glanced upward and shook his head. He should've known she would head to the top of the tower. It was her favorite place, a destination she went to when she needed to think.

Armir backed out of the room and shut the door before continuing up the last flight of stairs to the top of the tower. A gust of wind barreled into him when he reached the last step. He had to bend against the force so he wasn't blown back. Blinking, he raised his hand to block the wind and searched for Malene. He found her standing in the middle of the tower, her cloak billowing around her. But her long, flaxen locks set against the stormy sky were what captured his attention.

It was his duty as second in command to go out into the world and find a new Lady of the Varroki whenever one died. The fact that the magic chose young girls not in their city made it difficult to convince them to follow him. Some, he had taken by force. Because once they were chosen, they were the only ones who could lead.

He remembered the day he'd found Malene. She had been frightened and wary, but she had gone with him. Once in Blackglade, she had begged to return home. Under the weight of her duties, she had faltered several times. They all did. Many didn't even last a year. Those who did hadn't made it past five.

Then there was Malene.

After she'd accepted that she wouldn't be leaving, she had settled into her role as Lady, but she hadn't truly embraced it until the past year. And in that time, everything had changed for the Varroki. Because of Malene, they actually had a chance at survival now. Because of Malene, they would defeat Sybbyl and end the Coven once and for all.

Armir knew it in his soul. Malene was the first Lady in a very long time to have the blue radiance in both hands. It was a particularly strong magic that only existed in those chosen to lead the Varroki.

He braced himself against the wind and took the last step to the top. With his gaze locked on Malene, he walked to her, noting that she leaned into the wind with her arms out. When he reached her, he saw she was smiling with her eyes closed.

Only Malene would dare to venture to the top of the tower in such weather and bask in its perilous splendor.

But that's why she was so unique.

It was also why he loved her.

And why he could never have her.

Without opening her eyes, she shifted her hand and touched his arm. Her hand traveled down until she threaded her fingers with his. He didn't even bother to wonder how she'd known he was there. Malene was the epitome of all the Varroki stood for. She might not have been born one of them, but not a single soul in all of Blackglade didn't adore her and embrace her as one of theirs.

He let his gaze slowly move over her face. The delight etched into every crevice made his breath lock in his lungs. She looked at everything with love and wonder, welcoming it and enfolding it into herself so she could experience every beautiful and ugly thing about it. It was because of her that Armir had hope. It was because of her that he looked at everything differently now.

Even with the threat that loomed over them from Sybbyl and the Coven, and Lachlan's sword with the bone of the First Witch having been stolen, Malene didn't let that stop her. She simply shifted focus and tried to forge a new path.

Her eyes opened, her soft gray orbs moving to look at him. Armir was powerless against returning her smile. He tightened his hold on her fingers as their gazes held. Slowly, she shifted to face him. As she did, he moved closer to her. It was pure instinct to wrap his arm around her when she got caught by the wind. He knew dragging her against his body was the wrong thing to do. He knew he should release her or at least put some distance between them, but he couldn't seem to make himself do either.

As he looked into her eyes, he didn't try to ignore or push

away the feelings for her that had developed over the years. Once, his position had been one of celibacy. He hadn't cared because there had never been anyone he imagined sharing his life with. Then Malene came along and wormed her way into his heart little by little until he couldn't remember a time when she hadn't been a part of his life.

Many positions in the Varroki demanded celibacy. As a result, it had caused a decline in the Varroki numbers over time. Being the Lady of the Varroki, Malene had the ability to change that. Any of the other Ladies could have, as well, but Malene had been the one to read all the books bestowed upon those in her position. She was the one who'd learned how to change such laws, and then made sure to do it.

Because of her, Armir could have a wife now. Because of her, he could give in to the desires raging through him.

Touching the Lady was something no one was supposed to do. Not even him. And yet, he had found ways throughout the years to snatch small touches here and there. Like now. Except, each time he did, it became more and more difficult to let her go. Every fiber of his being bellowed at him to tell her how he felt, to kiss her and show her how good things could be between them.

Yet, he didn't.

He had been honed by too many years of rules. Then there was the fact that he wasn't sure how Malene felt about him. He liked his position and the ability it gave him to be near her. If he told her about his feelings, and she didn't return them, then she would replace him. And he would lose everything. If what he had with her now was all he could ever have, he'd take it. Because it was better than nothing.

A frown marred her forehead as she blinked up at him. "What's wrong?"

The wind yanked her words away, but he read her lips.

Armir shifted so the wind was to his back, blocking it from hitting her. "Synne and Lachlan are getting anxious."

"They have been for days."

"Something has changed."

Malene's gaze slid away as she let her mind wander. Armir knew she was letting her magic sift through everything. She had the uncanny ability to see things from distant places. Her visions had granted them access to things they otherwise wouldn't have known.

He remained silent until Malene's eyes jerked back to him. "What is it?"

"I'm not sure," she said warily. "Something has changed. I can't pinpoint exactly what it is, though. Did Synne say something specific?"

Armir shook his head. "She simply said the trees were irritated."

"They aren't talking to her?"

"Nay. They're giving off a feeling of impatience and frustration."

Malene was silent for a moment. "I missed that."

"You can't see or feel everything. You have many duties."

"My *duty* is to protect this city. Blackglade is our home."

He bent to capture her gaze and held it. "Your magic is what keeps us shielded from the outside world. Your magic has given us more power than we've had in generations. You have allowed us a giant leap in a new direction. Then there is everything you did for those fighting the Coven. Shall I list everything with Edra and Radnar, Leoma and Braith, Ravyn and Carac, Helena and Jarin, and Synne and Lachlan?"

"I didn't save Edra or Radnar or anyone else at the abbey."

"You've done so much more. Don't let the weight of the dead drag you down. Too many count on you to allow that to happen."

She blew out a breath. "You're right, but I'll never forget the sight of those bodies at the abbey."

"It's one of the many reasons we're fighting Sybbyl and the Coven."

"And the Gira," she added.

Armir had a particular dislike for the nymphs. They kept far from the Varroki, and the Varroki kept their distance from the Gira. When the two clashed in the past, the result was devastating for both sides. It was the prime reason the nymphs had never thrown in to support the Coven. All that had changed when Sybbyl took over.

Synne being at Blackglade had given the Varroki an advantage because she could communicate with the trees thanks to the half of her blood that came from the nymphs. No one in Blackglade had told her how a tenuous truce between the Varroki and the Gira existed, going back centuries.

With everything coming to a head soon, Synne would have to fight the nymphs. Since they were responsible for helping to kill everyone at the abbey, that wouldn't be a problem. The issue was Asrail, Synne's grandmother. The former queen of the Gira was being held by the Coven.

"You're thinking of Asrail," Malene said.

Armir nodded. "We need to make a decision soon before Synne takes it out of our hands."

"She was always going to take it out of our hands."

His brows snapped together. "You intend to let her go out there?"

"Let her?" Malene laughed. "I have no hold over her or Lachlan. They've been able to leave anytime they want. Lachlan has known that all along, but he, like us, has been buying time."

Once more, Malene had surprised him. Just when Armir thought he knew everything, Malene saw an aspect he hadn't.

He'd been fully prepared to tie Synne and Lachlan down to keep them from leaving. They were too important in the fight against the Coven to let them loose to try and free Asrail.

"For?" Armir pressed.

Malene shrugged. "That's just it, I don't know. It's only a feeling."

None of her feelings had ever led the Varroki wrong, so he wouldn't ignore her words. "What do you need me to do?"

"What you always do. Stand by me and protect Blackglade."

His prime directive was to help guide the Lady—and protect her at all costs. And he would adhere to that until his dying breath. "Always."

A soft smile curved Malene's lips. "I don't know what I'd do without you."

"You don't need me. You don't need anyone."

"That's not true," she said as her smile faded.

Her free hand came up to rest on his arm, her other still entangled with his. If anyone looked at them, they might think that he and Malene were lovers. Every night, his dreams were filled with him making love to her. And each morning when he woke and found his arms empty, he got up and sought her out to hear her voice, look into her beautiful face, and wait for a reason to touch her.

Malene cleared her throat as their bodies bumped together after a gust of wind caused him to shift forward slightly. "Synne wants to save Asrail, but the moment she steps through our gates, it's only a matter of time before Sybbyl finds her."

Armir's entire body buzzed with the brief contact he had with her. It was a heady feeling that made him hunger for more. "Sybbyl knows we won't let Synne go alone. She's counting on the Varroki to go with her."

"To weaken us. She believes with the Gira and her witches, they'll easily defeat Synne, Lachlan, and whatever Varroki go to battle. Then it'll be easy to take the rest of us down here at Blackglade."

"That's never going to happen."

Malene smiled. "Nay, it isn't."

"You have a plan?"

"I have a thought. I came up here to sort through it."

He quirked a brow. "And?"

"I think I have it figured out now. There's just one problem."

"What's that?"

Her brow creased. "I need to figure out if it's in our favor or Sybbyl's."

Armir grinned. "That way, we know how to use it to our advantage."

"Precisely." Her chin lifted then. "And I presume we'll continue having our lessons in battle magic?"

It was what he looked forward to most every day. It allowed him to touch her freely—and often. "Of course. You've made a lot of headway over the last week."

"Will it be enough?"

He never wanted her to leave Blackglade, but he knew it was pointless to continue that argument. All he could do was make sure he was by Malene's side when she left. She would be prepared for battle, and with the strength of her magic and mind, she would be victorious. He would make sure of that.

"Aye," he replied.

Once more, a smile was back in place. The wind was growing fiercer.

They should go inside, but neither moved.

13

She was here somewhere. Brom knew it. He swiveled his head from side to side as he looked through the forest. He'd given Runa a half-day's head start. With the clear skies, he'd been able to track her easily enough. She had crossed some rough terrain, over streams, and across sections of rock that held very little snow thanks to the cover of trees, but he had always managed to find her tracks.

Now, with trees all around him and snow several inches thick, her tracks had just stopped. It was like she just sprouted wings and flew off.

Brom's head lifted as his gaze took in the thick branches above him. From this vantage point, he could see how it would be easy to climb the trees and then use them to travel. The branches were plentiful, the limbs sturdy. It was the only plausible explanation that made sense. The problem with that scenario was that he had no way of knowing which way she had gone. She could have purposefully led him here, then used the trees as a means to shift her direction.

He sighed. From below, he couldn't tell if any snow had

been knocked off a limb as a means to track her. He debated whether to climb a tree himself to see if he could follow her, but at the sight of a red squirrel running across a branch and dislodging snow, he knew it might be futile to even attempt such a thing.

If he couldn't track her, what was he going to do? There was no way he would just return home. He didn't care if she had said she'd look for him until she found him. He had been meant to meet her now for a reason. Not later. Not after whatever she was about to face. Now. And if that meant he had to find her using whatever means were necessary, then he would.

Brom fisted his hand as his magic swirled, ready to be used, but he hesitated. He scanned the woods one more time. Runa had known about magic. While she hadn't said that she was a witch, she knew enough to tell him that she had been around it. All she had told him was that she had to help her family and that it was dangerous. Did that mean she was going to the Coven?

"Shite," he mumbled, realizing too late that's probably exactly where she was headed.

If he used magic now, the Coven would sense it. He'd listened to many stories from the Varroki of how the Coven tracked witches by their magic. If he used his powers now, he would be leading them straight to him, because he had a suspicion they were close.

"Runa," he murmured, wishing she had let him go with her.

If she didn't have magic, she didn't stand a chance against the Coven. But he wasn't sure whether she had magic or not. She hadn't used any to heal herself, but he hadn't given her a chance. After she had fallen, he had rushed straight to her and gotten them both out of there. Then, he had offered to heal her himself.

Had he been played for a fool? Had Runa instigated everything to get him to confess to being a warlock?

He didn't think so. There was much that had been out of anyone's control, and while he knew how powerful witches could be, he didn't imagine Runa was capable of that. Brom shook his head, wondering how he had gone from never trusting anyone, to barely knowing Runa and revealing his deepest secret.

What he felt in his heart couldn't be wrong, though. Could it?

No doubt, plenty of other men had claimed the same thing, only to be betrayed. He didn't want to believe that could happen to him, but just to be safe, he would be prepared either way.

If he had chosen the Varroki when Asa gave him the choice, he could be with them now. Of course, that assumed they allowed him into their city. Even if they had, there was no guarantee they would have granted him access to everything they were. Not that he needed it. He'd listened and learned enough through the years to gain sufficient knowledge. He would like more, but if he never got it, he'd survive. He'd come this far, hadn't he?

That didn't solve his current predicament, however. Somehow, he'd lost Runa, and he had a hunch that she had done it on purpose. She was too smart to just accept how he hadn't argued more about going with her. Not to mention, he'd warned her that he'd follow her. If she were trying to keep him off her trail, then doing something like disappearing would undoubtedly do the trick.

Brom turned in a slow circle, taking in the direction he'd come to where he was now and where the trail stopped. He looked at each tree, hoping one of them would tell him something, but it wasn't as if he could talk to the foliage.

He had to pick a direction. Runa had been on a direct route, headed straight on this course. It could be because she was trying to make up time. She had crossed terrain that most would've bypassed, but she had been in a hurry. Or, she could've done it to trick him, making him believe that she would continue on in the same direction. After he passed her, she would alter her course and turn another way.

There was only one way to find out if that was the case. Brom would have to continue on his present course for a little bit, then backtrack and see if she came out of hiding to continue on. Brom adjusted the pack across his body and started walking. He desperately tried to keep her out of his thoughts, but memories of their night together kept replaying in his head. Her words, her sighs, her smiles.

Her touch.

He was so lost in thought that he wasn't paying attention. Brom paused and looked behind him to see that he had traveled quite a significant distance, and he hadn't deviated from his course. But something had pulled him from his thoughts. He scanned the forest, noting how still everything had become.

Earlier, birds had flown, squirrels searched for food, and even a fox had darted across his path. Now, the very air seemed to stand still. Fear and alarm dripped from every tree and plant around him.

That's what had caught his attention. He had no idea how long that had been going on before it finally penetrated his mind, and that didn't matter now. All he cared about was discovering what was there and how to get away from it. If he could.

Just as he thought about slowly backing up, he heard it. A whisper. It was so faint that for an instant, he thought he had imagined it. Then he heard it again. Brom couldn't make out the words, but he didn't need to. He knew exactly what was there—Gira.

Brom could use magic and get away from them, but that would only alert them that a warlock was near. No doubt they would tell any witches nearby, and then he would be on the run from the Coven.

But if he didn't use magic, they would try to take him. He knew the ugly truth of what the nymphs did to anyone who got too close. They enveloped them, and while some toyed with them, tortured them with sex, it was only a matter of time before the Gira ate them. Brom would rather the Coven chase him for the rest of his life than be taken by a nymph.

His gaze moved to a tree to his right. He watched as the bark moved. The Gira turned, revealing herself. She was naked, her flesh resembling bark. Her hair was piled atop her head and also resembled the bark of a tree. Eyes as black as pitch met his as she smiled and beckoned him closer with a finger.

Magic gathered within him as he saw four more Gira show themselves. Just as he was about to release a spell that would kill them, something hit him in the back of the head. Pain radiated, and then there was nothing but blackness.

Runa waited until she knew Brom was unconscious before she moved away from the tree. The Giras' gazes snapped to her. The five didn't know what to do with her. Then the first who had shown herself to Brom pulled back her lips in a snarl.

Runa smiled as the attack came.

Brom grunted as he came awake. He pushed up on his hands and knees and winced at the pain that shot through his body. Gingerly, he reached up and felt the small knot forming on his head. Then it all came back to him.

He jumped to his feet, the world spinning for just a moment until he got his bearings. He had his magic ready to dole out punishment to the nymphs but there was no one there. No bodies, no Gira, no...nothing. Brom frowned as he turned in a circle, trying to piece it all together. Finally, he dropped his arms to his sides and shook his head. He hadn't imagined it. He knew the Gira had been there. His magic had been at the ready to kill them when something hit him from behind. Whatever it was had knocked him out cold. The nymphs never would've just left him there.

Unless something had come for them.

Brom dusted the snow from the front of his body and his hair and then carefully looked at the trampled snow. It was difficult to pick up footprints, but something had happened. Too much ground had been disturbed for him not to see that there had been an altercation of some kind.

What happened to the Gira and whoever came for them, he didn't know. For all intents and purposes, it appeared as if someone had saved his life. He just wished he knew who it was. And why had they wanted him unconscious?

Because they didn't want me to see them.

Witches and Gira weren't friends, but they weren't enemies either. The fact that the Gira had decided to join Sybbyl spoke of how fluid that relationship was. Witch Hunters were known to kill Gira when they encountered them. Anyone who knew of magic knew of the nymphs, so whoever it was had to know about magic, too.

His thoughts turned to Runa, but he realized that him

simply wanting her to be near didn't make it so. For one, she would've had no reason to knock him out. If anything, they would've worked better together to take out the Gira.

After going through the list of possibilities, he was no closer to knowing who it was than before. He realized he might never know. He'd gotten away from the Gira without having to reveal that he was a warlock. He was thankful for that, but he would have to pay better attention to not be caught unawares by the nymphs again.

Brom walked a few paces before he stopped and turned back to the area. From his vantage point, it was clear that there had been quite a scuffle. Something on a tree caught his attention. He walked to the side to investigate and noticed something dark. When he touched it, his finger came back red.

"Blood."

He looked around again, specifically searching for more blood. That's when he saw it on several other trees. Brom returned to where he'd been and kicked some of the snow aside. It didn't take long for him to find the copious amounts of red that stained the ground.

There hadn't just been an attack. Someone had been killed. The fact that he hadn't woken to find himself being held by a tree told him that whatever or whoever had knocked him out had killed at least one of the Gira—if not all of them.

Brom was glad that he didn't have to worry about those Gira again, but what bothered him now was that someone had gone to a lot of trouble to hide the fact that nymphs had been killed. Was it for his benefit? Or was it to conceal the signs from other Gira who might come through here looking for their companions?

It could be either one. Frankly, he was grateful to be alive, and the Coven unaware of his magic. That might be his only chance to scrape by, by the skin of his teeth. He might not be so lucky next time. Which meant, he had to get his head on right. He could think about Runa while asleep. For now, he had to imagine that everything and everyone was after him. It was the only way he'd stay alive as he looked for Runa.

14

Everything had nearly worked as Runa planned. *Nearly.*

She blew out a breath as she ran as fast as she could through the thick snow. The Gira who had gotten away traveled as swiftly as the wind. Runa was gaining ground, but not quickly enough. If she didn't do something soon, the nymph would reach the others and alert them to what Runa had done.

Twice already, Runa had thrown one of her blades at the Gira, but the nymph had managed to dodge the throws. Runa had gathered her swords as she ran past, her gaze moving ahead of the Gira. She had one last chance. The nymph was headed to a section of the forest where the trees narrowed. It was the perfect place for a Gira to disappear.

Or for Runa to find her target.

Runa tossed her sword into the air. The sun glinted off the blade as it flipped end over end with the blade landing in her palm. Her fingers closed around it, the sharp edges slicing her fingers. She ignored the pain as she locked her sights on the nymph's back. Then Runa reared back her arm and let the sword fly through the air.

She didn't stop running as the weapon somersaulted to land with a *thunk* in the Gira's back. The nymph collapsed, unmoving in the snow. Runa stopped beside her, breathing hard. Her gaze scanned the area, looking for anything that seemed out of place. Only then did she squat beside the nymph to see if her quarry had been eliminated.

Satisfied, Runa pulled her blade free and cleaned it off in the snow. She didn't bother to cover up the blood or remove any evidence of the attack to hide it from Brom. If he found his way here, it would be long after the animals had had their way with the Gira's body.

She looked back the way she had come. The last thing she wanted was to leave Brom, but there hadn't been another choice. Once she'd knocked him out and attacked the nymphs, the battle had been quick and vicious. She had sustained wounds that had impacted her ability to kill all five of the Gira, which was how this one had been able to make a run for it.

Runa closed her eyes as she leaned back against a tree. She hurt everywhere. From the battle, from the run, from nearly having everything blow up in her face. She slowly sank down to sit on the ground, resting against the tree. It didn't even matter that she was in the snow. Her body was exhausted, and she needed some time to regroup and see to her wounds.

But she couldn't stay here. Runa opened her eyes and forced herself to her feet. She put her swords in their sheaths and collected herself before she thought about what to do next. The Gira weren't far. She couldn't quite detect them, which meant they couldn't perceive her either. That was her only saving grace right now, but she'd take it.

If she had time, Runa would make a perimeter around the Gira to pinpoint exactly where they were and see approximately how many were with Sybbyl. Unfortunately, she didn't have that kind of time. It would make planning a decent attack even harder. In fact, Runa wasn't sure how she could do it at all. She was one against a horde—of Gira. She didn't stand a chance.

Even knowing that, she wasn't going to give up.

Then she thought about Brom and the life she might have had with him. She was most likely going to her death, choosing her family over him. She wanted nothing more than to rush back to him and fling her arms around his neck. To grow old with him. However, her origins prevented that. Not to mention, she'd never forgive herself for not going to her family.

She might not have been raised by Asrail, but neither had her sister. Her grandmother deserved to know that her family knew of her sacrifice and respected her for it. If that was all she could do, Runa would gladly do it. And if she were able to somehow make sure her sister stayed out of this mess, then their family line could continue. In Runa's book, that was a win.

Though her heart wept for the life she could've had.

Unfortunately, her road had been decided long ago. She wasn't sure how Synne had been able to find a place with the humans, but she was glad for it. Runa was tired of living between two worlds, never belonging to either.

Except with Brom.

"But I never told him who and what I am."

She couldn't help but wonder how he might have reacted if she had. The part of her that still held hope imagined that he would have accepted her. The other part, the cynical piece filled with despondency, knew exactly what would've happened. What had always happened.

Runa turned away, angry at herself for even going down that road with her thoughts. It only led to more heartache and sorrow, and she had suffered enough of that for two lifetimes. Maybe in her next life, she would find Brom and have the life she wished so desperately for.

But how could she—part human, part Gira—ever truly be content?

"I was. With Brom."

Saying the words aloud only made the situation worse. Runa had to stop. She couldn't allow her mind to keep dragging her into such despair. Squaring her shoulders, she turned back to face the direction the nymph had been running. It was the same route she had been on since she decided to help her family. If she kept going, she knew she would soon run into the Gira.

Runa turned to the right and decided to skirt around where she knew the Gira were grouped. There would be other scouts waiting to alert the nymphs and witches of any intruders. In order to stay ahead of things, Runa would have to be extra cautious.

She longed to look back over her shoulder for Brom, but she didn't allow herself that small indulgence. She made her way from the dead Gira, covering her tracks as she did. Only when she was far enough away did she pause to see to her wounds. The scratches on her arms throbbed. She packed some ice on them to deaden the torn tissue before she dug into her bag and pulled out her other shirt. She ripped it into pieces with one of her swords and used the material to wrap around each arm from her wrist to her shoulder.

Then she removed her sheaths and cloak and lay back in the snow. Runa hissed at the mix of cold and pain from the wound running down her right side. It would've been worse, but her sheaths had taken most of the damage given the marks on the leather. She couldn't see the injury properly, so she wasn't sure how deep the laceration was. It hurt like hell, but all back wounds did. When she could stand the snow no more, she sat up and did her best to wrap more of the strips of material around and across the wound. It wasn't a good job, but she didn't have much choice. Leaving it uncovered was an invitation for infection.

"I probably won't live long enough for that," she mumbled and forced a laugh as if to try and kid herself.

It didn't work.

Runa used the few remaining pieces of material to wrap around a slice on her left thigh. She was banged up more than she had ever been before. It wouldn't be her first time going after someone while injured, but it would be the first time she'd faced a mass of Gira while hurt.

Actually, it would be her first time facing a horde of nymphs period.

That made her laugh because she knew if Morea had the option, she would've been right here.

Runa gingerly fastened her cloak and returned her sheaths to lay against her back. Every breath made pain shoot through her. She longed for Brom, though not because he could heal her. Because she wanted to be with him.

Runa set out again, noting that she was losing daylight quickly. Her toes were so cold from walking in so much snow that she could no longer feel them. There would be no fire that night to warm her. There would only be planning and scouting.

15

Brom was about to give up on his route and backtrack when he saw the track. It had been hastily covered, but there was no doubt in his mind that it was Runa's. Once he found it, he uncovered a few more as he continued on his way. Then, all of a sudden, there were tracks to follow.

Runa must have figured that he would never get this far so she'd stopped covering her tracks. He squatted down beside the newest footprint, noting how deep in the snow it was, as if she had slammed her foot down. The snow was kicked up around it, a sign that she had been running.

He felt the back of his head that still pounded and knew then that Runa had knocked him out. But why? Why hadn't she allowed him to fight with her? Did she not think him capable? No, he realized. The only reason he had been unconscious was because she hadn't wanted him to see her. Though he still wasn't sure why.

She hadn't hesitated in pulling her blades on him.

That made him think as he followed the tracks with his gaze until they faded into the trees. He slowly straightened and wondered if she might have made sure he couldn't follow her because she really was worried about his safety.

The idea rankled him tremendously. And, somehow, it didn't quite fit.

Brom finally had to admit that he wasn't sure of anything. He didn't know Runa well enough. People sharing their bodies knocked down some boundaries, but that didn't mean they were open books to be read at will. Brom had made the conscious choice to tell her about his magic. If there had been any doubt in his mind that she would use it against him, it was gone now. Runa could've easily watched as he used his magic against the Gira and then made sure at least one of them got back to Sybbyl with the news. But Runa hadn't.

He looked at the tracks again. She had been running, that much was clear. Was she getting as far from him as she could? Or had she been chasing something? The fact that the area of the attack around him had been covered, and the bodies of the Gira were gone, told him that she was most likely getting away from him.

Unless.... He flattened his lips. There had been five nymphs. That was a lot for someone to take on alone, even using magic like he would have. There was a really good chance that one of the Gira had gotten away. It might have been injured, making it slow enough for Runa to clear the area where he'd woken up and cover her tracks as she chased the nymph.

Brom began running as he followed her tracks. One way or the other, he was going to find out why she'd done what she did. He really hoped that Runa was trying to put distance between them and not chasing after a Gira. His heart pounded as his mind came up with all kinds of scenarios. As he weaved through the trees, he glanced up at the sky and noted that the sun was beginning its descent to the horizon. There were still a few hours left, but clouds were gathering. Another snow shower could wipe out any trail he had, and he couldn't allow that.

Oddly enough, the tracks continued in almost the same direct line Runa had started in from the cave. There were a few deviations, but they had been around boulders on the mountain. His legs ached from the climbing, but he didn't slow. When he spotted a loch through the trees, he paid it no mind. With single-minded focus, he kept to the footprints.

It wasn't long until his lungs burned from exertion and the cold. He was getting a little rest as he made his way down the mountain after a rigorous climb. Brom glanced ahead to see the huge mountain ahead of him.

He paused when he got to the bottom to catch his breath. Brom used that time to look around and note anything important. After a few moments, he continued on. Just before starting up the mountain, he saw where the trees narrowed. And that's where he found the Gira's body.

Brom knelt beside it and noticed the single wound in the creature's spine from a blade. The weapon had sunk deep, denoting that it had most likely been thrown. There was a really good chance Runa had been chasing this Gira since the attack. The nymph's body was cold but not stiff. Runa was only an hour or so ahead of him. He might catch her before the sun went down.

Just as he was about to set out, he heard something. His head snapped to the side as he saw movement through the trees. Brom quickly looked around, trying to find a place to hide. He needed to get away from the dead Gira as well as cover his and Runa's tracks. The easiest way would be to use magic, but he hesitated.

Whoever was coming continued getting closer. He turned and sprinted back the way he'd come, hiding behind some boulders. Once he was concealed, he used a simple spell to cover his and Runa's tracks around the body.

He peered around the boulder and saw a group of witches come into view. One looked around intently. Almost immediately, the others did, as well. Brom grimaced because he knew they had sensed his magic. Still, they didn't start looking for him. Instead, they took particular interest in the nymph.

For several tense minutes, the witches stood close together, whispering amongst themselves. Brom wasn't sure whether they were looking at the body or determining where he might be. He didn't want to wait around to find out, but he didn't have a choice. He also didn't want to battle the witches. Not only would it alert others, but it would also put him farther behind Runa. He knew he needed to be there with her for whatever she had planned. She was in way over her head.

Brom kept his gaze on the witches, even as he recalled how steep the incline was. Their position gave them the higher ground. However, the dense trees and many boulders there also hindered them, giving him the advantage.

Minutes ticked by before the witches collectively took a step back and turned as one. Their gazes went directly to him. Brom inwardly groaned. There was no way out of this mess. He would have to fight them if he wanted to live. Or, he could play the fool and claim that he had just stumbled upon them. But he wasn't that good of a liar. It would be quicker and easier to dispatch the witches and get on to following Runa.

Just as Brom was getting ready to show himself, the witches started walking at a diagonal away from him. He followed them with his eyes, making sure none of them peeled away to come back and attack him. It wasn't long before they disappeared from sight, but even then, he didn't move. His mind screamed for him to start running, to catch up to Runa, but he needed to be more cautious.

The longer he sat there, the more daylight he lost. When he could wait no more, he cautiously moved away from his spot and went to the witches' tracks. Their route was much smoother, though still difficult through the mountain pass. He followed the trail a little to make sure that they stayed together. When he was satisfied, he turned and hurried back the way he had come.

Brom didn't even glance toward the dead Gira. The light was fast dipping behind the mountains. Twilight made it even harder to see, but that still didn't slow him. Brom's legs burned, his lungs ached, but he ignored it all to get as far as he could before the last of the light disappeared. Only then did he stop. He bent over and put his hands on his knees as he dragged air into his labored lungs.

He dug into his pack for the waterskin and drank deeply before replacing it and getting an oatcake. He used the time as he ate to allow his eyes to adjust to the growing darkness. Then he started walking slowly again, looking for any sign that the snow had been disturbed.

There were animal tracks, but no sign of Runa. Brom knew that she was near. Just as he'd known last time. He wasn't sure how she was hiding, but whatever she was doing, she was good at it. It meant that she could hide from her enemies. He wished he knew how she was doing it so he could find her.

He walked for hours in the direction she'd been headed. The longer he went with nothing to show for his efforts, the more he was convinced that she had changed course. Brom stopped near the top of the mountain as the temperatures dropped. There was no cave for shelter, just trees and rocks. He wrapped his cloak tightly around himself and huddled against the trees.

Exhaustion weighed heavily on him. Sleep pulled at him. He needed to rest his eyes, but after the grueling day he'd had, he would have to sleep so he could be ready for the morrow. If only he'd found Runa.

Brom wished he knew what secrets she kept from him. They must be huge for her to go to such extremes to stay away from him. Though, he couldn't get too upset by her not telling him. It wasn't as if he had been forthcoming to many people before her. He still wasn't sure what it was about Runa that had made him want to tell her that he was a warlock.

Maybe he wanted to see her reaction. Perhaps he wanted to know if magic was known to her. Or, he just wanted to share something with her besides his body. There was a deep connection between them. Neither of them could deny that, not with how much pleasure they had shared.

No one else had ever affected him the way Runa did. He wanted…well, he wasn't sure *what* he wanted other than to help her. Actually, that wasn't true. He wanted more time with her. Much, much more time. He wanted years with her, learning everything about her as she learned everything about him.

Did he yearn for something that had only been there in the cave? Was something greater between them? Something like…love?

Brom sighed heavily. He'd have to wait to discover that. First, he had to find Runa.

16

Things were worse than Runa had imagined. Having Gira blood allowed her to know when she was getting close to them. Unfortunately, the nymphs were everywhere. If she had sensed them, then they knew she was here, too.

Runa had done her best to stay just to the edge of where the Gira congregated, but she had made a mistake. And it might very well cost her her life. But what was done was done. All she could do now was prepare for the inevitable.

She leaned her back against a tree and closed her eyes. Her entire body ached in some form or fashion. And all she wanted was to be in Brom's arms as they lay together. She wasn't sure how it had happened, but she had developed intense feelings for the warlock. Very deep.

In fact, it might be love.

And yet, you left him.

She had left him because bringing him with her meant his death.

You don't know that.

Runa hated when her conscience argued with her. The simple fact was that she *did* know that. Brom didn't need to get mixed up in her family drama—no matter how much she wished he was beside her.

How odd that she had always preferred to work alone. She didn't want just anyone with her. She wanted Brom. And she kept finding ways things would be easier if he were with her. But he wasn't, and she had made sure of that.

He isn't stupid. He's going to figure out that you knocked him out and killed the Gira.

She turned and hastily climbed the tree to a sturdy branch that split into two sections. Runa settled herself comfortably on them after removing the snow. She tried to think of an attack strategy, but her mind kept going to Brom. Though she hadn't wanted to admit it at the time, she had been pleased that he had followed her.

Yet when given the opportunity to travel together, she had chosen instead to knock him unconscious and then take out the nymphs. She hoped that when he woke, he returned to his home. It was as if he could pick up her trail again. She'd made sure not to make that mistake a second time.

He's following you because he cares.

Oh, how she wished that were true. She wanted it so very much, that it would be easy to convince herself of that very thing. If she weren't going up against the Gira and the Coven, if she didn't have Gira blood in her veins, if her life was different in any way…then she would've grabbed hold of Brom with both hands and never let go.

Maybe he wants you because you're different.

Runa bit back a laugh. She knew that wasn't true, but it was nice to imagine. And even though it was folly for many reasons, she allowed herself to imagine what life would be like with her and Brom together. There would be many nights of lovemaking, lots of laughter, arguments that led to them making up with long kisses and lying in each other's arms every night.

It was a life so many others in the world had and took for granted. It had been a life that Morea urged her to find. That's how Runa had discovered that she would never fit in with the humans and realized that nothing about her was normal—and there wasn't a place for her anywhere.

You want to pity yourself? Look at what you can do. There isn't another like you.

That wasn't strictly true. There was her sister, Synne. They shared the same mixture of blood, but Runa didn't know if her sibling had the same gifts as she. Not that it mattered. Synne knew nothing but the human world. That's where she belonged.

Runa blew out a breath and thought of the layout of the forest. She had already seen a small group of witches headed out of the woods. They didn't look as if they were leaving the Coven, rather like they were on some kind of mission. She could only imagine what Sybbyl had sent them to look for or do. Hopefully, more witches had left. The fewer there were, the better.

But they weren't Runa's only problem. The biggest one was the Gira. She might have some gifts, but in the end, she was half-human. That part would slow her down in the end. All the nymphs had to do was converge on her, and it was over. She was good at fighting a handful, but more than that would mean the end of her.

The only way she could ensure that didn't happen was to keep her distance. But she couldn't do that and still get to Asrail. She wasn't even sure this was the right thing to do. There was no way she could free her grandmother. The odds had been stacked against her from the very beginning, but even knowing all of that, she still wouldn't walk away. She couldn't.

Things might be different if she'd had time to find her sister and talk to Synne, to devise a plan that actually had a chance of succeeding. Wishing was a waste. Runa had run out of time. The Gira would come at her soon, and they wouldn't wait for dawn.

Despite that knowledge, she couldn't keep her eyes open. It was like something was lulling her to sleep, and the more she fought it, the more it pulled her under. Runa finally surrendered. In a heartbeat, she stood in the middle of the forest in summer with bright sunlight streaming through the trees. The ferns on the ground sparkled with droplets from a recent rainstorm.

Runa turned in a circle, looking for whoever had brought her to this place. She wasn't sure if it was in her mind, or if it was real. Either way, she wanted to know what she was up against.

"Who's there?" Runa called out.

A Gira pulled away from a tree and came to stand before her. "You are a beauty."

She eyed the nymph, unsure how to respond.

The Gira chuckled and shook her head. "Forgive me. It might be better to introduce myself. I'm Asrail, your grandmother."

Morea had taught her that magic could be used for many reasons, including tricking someone. Runa wanted to believe this was her grandmother, but she needed proof. "How are we here?"

"I felt you," Asrail answered. "The others did, as well. Your presence took their interest off me long enough so I could connect with you."

"How do I know you aren't lying?"

Asrail smiled. "You're right to ask. The simple answer is, you don't. You can either talk to me, or you can leave. It's entirely up to you."

"What do you want?" Runa asked to give herself time to make a decision.

The nymph drew in a long breath and then released it. "That day Morea and I saved you and Synne altered all of our lives. I wouldn't change a minute of it, however. Just knowing that you and your sister lived was enough for me."

"Why didn't you ever come to see me?" The minute the words were out, Runa realized how much she needed the answer.

"Because I thought you were dead. When Morea disappeared with you, she never made contact with me again. And no matter how hard I looked, I couldn't find her. I believed the Gira had gotten to both of you. Just recently, I saw Synne for the first time since I left her in Edra's care. There were times I wanted nothing more than to have both of you in my arms, to tell you both how much I loved you. I wanted to share everything about your father and what I knew of your mother. But I didn't. Because I loved you both so dearly."

Runa glanced away as emotion welled up within her. "Morea was good to me."

"I know," Asrail said with a grin. "She was my closest friend. More like a sister than anything. I can never repay her for what she did for you. Runa, my dear, it warms my heart more than you can imagine that you're here, but why?"

"To free you."

Asrail shook her head, sadness filling her eyes. "I've lived my life. There is still time for you to leave and get as far from here as you can. Go find your sister with the Varroki."

"I owe you and Morea. This is how I can repay that debt."

Asrail took a few steps closer, her voice lowering as urgency filled her words. "Please. Leave while you can."

"Because you don't think I can win against the Gira?"

"Because to win against Sybbyl and the Coven, you need to join your sister and the others."

There was more, Runa was sure of it. But, for whatever reason, Asrail didn't want to tell her. "I'm already here. The Gira know I'm here. I'm sure Sybbyl does, as well."

"Not yet," her grandmother stated. "The Gira don't tell Sybbyl everything, even though she likes to believe they do."

"Where are they holding you?"

Asrail shook her head. "You aren't listening to me."

"You and Synne are the only family I have. Please don't ask me to walk away after just discovering both of you."

"Dear child." Asrail started to reach out a hand to touch Runa but hesitated. Her arm lowered to her side. "Your parents loved you and your sister more than anything. I wish I could've saved them, but I couldn't. I relive that day often. You might not have known about me or Synne, but I've kept both of you in my thoughts daily. I only got a little while with your sister. I'm glad I got this time with you."

"Tell me where you are so I can come for you. Even if you don't, I'm going to go looking."

Asrail sighed loudly. "Please. I'm begging you. Leave now while you still can."

Runa narrowed her eyes on the Gira. "Either you want to die, or you aren't Asrail and you're trying to convince me to leave so you can kill her."

"I am your grandmother."

"Then why not let me help you?" Runa shouted.

"Because you're doing exactly what they want!"

Runa blinked, taken aback not just by Asrail's explosive tone but also her words. "What?"

The Gira squeezed her eyes closed and shook her head. "Don't ask."

"You can't say something like that and not expect me to demand to know what you're talking about."

When Asrail opened her eyes again, there was resignation in her gaze. As well as a wealth of sadness. "There are things at play here that you don't know. Not even Sybbyl knows."

"You're telling me the Gira are doing all of this?"

"Not all of it," Asrail said with a half-hearted shrug. "As soon as the Blood Skull was found, they began plotting."

Runa was getting more confused by the minute. "I assume it's because they know that whoever has the bones has the most power."

Asrail chuckled. "You give us too much credit."

"Then explain it to me. Please," Runa implored.

"Your stubbornness is so much like your father's and mine. I can't even be angry because if I were in your shoes, I'd be doing the same thing."

Runa waited impatiently.

Asrail's shoulders slumped. "I'm sure Morea told you I was once queen."

"She did."

"I was removed from the throne when they discovered I allowed my son to marry a human. Your father would've done anything to be with your mother. When I saw your parents together, I couldn't refuse them. I'd never seen my son look at someone as he did your mother. And your mother, she adored him with every fiber of her being. It was the kind of love others dream of. And there it was, right before my eyes. And I did what any mother would do for her child. I found a witch who used a spell to turn him human so your parents could be together."

Runa took in every word, putting it to memory so she could look back on it later. And eagerly waited for more.

"What I allowed for my son and your mother was seen as a true transgression by my people. They wanted me dead, and I was willing to give up my life if they left your parents alone. Except they went for your parents first. Unfortunately, they saw me take Synne and hunted us relentlessly until I found a place for her with the Hunters. Then I went into hiding. It wasn't until the bones of the First Witch began surfacing that everything changed."

"How?" Runa asked.

Asrail went silent for a moment before she said, "There hasn't been another queen since I was removed from the throne. And only females rule the Gira."

When her grandmother didn't continue, Runa said, "Go on."

"The Gira have found a new queen."

"Does that mean she's going to kill you? Tell me so I can stop her."

Asrail smiled sadly. "That would be rather difficult since it's you."

Runa was so shocked that she couldn't speak. She tried to grasp what her grandmother had just said, but her mind wasn't accepting it. "But...I'm only part Gira. And so is Synne."

"Synne has some amazing skills that include communicating with trees, but she can't do what you can."

Runa shook her head. "You must be mistaken."

"I'm not. They took me to draw both you and Synne out. They want to deliver Synne to Sybbyl. You...they want to make their queen."

It was Runa's turn to squeeze her eyes shut. "Wait. Just... wait." Her eyes snapped open. "I've mingled with the Gira for years, even taking jobs from them. If what you're saying is true, they would've done something sooner."

"Not exactly. The magic of the First Witch is extremely powerful. When Sybbyl took over as leader of the Coven, the Gira went to her. They used their seductive skills to divert her attention so they could use the staff's magic to locate their next queen. That's when it pointed to you."

Runa swallowed and put a hand on a tree to lean against it. This couldn't be happening. Could it?

"I don't have much longer," Asrail said. "My power is draining quickly. Please, get away from here."

Runa looked into her grandmother's dark eyes. "Will it do any good? Or will the Gira hunt me down for the rest of my life?"

Asrail didn't reply, which was answer enough.

In the next instant, Runa jerked awake. Her breath billowed out from her mouth as she shivered from the cold. She wasn't sure if the dream had been real or not. All this time, she'd come here thinking she was meant to save Asrail. But was it because her Gira blood had known what she was destined for?

She could feel the nymphs getting closer. It was time for her to run. Runa put her hand on the tree and leapt from the branch to the pile of snow below.

17

Blackglade

"You can't keep me here," Synne stated.

Armir stood up immediately. "Remember who you are addressing. She's our leader."

Lachlan got up from his chair near the hearth in the tower, glaring at Armir for speaking to Synne in such a manner.

Malene put her hand on Armir's arm. That's all it took for her second in command to back down. She took in his blond hair pulled back in its long queue. The sides of his head were shaved, showcasing intricate tattoos on either side. His pale green eyes met hers briefly. Malene then eyed Synne, who stood with her arms crossed over her chest. She was ready for battle, as anyone in her predicament would be. Malene could, in fact, keep Synne and Lachlan there for as long as she wanted. Her refusal to open the gates for them to leave ensured that.

"It's a trap. We've gone over this," Malene said.

Lachlan ran a hand down his face. "We know. However, it's our decision."

"It's not just your decision," Armir said. "Because it won't be only you who goes."

Synne sighed loudly. "I understand that a battle is coming, but it doesn't have to be now. Let us leave. Lachlan and I might be all that's needed to get to Asrail."

"That's wishful thinking," Armir snapped.

Malene had noticed that Synne had become increasingly agitated with each day that passed. To the point where she was beginning to suspect there was something else at play. "Is this about finding Elin?"

Synne dropped her arms to her sides. "She will absolutely pay for what she's done, but that's for another day. More important matters are at hand."

"Then it must be Avis," Armir said.

Lachlan pulled back his lips in a sneer. "That witch will die by my hand when we're finished with what we must do."

Malene looked between the couple. "There is something neither of you is telling us. I've opened Blackglade to you. A Coven witch was within our walls and escaped, something that has never happened. I will right that wrong, but if you want us to continue helping you, then you need to be straight with us. Now."

Synne and Lachlan exchanged a look. Synne licked her lips and swung her gaze to Malene. "I learned something from the trees."

"Well?" Armir asked with a quirked brow.

Lachlan answered. "Synne has a sister."

Malene hadn't been expecting that. It explained a lot, however. What it meant for them, she wasn't sure. "Where is she?"

"Elin told me she was dead," Synne said. "Even Asrail believed she was deceased. I don't know if they both lied to me. It doesn't matter. I have to get to her."

"Where is she?" Malene asked again.

Synne pressed her lips together. "She's headed to the Gira and Sybbyl."

"Bloody hell," Armir said as he turned to pace.

Lachlan widened his stance as he crossed his arms over his chest. "It's no' ideal."

Armir snorted loudly. "Not ideal? Do either of you know if she's sided with Sybbyl and the Gira?"

"She wouldn't do that," Synne said.

Armir quirked a blond brow. "In other words, you don't know what she's doing."

"Synne is certain her sister wouldna side with the Coven."

Malene listened to the three of them arguing for several minutes. Finally, she raised a hand, and everyone fell silent. Her gaze slid to Synne. "I can't imagine how you must feel learning that your sister is alive. The need to get to her must be tremendous. You want to help her, join her even, but the simple truth is…you don't know her. She could be your ally. She could also be your enemy."

"That's for me to determine," Synne stated, lifting her chin.

Malene let those words hang in the air for a beat before she replied. "A war is on the horizon. It's imminent. When you and Lachlan came here, it was because Sybbyl was after you and the bone Lachlan had. We gave you sanctuary. We all planned how we would deal with the Coven and Sybbyl. And while I will still hold to that promise, what I refuse to do is allow anyone to leave with either of you if you go now."

"You can no' be serious," Lachlan said in a shocked voice, his arms falling to his sides.

Armir nodded once. "She is."

Synne said nothing, her gaze locked with Malene's. She had no idea what the Hunter was thinking, and it didn't matter. Malene had more than just two people to think about. She had an entire city and its occupants to keep safe, even if the Coven won.

"The two of you can leave now. Today," Malene continued. "Or, you can wait, and let us see what we can learn about your sister."

Synne shook her head sadly then looked at Lachlan. "I just found Asrail when Sybbyl took her. Though we lost your sword and a bone of the First Witch, by some miracle, you survived Avis's magic. I discovered that my younger sister is still alive, and I'm supposed to wait? I can't do that."

"Malene has a point," Lachlan said. "I'll stand with you no matter what you decide, but more information is always better."

"The trees told me nothing else."

Armir shrugged. "Ask them again. Ask them over and over. Maybe they didn't tell you because they didn't know yet."

Malene frowned as she had the distinct feeling that someone was listening to their conversation. She walked to the door of her chambers and opened it to look out into the darkness. No one was on the stairs outside the tower.

"What is it?" Armir asked as he came up behind her.

She peered into the darkness. "I thought someone was out here."

"Knocking?"

She shrugged, not wanting to say anything just yet.

Armir gently pulled her aside and looked out himself. Then he shut the door and faced her. "This door is spelled so no one can get in unless you want them here. No one can hear what's happening inside either."

"I know." Yet none of that rid her of the feeling within her.

Lachlan caught their attention. "Is everything all right?"

"It's fine," Armir said.

Malene followed Armir back to the others. "Synne, you were destined to find us because you were meant to fight alongside the Varroki when we go up against the Coven."

"What if there isn't a battle?" Synne asked.

Armir propped a hip on the table. "No one wants a war, but that doesn't mean we can stop it."

"We can if we free Asrail and my sister joins us."

Malene smiled and tried not to look over her shoulder like someone was there, eavesdropping. "That is a lovely thought. How do you think you can get to Asrail, who is no doubt surrounded by Gira? Not to mention finding your sister during all of that."

"Then there's the Coven," Armir added.

Synne threw her hands up as frustration filled her face. "I don't know! I'm willing to try whatever is necessary, though. Is either of you? Or do you both just want to hide in the tower and pretend that none of this is happening?"

"Lass," Lachlan said in a soft voice as he moved to stand before her. His hands came up to grasp her shoulders as his voice lowered so only the two of them could hear.

Armir caught her eye. "What is it?"

Malene shook her head. She was sending out a little magic at a time, trying to determine if someone was trying to invade the tower or her head. She didn't think Sybbyl had that kind of magic, but she wasn't going to be taken unawares if she could help it. Her instincts told her that someone was listening. She'd never had such a strong reaction before, but the more she thought about it, the more she realized that this wasn't the first time she'd felt something like this. The times before had been so slight that it had nearly gone unnoticed. If this time hadn't been so intense, she probably wouldn't have recognized it now either.

Armir wasn't taking her silence. He straightened and

walked to her. Without saying a word, his fingers wrapped around her wrists, and he lifted her fisted hands so her palms faced her. The blue radiance filtered through the cracks between her fingers. Malene pulled her arms away and put her hands behind her back. She frowned and shook her head at Armir. He got the hint and remained silent as he returned to his position by the table.

A few minutes later, Lachlan moved aside and nodded to her and Armir. "A lot has happened in a short period. Synne just wants to help her family."

"As anyone would," Malene said. "If your sister is against the Coven, then I'll be standing right beside you to help find her. But you must understand that I have to think of more than just what I want."

Synne flashed her a quick smile. "I know. I apologize for my outburst. I just feel like time is slipping away."

"Because it is." Malene hadn't wanted to tell them so soon, but she realized she could no longer put it off. She glanced at Armir to find him frowning at her. "I know where Sybbyl is. She's called the entire Coven to her."

Lachlan smiled. "Then we know where to attack them. Unless you want her to come here."

"She'll never find this place," Armir declared.

Malene swallowed. "Avis and Elin both managed to get out of Blackglade. Avis will have a difficult time returning because she was considered an enemy. Elin, however, is another story."

"You think they took the sword to Sybbyl and will come here," Synne said.

"That's a possibility, but if what Avis told you is true, she intends to keep the sword herself."

Armir's voice was filled with fury when he said, "Then she'll be easy to find and kill."

"We can no' go after three different people," Lachlan said.

"We need to focus on one. And right now, the biggest threat is Sybbyl and the Coven. If Sybbyl is defeated, then Avis can step right in."

Synne's lips twisted. "I'm sure she's hoping for exactly that."

"No matter what we do, the Coven will always be around in one form or another," Malene said. "It's balance. Where there is good, there must be evil. And where there is evil, there needs to be good. We were able to keep the Coven in check for the most part. Edra and Radnar's Hunters helped a lot. Was it a perfect solution? Not by any means. But it was something."

Armir's brows snapped together. "What are you suggesting?"

"I don't know," Malene admitted as the prickling sensation on her neck intensified. "There is something...just out of reach. If I can get a handle on it, then I may know what our next step should be."

Synne studied her for a moment. "Are you saying that we shouldn't attack the Coven?"

She parted her lips to reply when she stilled. Her gaze jerked to Armir as chills raced over her body. She whirled around, hands up as she stretched her fingers. "Someone is listening."

18

"*S omeone is listening.*"

Brom came awake as he jerked his hands up to shield his face from the blue magic. It was the first time he'd ever seen a face as he listened in on the Varroki. This was the second time it had happened without him trying to connect with them. It felt as if he were in the room with Malene, Armir, Lachlan, and Synne. Their voices had been so clear and loud. But he had seen nothing.

Until Malene spun around. He'd looked into her gray eyes, shocked to see that she was much younger than he'd expected. And beautiful.

When he realized that he wouldn't have to defend himself against the magic of the Lady of the Varroki, Brom ran a hand down his face. He blinked into the darkness, trying to get his bearings. He shook off the light dusting of snow and got to his feet to get his blood flowing to warm up.

As he did, he thought over the conversation he'd heard at Blackglade. Synne needed to know about Runa. The problem was, he wasn't sure what to tell her, even if he could. Then his gaze landed on a tree.

Synne had said the trees had told her she had a sister. How was it that she could speak to trees? Then there was Asrail. That must be the family member Runa had spoken of helping. But if the Coven had Asrail, then there was no help for her. Unless she was being held to get to Synne or Runa.

Or both of them.

But…why? What was it about Runa and Synne that was so important? The more Brom tried to figure it out, the more confused he became. Runa had known of magic, but he didn't think she was a witch. Even if she had been, once he told her that he was a warlock, there would have been no reason for her *not* to tell him.

"Then what?" he asked.

Brom shook his head. He'd have to think on that some more. For now, he had another idea. He faced the nearest tree. "I know you can hear me. I wish I could hear you, as well, but that will have to wait for another day. There is something important I need you—all of you—to do. Carry a message for me." He put his hand on the tree, hoping that it would sense how imperative this was. "Please tell Synne, the Hunter with the Varroki, that her sister, Runa, is going to help their grandmother, Asrail. Runa is alone, and she will need help."

He stood there silently for another few moments before he dropped his hand and stepped back. "Please hurry. I think we're running out of time."

If he thought the trees might respond in some way, he was vastly disappointed. Brom had no way of knowing if his plea had worked or not. Maybe the trees couldn't understand him as they could Synne. Regardless, it was worth a try.

He drew in a breath and looked around. There were still several hours before dawn. He doubted that he would get any more sleep, but trying to find signs of Runa now would be folly. It was too dark. Yet the dusting of snow might very well hide anything he could have found anyway.

It felt as if obstacles were being put in his way to slow him —or to stop him. If that were the case, then whoever was doing this had no way of knowing how stubborn he was. But even he had to see that his only course of action for the present was waiting until dawn. The mountain was too treacherous, and he didn't know it well enough to move about in the dead of night. Especially when there was no moon to help light the way.

If he weren't so near the Coven, then he'd use magic. Instead, he had to keep that hidden, as well, and use his other skills. It made things difficult and took him twice as long, but the alternative wasn't an option.

Brom situated himself against the boulders once more. He flexed his fingers to help stave off the cold, but it permeated everything. It was easy to say that winters weren't that bad when there was a cottage with a fire within. Being in the elements had him wishing it was any other season.

He leaned his head back and closed his eyes. Almost immediately, he felt the pull of his mind toward Blackglade. Brom tried to withstand it, but he was powerless to resist. Asa had warned him that being so close to the Varroki would mean he couldn't control it. She was right.

There was only silence now. No conversations, laughter, or the battle magic lessons Armir had begun with Malene. Brom didn't realize how much he had come to enjoy the small peeks he had gotten into those at Blackglade.

"Who are you?" Malene asked, breaking the quiet.

The darkness Brom usually saw began to lighten gradually. He'd never tried to talk to them before. He wasn't even sure he could. "Brom."

"How long have you been listening to me?"

He drew in a breath and slowly released it as Malene's face came into view. She had long, flaxen hair done up in a myriad of different-sized plaits. Gray eyes the color of a stormy sky stared at him from a face of unearthly beauty. The wisdom he saw in her gaze left him dazed.

"The first time was when I was a small child. It took a great deal of effort," he admitted, still astounded that she could hear him.

"But it's gotten easier, hasn't it?"

Brom paused, unsure how she knew that. Then again, this was Malene, the Lady of the Varroki. "Aye."

"I know what you have."

He remained silent, not wanting to admit or deny anything.

Malene sighed loudly. "I understand why you don't wish to reply. However, it would behoove you to tell me."

Though she hadn't said the words, Brom knew that Malene could send one of her Varroki warriors after him. He had no reason not to trust her, but since he had never told anyone—not even his mother—what he had found, he was hesitant to do it now.

The silence lengthened as Malene watched him intently. Finally, he asked, "What is it you think I hold?"

"A bone of the First Witch," Malene replied immediately.

Brom nodded.

Malene quirked a brow. "You were able to listen to us for a long time without the bone. That means it wasn't the bone that gave you the power to do so. That means you are a warlock."

"I am."

"Why do you not live with us?"

He licked his lips and shrugged. "My father spent time

with my mother one summer. She didn't find out that she carried me until after he left."

"You could've come to us."

"I know. I almost did."

"What stopped you?"

Brom looked away, unsure how much to say.

"I don't know how many of our conversations you overheard, but you know quite a bit about us and what we're planning. It's only fair that you share, too," Malene told him.

He knew she was right, but his instinct to protect Runa was strong. His gaze slid back to Malene. "I chose to follow someone instead of coming to Blackglade."

"That someone wouldn't happen to be Synne's sister, would it?"

"How do you know that?" he demanded.

Malene smiled, her eyes crinkling at the corners. "You aren't the only one with magic. Besides, the request you sent out via the trees carried much farther and stronger than you could have imagined."

"You can talk to the trees?"

"Unfortunately, I can't. But I heard you just the same. You have significant magic, Brom, despite being only half-warlock. That, coupled with the bone of the First Witch you carry, has added much to your power."

He'd never thought of that. His hand slipped into his bag, where his fingers curved around the rib bone. "Runa needs my help."

"Do you have any idea how close you are to the Coven and the multitude of Gira?"

"Pretty close by your tone," he replied.

Malene gave him a hard look. "How much do you know of Runa?"

"No' a lot. I had a dream with her face in it and a

woman telling me to find her. It didna take me near as long as I expected. I continued following her until I saw her injure herself during a blizzard. That's when I helped her. We spent a night holed up in a cave until the storm passed."

Malene nodded slowly. "You healed her."

It wasn't a question. "I did."

"And you didn't worry about her telling others you're a warlock?"

"I've never told another person what I am, but it felt right to tell her. I can't explain it."

Malene's expression took on a faraway look. "You don't have to. I understand perfectly."

Brom watched her for a few moments until she blinked and focused on him once more. Then he said, "Runa knew of magic. She told me she was going to save her family."

"When did you figure out that Synne and Runa were sisters?"

"Only recently. Runa is doing her damnedest to keep me from tracking her. I'm not sure how she's doing it, either. She must be skilled at climbing trees. That's the only way I can see her disappearing like she does."

Malene frowned. "Runa didn't tell you of her origins."

"You say that as if it's bad."

"You speak of her as if she means something to you."

Brom shrugged, briefly looking inside himself to gauge his emotions. "I'd be lying if I said I didna care about her."

"After spending only a short time with her?"

"Aye. When you meet someone you connect with instantly, you just know."

Malene smiled, though there was a hint of sadness in her eyes. "That you do."

"If you know something about Runa, please tell me."

"I'm wondering now if I should. It might change your mind about helping her."

Brom shot the Lady of the Varroki a flat look. "That could never happen."

"Runa's father was a Gira."

The words were so shocking that, for a moment, Brom couldn't digest them. He blinked, letting them turn over in his head. "She's a...Gira?"

"Half," Malene corrected. "Just as you're part Varroki."

"A Gira," he repeated, then thought about the time they had spent together. There wasn't anything Runa had done or said that made him think she was anything but human. But he'd known she wasn't a witch.

Malene called his name in a gentle voice. "That doesn't change who Runa is."

"I know," he stated, anger infusing him that Malene would think otherwise. "I never saw anything that said she was half-nymph."

"She probably made sure you didn't."

Brom ran a hand down his face, his other hand holding firm to the bone. "She's going to the Gira, isn't she?"

"Her grandmother is a Gira."

"Asrail," he said, putting the pieces together.

Malene bowed her head in acknowledgement. "Synne just discovered Asrail."

"And thought Runa was dead," Brom finished. "But Runa knew of Synne. I doona know for how long, but she's known."

"You believe Runa is going to help Asrail and not join the Gira?"

Brom started to answer but hesitated. "She never mentioned the Gira or the Coven. She said only that where she was going was dangerous, and that I shouldna come. I took that to mean that she was going to help her family as she told me."

"Yet there is a chance she's going to join them."

"Why would she do that?"

"Because they're powerful. Because they have her grand-mother, and it might save her sister. Because there was no way she could go there and not be killed almost immediately."

Brom wanted to shout his frustration. Instead, he swallowed the bellow and pressed his lips together. "Runa is a good person. She wouldna join the Coven."

"Joining the Gira isn't the same as aligning with the Coven."

He got to his feet. "Can you tell me where she is?"

"The magic Sybbyl uses prevents me from pinpointing anything near the Coven, which is where Runa is. It's how I know how close you are. The last thing you want is any of the Coven learning you are a warlock. Sybbyl wanted one of my fiercest warriors, Jarin, as hers. He managed to get away, and I doubt Sybbyl will allow a second warlock to slip through her fingers."

"I can't leave Runa."

"She might be gone from you."

"I'm not leaving her," he stated.

Malene sighed and shook her head. "Stay where you are."

19

Runa didn't get far before Gira surrounded her. She stared at the nymphs, daring them to attack her. But they didn't. They just stood there, watching her.

"What do you want?" she demanded.

As one, the Gira went down on their knees in the thick snow and bowed their heads. "Our queen," they said in unison.

Runa shook her head. She hadn't wanted to believe Asrail's words because they had seemed too preposterous. Now, she realized she should've heeded her grandmother. "I'm not your queen."

Five of the Gira got to their feet and came to stand before her. The number of nymphs around her was staggering, but she had a feeling this was only a fraction of them. She steeled herself as the five blinked back at her. Four of them were women. There were very few male Gira. She didn't want to think about the reasons for that at the moment. Not when there was so much more to fill her head.

"We've been waiting for you," the male said.

Runa lifted her chin. "The Gira murdered my parents and

tried to kill me and my sister. You've not been waiting for me to claim a throne. You've been lying in wait to finally take the life you sought to end so many years ago."

"Maybe," one of the four females said. "It would've been our mistake."

Runa didn't believe that at all. "You killed my parents," she stated again.

The female on the end shrugged. "It isn't allowed."

"What? A human and a Gira?" Runa asked.

The male nodded. "That's right."

"But I'm a product of that. How does that make me your queen?"

"You were chosen," another female said.

Runa wanted to laugh at the irony. "If you had succeeded in killing me, you would find another queen."

"Synne," the entire Gira crowd said in unison.

Runa's blood went cold. "Neither of us will be your queen."

The female on the end smiled. "One of you will. You were chosen."

"Why?" Runa demanded. "Tell me."

"Do you really need to ask?"

Runa's hands itched to hold her swords. "I've killed your kind."

"Which makes you perfect," another female said. "You are feared for your skills at tracking nymphs down."

"I've killed you because of what you did to my parents."

The male smiled. "You've shown every Gira your courage and triumph and power. We were beginning to think we'd never have another queen until the bones of the First Witch were found. It was her magic that allowed us to find you."

Unease rippled through Runa. "Any of you could've come

to me at any time. I just recently accepted a mission to hunt one of you down. Why wait?"

"We were waiting on something," a female said with a smirk.

The more Runa spoke to them, the more uncomfortable and nervous she became. Something was going on. Asrail had warned her to get away, and now, it was too late.

"Get your hands off me!" a woman shouted.

Runa peered into the darkness through the trees to try and see who it was. The Gira parted as a group of nymphs held a woman by her arms and legs as they carried her. The woman struggled, but it did no good since the Gira's hold was nigh unbreakable once they latched on to someone.

When the nymphs and the woman came closer, Runa glanced around, wondering if she could get through the Gira and break free. She didn't get the chance as the Gira threw the woman before her. The human rolled in the snow, tangled in her cloak and skirts. Her hood came up, covering her head. On instinct, Runa reached back and grasped her swords. She pulled them free of their sheaths and twisted her wrists as she pointed the blades at the newcomer.

The woman yanked the hood away and got to her feet, facing the Gira. "I'm going to rip every one of you vile creatures apart!"

The five Gira stood together, smiling, not the least bit afraid. In fact, from what Runa could see, none of the nymphs appeared worried about the threat at all. That made Runa take a closer look at the woman. She noted the blond hair, but she knew the woman wasn't Asa because of the shrill voice and the English accent.

"Do you know who I am?" the woman demanded.

Runa said, "Why don't you tell us?"

The woman whirled around and looked Runa up and down, dismissing her immediately. "Who are you?"

"No one."

The woman rolled her eyes and glared at the five nymphs. "Give me back what was taken."

"You mean what you stole, Avis?" one of the females asked.

Runa was instantly intrigued. The Gira appeared to have some grudge against Avis, and they clearly wanted Runa to witness this. While she was curious, she knew the Gira didn't do anything without reason.

Avis crossed her arms over her chest and glowered at the five. "I killed to get it. Sybbyl did the same. You follow her, but attack me? Why?"

Instead of answering, one of the five motioned with a hand. Once more, the nymphs parted as a male made his way through the throng. Once he passed them, they closed ranks behind him. The moment Avis saw him, she dropped her arms and formed magic. Without missing a beat, the five quelled her magic in an instant.

Runa looked between the witch and the five. The power struggle had been short-lived. Runa wasn't sure why Avis believed she stood a chance against the nymphs. Maybe it was because of exactly what she said. The Gira followed Sybbyl, so why not Avis? Although, Sybbyl had killed to get the Staff of the Eternal.

Runa's mind halted as her gaze swung to the male coming toward her. She noted that he carried a sword. Her heart skipped a beat as he held the sword in both hands and offered it up to her as he fell to his knees.

"The finger bone of the First Witch is within the pommel," the male told her.

One of the five said, "It's our gift, Your Highness."

"Highness?" Avis repeated shrilly. She looked between the

five and Runa twice before her eyes widened and she tried to take a step back.

But the nymphs were there to stop her.

Runa didn't take the sword, though she wanted to. A bone of the First Witch. For her. It didn't seem possible. She pulled her gaze from it and looked at the five. "Why not give it to Sybbyl?"

"We have as much right to a bone as anyone," they said in harmony.

Runa wanted to refuse it, but if she could free Asrail and make sure her sister wasn't harmed, she would need the sword. She returned her weapons to their sheaths. Yet she still didn't grab it.

"Why do you hesitate?" the male before her asked. "We tracked down Avis and got this for you."

Runa looked at the five. "If I take this, it means I accept being your queen."

They nodded.

"And if I refuse?" she asked.

One of the females said, "As we said, we have a second option."

What choice did Runa have? While they hadn't said they would kill her, she didn't think the nymphs would allow her to decline their offer and then just walk away. They would take her life.

At least, if she were queen, she could halt anything done to Asrail as well as keep the Gira away from Synne.

"I have stipulations," she announced.

The five smiled. It was the male who asked, "And they are?"

"First, tell me what you'll do with her," she said, pointing to Avis.

One of the females said, "She betrayed Sybbyl. We'll turn her over to the Coven leader."

"Without the sword?" Runa asked. She shook her head. "Not smart. Sybbyl will ask for it. If she suspects we have it, she'll attack."

The nymphs laughed at her remark, but Runa didn't find anything she'd said humorous.

"The Gira are stronger than witches," one of the females said. "We aren't afraid of them. Not even Sybbyl."

Runa thought that was idiotic, but she kept that to herself. "The Gira should deal with Avis."

The five looked among themselves before they faced her and nodded together.

Well. That was easier than she'd expected. Though she didn't think everything would go that well.

"Wait," Avis said and gave Runa a pleading look. "You can't mean to let them kill me."

Runa cut her eyes to the witch. "Where did you get the sword?"

"A Highlander."

"Just some man you came across?"

Avis frowned and shook her head. "Of course, not. I was after a Hunter. He just happened to be with Synne."

The moment her sister's name was mentioned, rage filled Runa. "Did you hurt either of them?"

Avis shrugged. "Of course, I did. I killed the Highlander and made the Hunter watch his life draining away."

"Why?" Runa asked in a soft voice.

"Because she dared to hunt us. She was one of the last of her group, and Sybbyl sent me to dispatch her."

"But you didn't kill Synne, did you?"

Avis narrowed her eyes on Runa. "I got more satisfaction

from ending the Highlander's life. The two had fallen in love, so Synne will feel the pain of that for a long time."

One of the five said, "Except Lachlan isn't dead. Synne and the trees saved him."

Runa couldn't dismiss the fury that swirled through her at what Avis had attempted. She stalked to the witch. "You went after my sister."

"Sister?" she asked with a frown. "Elin said you were dead."

Runa stared down at Avis. "Where is your sister?"

"I don't know," Avis said, fear filling her visage.

Out of the corner of her eye, Runa saw the nymphs begin to crowd around them. They seemed to sense her rage and were feeding off it.

Runa held Avis's brown gaze. "Anything else you'd like to add?"

"I can be an ally. I know much about Sybbyl."

"So do the Gira," Runa said as she stepped back.

The nymphs quickly converged on Avis. Runa turned her back on the witch and walked away, even as Avis's screams filled the forest. Runa's stomach tightened. In all her years, she had never killed a human. And while it wasn't her hands taking the witch's life now, she hadn't stopped it either. Which made her as much to blame as the Gira.

If she were to see this through, she would have to remember that this wasn't about her. It was about her family. Even as that thought went through her head, an image of Brom filled her mind. How she longed to be back in the cave with him. None of this was what she had expected, and she wasn't sure she was doing the right thing. Yet, when all her choices were taken away, there was nothing left for her to do.

Maybe things would be different if she had let Brom come with her. She wanted to kick herself because she knew that for the lie it was. She hadn't let Brom come because she knew it would've meant his life. The Gira wanted her, and they had done everything to make sure they had her right where they wanted her.

She walked to the male who was still on his knees, holding the sword. Her hand hovered over it for a moment before she wrapped her fingers around the pommel and claimed it. There was no rush of power or anything to signify that what she held was a sword containing a bone of the First Witch, but that didn't matter. Not now, at least.

The Gira had chosen her as their queen, and they had given her the sword. That meant she had the power now.

20

Brom fidgeted. He wanted to go, but Malene told him to remain. He wasn't sure why, but he was beginning to wonder if it was her way of keeping him from going after Runa. If that were the case, she would be disappointed because nothing could keep him from Runa.

He got to his feet and looked around. The snowfall continued with some flurries dancing through the air as if they couldn't decide which direction to go. He looked through the trees to the sky, but it was still too dark to see anything. With no moon available, he had to either remain where he was until dawn or use magic.

He heard a sound behind him. He whirled around to see a woman bent over, a hand on the tree to steady herself as she coughed and emptied her stomach. She started to straighten before she fell sideways into the snow.

Brom rushed to her. As he knelt beside the woman, he found himself looking into the face of the Lady of the Varroki. "Malene?" he asked as he put a hand beneath her nose.

She was still breathing, but the fact that she was unconscious wasn't a good sign. He wasn't sure how she had gotten here, but he suspected she'd used magic, which meant it would send a call out to every witch in the Coven. He had to get her up so they could get away.

"Malene," he said, tapping her face. "Wake up. Come on. Wake up."

He lightly slapped her face twice more before her lashes fluttered, and she opened her eyes. As she looked up at him, she seemed to realize where she was and sat up. "You stayed."

"I did," he said as he helped her to her feet. "We can't remain here."

"We won't."

"Which direction do you want to go?" he asked, looking around.

Malene's hand wrapped around his wrist. In the next blink, he was falling through the sky. Just as quickly as it had begun, it ended. He tried to remain on his feet, but the room started to spin, and his stomach rebelled. All while his head felt as if someone had split it in two. Brom bent over just as someone shoved a bucket beneath him.

He managed to lift his head to see a man striding into the chamber, heading straight to Malene, who he caught in his arms as she collapsed. That was the last thing Brom saw before the darkness took him.

It could have been an hour or ten years before Brom finally opened his eyes again. He was still shaken by what Malene had done. As he stared up at the ceiling of the chamber, he began to comprehend that she had used a very rare, very difficult spell that allowed for huge jumps over land. The reason it was rarely used was because it not only took a great deal of magic, but it also took a massive toll on those who used it.

Given the pain in Brom's skull, the spell also took its toll on passengers. He gripped his head as he swung his legs over the side of the bed and sat up. His stomach churned, but he managed to keep from being sick. Barely.

"You're finally awake."

He knew that voice. Armir. Brom lifted his gaze to find the Varroki sitting at a table before the hearth. Armir was furious. Brom wasn't entirely sure the anger wasn't directed at him. "Why did she bring me here?"

"To save your bloody life," Armir stated and slammed his hand on the table. "And nearly took her own in the process."

Brom winced at the pounding Armir's fist caused in his head. Then he followed the Varroki's gaze to a chair where Malene sat, looking pale and in as much pain as he was.

"I didn't have time to get you," Malene said. "Besides, bringing you would've caused me more pain."

Armir rose swiftly, his anger palpable. "You left without me because you knew I'd stop you."

"Yes," she admitted, looking him in the eye.

Armir shook his head and stormed from the chamber.

Malene sighed and looked at Brom. "Forgive him. He's a little protective."

"You are the Lady of the Varroki."

She smiled swiftly, but it didn't quite reach her eyes. "Sometimes, a person in my position must put themselves in danger for the greater good."

"I'm no' sure I understand."

Malene moved a lock of flaxen hair from her face and shifted in her chair. "If you had remained in the forest, the Gira would've found you."

"I might have been able to get them to bring me to Runa."

Malene shook her head. "I doubt it."

His gaze narrowed on her. Despite his aching head, he realized she was leaving out important details. "What do you know?"

"The Gira found Runa."

"Is she hurt?" He was immediately on his feet, about to demand that Malene take him back to the forest.

The Lady's gray gaze dropped to the floor for a heartbeat. "Nay, she isn't."

"You are no' making me feel better. Whatever you know, just tell me."

"The Gira have chosen a new queen. Runa."

Brom blinked then shrugged. "She doesna have to accept, does she?"

"You know the nymphs, Brom. Do you honestly believe they would put someone in such a position and allow them to refuse?"

His mind was going in all different directions, trying to think of something, *anything*, to say.

"If you had remained in the woods, the Gira would've found you. If they didn't kill you immediately, they would've brought you to Runa, where they would've urged her to end your life."

He frowned. "She wouldna have done that."

"You said yourself that you don't know Runa that well."

Brom was thinking of something to say when the door flew open, and a couple stormed in, followed by Armir. The woman had blond hair pulled back in a thick braid. Her amber eyes fastened on him. In her face, he spotted similarities to Runa. Without hearing the woman speak, he knew this was Synne. The Hunter wore brown pants, a beige tunic, and a dark leather vest and boots.

He looked past her to the towering man who had his hand on Synne's lower back, which must mean he was Lachlan. The Scot's long, black hair was pulled back in a queue, and his gray eyes dared Brom to irritate his woman.

"I thought they should know," Armir said to Malene as he

walked around the couple and returned to his seat near the fire.

Synne's chest heaved as she took a few short steps toward Brom. "Is it true? Do you know my sister?"

"Aye," Brom replied. "Her name is Runa."

"I know. The trees gave me your message." Synne smiled and looked back at Lachlan. Then her gaze swung to Malene. "This is a sign. Brom said Runa would save her family."

Malene used the arms of the chair to push herself to her feet. Out of the corner of his eye, Brom saw Armir stiffen as he got ready to jump up and rush to Malene. There was more than just respect and admiration in Armir's gaze. There was something else there, something that was barely veiled—love. Brom wondered if Malene knew it.

"I did what I thought was the wisest thing to do," Malene told the room.

The door opened for a second time and another couple came in. The woman had dark red hair and vivid green eyes. Beside her was a Varroki warrior. Brom wasn't sure how he knew exactly, he just did. Perhaps it was the man's stance, or the way his blue eyes so pale they were nearly white watched Brom.

The woman smiled. "You've made a grand entrance."

"No' something I intended," Brom replied.

The warrior gave a nod to Malene and walked to Brom. He stopped a foot away, his unusual eyes sweeping over Brom. "You're a warlock, then?"

"I have magic from my father, who was a Varroki, if that's what you're asking."

The man suddenly smiled and glanced at Armir. Then he held out his arm to Brom. "I'm Jarin."

Brom was so shocked to finally meet the warrior that, for a

heartbeat, he didn't reply. He clasped Jarin's forearm and smiled. "It's good to meet you."

"And I'm Helena," the woman said as she came to stand beside Jarin.

Brom bowed his head to the witch, recalling the conversations he'd heard that included her. Jarin wrapped his arm around Helena and looked down at her with such devotion that Brom felt he should look away.

"Sybbyl will no doubt know what you've done," Armir said into the silence.

All eyes turned to Malene, who looked directly at Armir. "I knew that."

"You put yourself in danger for him." The fury in Armir's voice filled the chamber and grew with each moment.

Malene quirked a flaxen brow at him. "Brom is the key."

"The key?" Synne asked. "The key to what?"

Brom wanted to know the same thing. Everyone began to talk at once, asking Malene all sorts of questions, with no one paying any attention to him. Frankly, he wasn't going to stand for it.

"Enough!" Brom shouted. When everyone went quiet and looked at him, he drew in a breath and tried to collect his thoughts. "I understand there is a lot at stake here, but I am able to make my own choices whether you agree with them or not." He pointedly looked at Malene. "You may have had good intentions by bringing me here, but you should've asked."

She lifted one shoulder. "You wouldn't have agreed."

"As he said, that was his right," Jarin replied, no heat in his words.

Brom shook his head. "Runa is out there on her own. She needs an ally."

"And that's you?" Synne asked.

Brom's gaze slid to her. "It is."

"And what of the Gira and the Coven?" Armir asked. "How did you think to get through them? Do you even know what Sybbyl tried with Jarin?"

Brom glanced at the warrior and nodded. "I heard conversations."

"We've not even gotten to that part," Armir added, his tone dripping with ire.

Malene held up her hands, quieting everyone. "While I don't like that Brom listened in on our conversations, not once did he share any of the details with anyone."

"And you don't think he will if Sybbyl gets hold of him?" Helena asked. The witch shrugged. "No offense, Brom, but Jarin and I know firsthand what Sybbyl will do to get what she wants."

Brom shifted his feet, beginning to feel slightly better with each passing moment. "I can no' say what I would or wouldna do, especially if Runa's life was in danger."

"My point," Armir stated icily.

"However," Brom said, drawing out the word as he glared at Armir, "I would do everything in my power to keep any knowledge of you or Blackglade from Sybbyl."

Synne twisted her lips. "I think we all appreciate your words, but you've not come up against Sybbyl. You don't know what she's capable of."

"You're right. I doona." Brom left it at that since there wasn't anything he could say that would help matters. The fact that he had been taken farther away from Runa only irritated him more.

Malene sank back down to the chair. Her face was pale, and she looked like she needed to sleep, but she remained. "I'm sorry I brought you here without asking your consent, Brom. I knew you would refuse, and I needed you here."

"Why?" Armir asked as he rose and walked to lean against the wall near Malene.

It was as if he had to be near the Lady of the Varroki, and the more Brom looked, the more it was obvious that Armir was in love with her. What Brom couldn't determine was if Malene felt the same way about the commander.

But Malene didn't answer Armir. Instead, she drew in a breath and slowly released it. It appeared as if she carried a great weight, something that was slowly crushing her. And he had the distinct impression that it involved him. Suddenly, he didn't want to know any more. He wanted to rewind and take back every question he had. If he hadn't spoken to Malene, she never would've come to get him, and he would still be out there searching for Runa.

As much as he wanted to believe all of that, he knew it was a lie. Malene had said that he was the key. Regardless of whether he had or hadn't spoken with her that first time, he knew without a doubt that he'd be in Blackglade eventually regardless.

"You said I was the key," Brom spoke into the silence.

Malene blinked rapidly and nodded. "Ever since the Blood Skull was found, I've been getting snippets of things. Sometimes, they're in my dreams. Other times, they appear when I'm awake. I couldn't tell at first if I was seeing something important or if I was just getting used to the magic."

The more she spoke, the deeper the frown on Armir's face became. Brom could well understand the distress filling Armir's gaze. It was pretty much the same thing Brom had felt since Runa left.

"What did you see?" Brom asked when no one else spoke.

Malene licked her lips and shot a quick glance behind her to Armir. "Snow. Magic. Death. Fire. Trees. And a man's back.

I began to suspect over the last few weeks that they were all connected."

"The roof of the tower," Armir said, more to himself.

Malene paused for a heartbeat. "I might have fought my magic and position at one time, but after I accepted it, the power doubled. With it came certain…abilities."

"Like traveling over vast distances in moments?" Brom asked.

"Just like that. Also, I've heard Trea's voice, the First Witch. The more I heard, the more I could piece a few things together. Though I never saw the face of the man in my vision, I did hear his voice. It was you, Brom."

What did one say to something like that? Brom couldn't think of anything, so he remained silent.

"Then," Malene continued, "when you spoke to the trees and sent out that message, I knew for sure."

Brom frowned and slid his gaze to Synne for a moment. "I knew from overhearing a recent conversation that Synne was worried about her sister. I didna know much, but I figured what I did know could help."

"Exactly," Malene said with a wide smile. "Except, your actions were much greater than you realize."

Brom nodded as he recalled those words from earlier. "You said that before. What do you mean?"

"You said you wanted the trees to give Synne your message. Is that all you intended."

"Aye. What else could I have done?"

Malene's smile grew. "You used no magic when you spoke to the trees."

"Nay." Brom was getting frustrated. He just wanted an answer. But for whatever reason, Malene was leading him somewhere instead of telling him what he wanted to know.

"Why?"

Brom sighed loudly and looked at the floor as he shook his head. "I didna think I needed to. I'd heard Synne say the trees told her where her sister was, so I hoped they could hear me. Then there was the fact that I didna want anyone to know of my magic. By no' using any, I remained hidden."

"You forgot that which you carry. The object that called to you all those years ago."

Brom reached for his bag, only to realize that it was gone. His gaze quickly moved around the circular chamber, searching for it.

"Easy," Armir said as he walked around Malene and moved to the table and benches. There, sitting on the pew, was his bag. Armir grasped it and took it to Brom.

Brom accepted it and looked inside. The rib bone was still there, but just to be sure it was from the First Witch, he touched it. The moment he did, the magic zinged through his palm and up his arm.

"For months now, I've believed that the Blood Skull finding its Warden began everything, but that isn't true. The Blood Skull wasn't the first relic since the finger bone had been in the sword passed down in Lachlan's clan for generations. The Staff of the Eternal has also belonged to a family for generations." Malene's gray eyes caught and held Brom's gaze. "What began all of this was you. Trea coming to you and leading you to the rib bone."

Brom felt the weight of everyone's eyes on him. He wanted to deny everything Malene said, but he couldn't. "Aye."

"You knew where to find the rib bone because Trea spoke to you, as well."

He slowly nodded. "She first came to me in a dream when I was but a lad. The older I got, the more she appeared. She never spoke, but I knew her name. I used to go up into the mountains in a cave every so often to be by myself. It would take me hours to connect to Blackglade. I learned spells and how to do magic simply by listening to everyone here. During one of those times, she spoke to me. She told me exactly where to find the bone."

"Did she say anything else?" Helena asked.

"Nay," Brom answered. "But I didna hesitate to strike out the next day to go and find it. It took me months, but I retrieved it. I've kept it with me ever since, telling no one, no' even my mother."

Jarin caught his attention. "Did you hear from Trea again?"

"She didna speak again, nay. However, she appeared a day before I saw Runa's face in a dream."

Synne perked up. "Was it Trea who showed you my sister?"

Brom hated to disappoint her. "Actually, it was Asa."

"Asa?" Synne repeated, her eyes going wide. "The Asa from the abbey?"

"The same," Brom said. "I saw her in my dreams as a lad. It had been many years since I had seen her, so I didna recognize her voice in my dream when she told me to find your sister."

Lachlan's brows were drawn together. "But you went after Runa anyway?"

"I did."

"Two witches speaking to you in your dreams. Two of them giving you direction." Armir looked at Malene. "You knew all of this?"

The Lady of the Varroki shook her head. "I had no idea Asa had such magic."

"Neither did I," Synne added.

Armir returned to Malene's side. "You've kept a lot to yourself."

It was said in a low voice, but everyone heard it. Brom noted there was no censure in Armir's tone. Instead, there was hurt. Malene noticed it too, because she turned to him, her gaze searching his face.

"What I did wasn't because I didn't trust you. I kept it all to myself because I didn't put the pieces together until I spoke with Brom. Then, well, you know why I didn't tell you I was going for him," Malene said.

Armir nodded. Whatever hurt had been in his gaze before was gone. But Brom didn't believe for an instant that Armir had forgotten about it. Instead, the pain was carefully concealed, hidden away so no one could see it.

"What does any of this have to do with me having the rib bone?" Brom asked, bringing the conversation back to him.

Malene drew in a breath and turned her head to him. "Because when you sent that message through the trees to Synne, it went even farther."

Now, Brom was even more confused. "What do you mean?"

"The trees carried the message to Synne, but they also sent something else out into the air. Think of it as a call to action."

"I didna intend for that," he said, wondering if he had done more harm than good.

Malene shook her head and shifted to face him. "We here at Blackglade have known for some time that Sybbyl and the Coven would come for us. We've been preparing for it. We also made the decision not to bring any of the other bones here in case we lost. Helena is the most powerful of anyone who carries a bone of the First Witch since she's a direct descendent. Next is the Blood Skull that is currently far from here and will never fall into the Coven's hands."

He watched her, waiting for Malene to continue.

"We had Lachlan's sword and the finger bone, which would've given us an advantage. However, that is now lost."

"Stolen," Brom corrected.

Malene shrugged. "The only instance of Trea choosing someone to guard a bone that we know of is Braith as Warden of the Blood Skull. Yet, here you are. She chose you, showed you where to find the bone. She did that because she realized how powerful you are. Combining your magic with her bone raises your power considerably."

"I'm only half-Varroki," he argued, frowning.

Armir twisted his lips. "Be that as it may, you've done what no other Varroki has. I say that because we're a very powerful group, and if none of us have connected our minds to an entire city before, then you have something special."

"That is if you wish to fight with us," Malene said.

Brom lowered himself back to the bed to sit. He put his hands on either side of him and looked at the floor. "For so long, I dreamed of coming here. Even before I knew there was a war on its way. I heard enough about the Coven to want them gone." His gaze lifted to Malene. "I'm against them wholly."

"But?" Jarin asked into the silence that followed.

Without looking away from Malene, Brom said. "Runa."

21

She had no idea what she was doing. Runa's hands shook, but she gripped the sword even tighter. Accepting the Giras' demand to be their queen might give her power, but how much? She didn't think the nymphs would hand over the sword without thinking they could claim it again. After all, they had tracked down a Coven witch and had taken the sword from her.

No matter what happened, Runa knew that this was the right choice. Whether she succeeded or died, she did it knowing that she was doing everything she could. It wasn't that she feared death. She never understood why so many did. Sure, it was an unknown, but so was every day that dawned.

Her feet crunched in the snow as she walked through the forest, the Gira surrounding her. She felt their eyes on her, but she kept her gaze straight ahead. Not once did they stop, but she was glad. Halting would cause her to have to talk to them, and she wasn't prepared for that. Not since she still wasn't sure if her plan had even a marginal chance of succeeding.

They walked until her feet were numb, and the sky began to lighten with the coming dawn. Runa wasn't sure where they were taking her, but she hoped it wasn't to Sybbyl. She wasn't prepared for that. Actually, she wasn't sure she was prepared for anything. How she wished she could speak to Asrail once more. Maybe her grandmother would be able to guide her.

The trek up the mountain was arduous. Her thighs burned, and a headache had begun from the worry and fear churning violently inside her. She knew how to hunt and track nymphs. She knew nothing about being a queen.

When they finally reached the top of the mountain, Runa looked down and saw the loch that was frozen around the edges. A rather large group of nymphs stood near the water, though they kept giving the loch a trepidatious look. She tried to see what they were doing, but it was difficult with the sun still hidden behind the mountain. On the way down, more Gira joined. Some stood waiting to see her but most merely leaned away from the trees they had chosen.

Runa's nose was numb from the cold, as were her fingers and toes. She wanted a fire. No, what she wanted was Brom. As if thinking of him could conjure him to her side. No matter how much she wished for him, she knew that it was better that he wasn't here. She wasn't sure what the nymphs would've done to him if he were, and she didn't want to find out.

As the loch came closer, she realized that the group of nymphs she had seen were standing around something. Her stomach fell because she knew without looking that it was Asrail. Runa had to prepare herself. She couldn't let anything show to the Gira. Not anger, not fear.

Not yet, anyway. She needed to establish what kind of power she had and how to wield it before she let them know precisely what she intended.

When she and the other Gira reached the group, the nymphs parted, giving Runa her first glimpse of what they had done to her grandmother. Asrail was tied to the ground in the loch, her nose barely above water. Runa wasn't sure if they wanted her to drown or freeze to death. By Asrail's blue-tinged lips, she was on the verge of freezing already.

Runa stared at her, unsure of what to say. Asrail's eyes were closed. Runa wanted to go to her grandmother and nudge her to see if she was still alive, but perhaps it was better if she didn't disturb Asrail.

Hundreds of eyes were on her. Runa wanted to scream at them to leave Asrail alone, but she remained calm. She turned to the five who had remained directly behind her for the entire walk to the loch and quirked a brow at them.

The male asked, "What is that look for?"

"What are you doing with her?" Runa asked.

The female next to him smirked. "What does it look like?"

"It appears as if you're freezing her."

Another female stared at Runa intently. "Do you know her?"

Runa shot her a flat look. "I do not. If you're doing that to get a reaction out of me, then you're wasting your time."

"She's your grandmother," another female stated.

Runa's gaze slid to the Gira who had spoken. She had suspected that they might use someone against her. She wasn't sure if it would be Asrail, her sister, or even Brom, but she thought through every way she could reply. In order to remain on course, she needed to rely on her skill for reading people and keeping track of the lies she was going to tell.

"I was raised by a nymph. Of that, you already know. Which also means you're aware that I recently learned I had a sister," she stated.

The last female said, "As well as a grandmother. Asrail." She pointed at the loch.

"I learned of her the same time as I did my sister. Just a few days ago. I feel nothing toward people I don't know."

"No need to save her?" the male asked.

Runa turned and walked away. She prayed that Asrail was unconscious. She didn't want to hurt her grandmother, but in many ways, she hadn't lied. She didn't know Asrail or Synne. Runa felt responsible for them, but she wasn't sure why. They had never reached out to her. She'd risked everything for two people who didn't know her any more than she knew them.

She had no destination in mind, but she couldn't look at Asrail anymore. Hopefully, the Gira would think that she wasn't interested in saving her grandmother or condemning her to death. But in her heart, Runa knew there was little chance of saving Asrail. Tears pricked her eyes. It took everything she had not to cry over a woman she'd never met, someone who had only spoken to her once in a dream.

Still, she was a woman who had done everything in her power, along with her friend, to save Runa and Synne.

Runa wanted to go to a tree, but she couldn't stand to look at one right now. Too many nymphs were around. She needed to go somewhere they wouldn't be hiding. Her feet took her along the edge of the loch. With all the snow, it was difficult to know where the land ended, and the ice began. Since she wasn't keen on falling into the freezing water, she remained far enough away to be safe, yet also distanced from the edge of the forest and the Gira.

She stood looking out over the still waters of the loch to a small island that had a large defensive wall. Runa couldn't see what was on the other side, but she found she was curious to see what it was. If it was summer, she would've swum out there and taken a look for herself. Now, she would just have to use her imagination.

For a brief time, she forgot that she was now queen of the

Gira, forgot that she missed Brom, forgot that her grand-mother was closer than ever before and dying. But it was just a blink in time. Not long after, it all came crashing back down around Runa. She drew in a breath and realized that the five Gira were behind her. She was really beginning to hate them.

"What do you want?" she asked.

A female said, "We're waiting on you."

She should probably get their names, but she didn't care enough to do that now. Maybe not ever. "To do what?"

"Guide us," the male answered.

Runa turned and looked at them. "You want me to issue orders?"

"Aye," the older female said. "You have the sword."

She looked down at the weapon in her hand, the one she hadn't let go of since she had taken it. "You want an order? I'll give you one. I've claimed the throne. That means you'll leave my sister alone."

"As we said we would," the five replied together.

That was easier than she had thought. The next one wouldn't be. "Release Asrail."

Just as Runa expected, the five hesitated and looked at one another.

Runa raised a brow. "If I'm your queen, as you've made sure I would be, then you will listen to my directives. Asrail ruled you once, and she saved my sister as Morea saved me. Yet, you would have me or Synne as your queen. Instead of punishing Asrail for what she did, you should be thanking her. So, get her out of the water and warm her. Now!" she shouted when the five didn't budge.

One of the females turned and snapped her fingers toward the other nymphs, who watched. To Runa's shock, Asrail was immediately taken from the water and dragged to the nearest tree. For several minutes, her grandmother didn't move. Then, finally, she curled around the base of the tree, blending into it effortlessly.

"When Asrail is healed, she will be allowed to do whatever she wants. If anyone so much as looks at her crossly, I'll kill them," Runa said in an icy voice. None of that was a lie.

The five bowed their heads as the rest of the nymphs did.

Runa drew in a breath, feeling marginally better than she had a moment before. But this would be an uphill climb. These were only two steps she needed to take. She couldn't falter after this. Not even a little.

"Now," she said, "if we're going to use this sword and the bone of the First Witch, I need to know what Sybbyl plans."

The five Gira exchanged worried looks.

Runa sighed loudly. "If you already knew what you wanted to do, then you didn't need me or anyone to lead you. That means if I'm to make a decision, I need details. All of them."

One of the females grinned. "And this is why you're our queen."

Runa nearly laughed out loud. She was drowning in uncertainty and panic. Everything she was doing was all bluster in an effort to learn what the Coven was going to do so she could thwart it and give her sister and the Varroki a chance.

The mere thought of the Varroki brought Brom to mind. She would cry later for what could have been. For now, she had to push him from her thoughts and concentrate on remaining queen and staying alive.

The male Gira said, "Sybbyl thinks we're using Asrail to draw out your sister so she can kill her. Synne wasn't in the abbey with the other Hunters, and Sybbyl wants to make sure there are none left."

"Since I've decreed that Synne will be left alone, Sybbyl's plans matter not." Runa felt the first rays of the sun on her face. She wished it would heat her as it did the earth, but it would take much more than that to rid her bones of the chill. "Do Sybbyl and the Coven stand a chance at winning without us?"

The smile on the five's faces at her calling herself one of them was just the touch Runa had been hoping for.

"No," answered one of the females.

"Without Avis being found, Sybbyl will believe the witch went far away." Runa shrugged. "That could be to our advantage."

Another female shook her head. "Sybbyl sent witches out looking for Avis."

"They won't find anything, will they?" Runa asked.

The five shook their heads.

"Good. If we're not joining Sybbyl, then we need to prepare for her attack. Because it will come."

The male tilted his head. "You could go to her and tell her you're our new queen."

"If I did that, she'd likely attack right then." But that might be just what Runa *should* do. If only she could talk to Synne about everything and coordinate. That wasn't possible, and she wasn't sure if the Gira were powerful enough to take out the Coven and Sybbyl. Yet, that might be exactly what it came to.

Runa looked at the forest. She had always found sanctuary within the trees. She needed time to think and plan, and there was no better place.

Her gaze swung back to the five. "I need a fire, food, and a place to sleep."

"It will be seen to," they replied.

She gave them a nod and headed toward the nearest tree.

22

The pain was becoming unbearable. Sybbyl could find no rest, no respite from the wounds Helena had inflicted upon her during their battle. With the Staff of the Eternal and her own considerable magic, she should've been able to heal herself. But for whatever reason, the injuries on her wrist and neck continued to fester and cause her unbearable agony.

She paced, she sat, she slept, but the hours crawled by with excruciating sluggishness. Sybbyl now began to doubt if she would even be alive when it came time to face the Varroki.

"Nay," she mumbled to herself. "I hold a bone of the First Witch."

If she thought the bone would talk to her as it often did, she was mistaken. That made her immediately wary. The bone hadn't hesitated to take jabs at her any chance it got. Why was it quiet now?

Sybbyl set the staff in front of her where she sat in the middle of the Witch's Grove. She drew in a deep breath, feeling the relief of letting go of the bone. It was an incredible weight to bear, but she was prepared to carry it for the rest of her life. She was, after all, the one born to rule the witches and the new world where they could live as they wished.

Her gaze moved around the trees. For the first time, she realized how quiet the Grove was. There were no whispers, not that the Gira spoke to her much. Having the nymphs follow her was a boon she hadn't counted on, but one that would turn the tide in her favor.

Sybbyl debated whether to get up and walk around, but she decided to conserve her energy. The Grove helped to restore a witch's magic and intensify any spells used. She decided to give a healing spell another try. Though this time, she decided to do it without touching the staff.

The words tumbled from her lips in a flurry as she closed her eyes and felt her magic swirl inside her then move throughout her body. The magic focused on the two wounds. Sybbyl clenched her teeth as the pain intensified. Just when she didn't think she could handle any more, it began to ebb away.

The longer the spell worked, the better she felt. Why hadn't she tried this before? Why had she been so insistent that the staff would help her?

Because it *should* have.

She carried it now. Which meant, it answered to her. It shouldn't be doing anything to hinder her magic. And as far as she knew, it hadn't, other than with her wounds. Sybbyl waited until the spell was finished before she opened her eyes. She glanced around to see if any witches were looking her way before she pulled up her sleeve and checked her wrist.

The wound was still there, but it was much better. It was no longer red and filled with puss. The pain was minimal now, bearable enough that she could easily continue on. Now she knew that to heal herself, she had to set aside the staff—even if that shouldn't be the case.

But the more she thought about it, the angrier she got. The staff was hers to command. It didn't get to choose when and if it obeyed. It merely gave her its magic to mix with her own. That's why it had been so imperative that she do whatever necessary to get the staff from the elders.

Anyone could pick up the Staff of the Eternal and use the bone. Same with any bone from the First Witch. Well, just about any bone. The Blood Skull was an exception, one that rankled Sybbyl to no end. Although, had the elders gotten their greedy little hands on it, she would never have been able to kill them and get the staff for herself.

She looked at her wrist again. What was it about Helena's magic that caused such a reaction? The witch was powerful, but no more than Sybbyl. The only difference between them was that while Sybbyl had a bone, Helena was a direct descendent of the First Witch. A living, breathing person might be considered stronger than a single bone.

Though Sybbyl would've had more than one bone if Avis hadn't turned against her. Sybbyl wasn't a fool. She knew the moment the witch hadn't returned that Avis had taken the sword for herself. Not that it mattered. Avis wouldn't get far.

Sybbyl almost felt sorry for the witches she'd sent out to look for Avis. The only way Avis would return was if she wanted to. Anyone who forced her would feel her wrath magnified by the sword she'd stolen.

While Sybbyl wasn't pleased she had been deceived, she had to admit that what Avis had done took courage. It was precisely something Sybbyl would've done in her place. Perhaps she should've seen what Avis was about. Then again, Sybbyl wasn't worried about Avis. Bone or not, Avis was no match for Sybbyl one on one, and Sybbyl wasn't alone. She had the Gira.

The more time that passed after the healing spell, the

better she felt. With her mind cleared from the pain, she could think about her plans for the Varroki and how she was going to find more bones. She could take the time now to search out more of the First Witch, but she would rather deal with the Varroki first. Then there would be nothing standing in her way.

Her gaze dropped to the staff. This was usually the time when it told her that of course something would always stand in her way. She didn't have all the bones, nor would she ever get her hands on the Blood Skull. Which meant there would always be someone opposing her.

That used to bother Sybbyl. Now, she didn't care. If the Blood Skull was so powerful, why wasn't the Warden, Braith, here with the relic and his wife, the Hunter, Leoma? They weren't here because everyone knew she was unstoppable.

"My queen."

Sybbyl's head turned to the side to see a petite witch with mousy brown hair and eyes watching her. "Aye?"

"A group of witches has returned."

Sybbyl nodded, feeling the weight of the large, black crown atop her head. "Send them to me." When they came into the clearing, Sybbyl looked them up and down. "Did you find anything?"

"We had Avis's trail," an older woman with salt and pepper hair said. "Then it disappeared."

Sybbyl frowned. "Disappeared how?"

"She just seemed to vanish," a tall redhead said.

The rest nodded in agreement.

There were only two ways to disappear. One was with a spell, but Sybbyl knew it left a witch weak to use it for traveling great distances. Avis had been unwavering in her desire to lead the Coven one day. There was no way she would travel away from the coming war. Her only option was to join

Sybbyl in a bid to jointly take out the Varroki. Sybbyl wasn't a fool. She would've taken that offer, then killed Avis the first chance she got. Which, no doubt, the witch planned to do with her, as well.

The other way was with the Gira. No other creature in the world could make someone vanish like the nymphs could. And they knew what Avis had done. They also knew that Sybbyl was looking for the witch.

Sybbyl wrapped her hand around the staff and anchored it in the ground to use to help her rise. She braced herself, hoping her wounds didn't start to fester again. To her delight, they didn't. Feeling better than she had in weeks, Sybbyl knew she had one place she needed to go.

She nodded to the witches. "Thank you for returning so quickly with the news. Rest and recharge with the others. It won't be long now before we face the Varroki."

When the witches turned away, Sybbyl walked from the Grove into the thick, twisting branches of the trees surrounding it. She walked past trunks, noting only a few Gira remained. There had been great excitement when she allowed the nymphs to take Asrail and use her to get Synne's attention, but she hadn't expected so many of them to leave.

Sybbyl wound her way through the forest, looking for the Gira. The farther she went from the Grove without finding them, the more concerned she became. Just where had the nymphs gone? Out of the corner of her eye, she spotted a Gira, who had turned her head from the tree, watching her.

"Where are they?" Sybbyl asked without looking at the nymph. When the Gira didn't answer immediately, she looked at her.

The nymph dropped her arms from around the tree and stepped back before facing Sybbyl. The Gira held her head high, uncaring that she was naked, and her skin looked and felt like bark. "Follow me."

Sybbyl didn't like the uncertainty she felt. Something had changed, and she wasn't sure what. Or even when it had happened. But there was no denying *something* was different. How that would affect her in her bid to take out the Varroki, Sybbyl didn't know. It was another reason to track down the Gira. There was a good chance she would find out what she needed from the nymphs.

The Gira she followed took her farther up the mountain and then over it before they began their descent. Halfway down, Sybbyl spotted the loch and some of the nymphs. She tried to think about what could've changed with the Gira, and the only thing she could think of was Avis. Had she gone to the nymphs? Had they aligned with the witch? That couldn't be possible. Avis wasn't the leader of the Coven. Which meant, she didn't have the power Sybbyl did.

No matter how hard she tried to find the answer, Sybbyl kept coming up empty. As she neared the loch, she noticed that some of the Gira didn't even look her way as if she didn't matter. They were the ones who'd said they would follow her. She hadn't gone after them to join her, so it shouldn't bother her so much that they didn't seem to care that she was here now. But it did.

Sybbyl came to a halt when five Gira—four females and a male—stood before her. Some might think the five had come forward to greet her, but she knew they had situated themselves so she couldn't go any farther. Sybbyl looked over them to the loch and the forest that curved around it. What was in there the nymphs wanted to protect? Or keep hidden?

And where was Asrail?

Just a day ago, Sybbyl had known she could command the Gira. She had captured and held Asrail. She had given the nymph to the Gira to call out Synne. So, why did it feel as if they were simply humoring her now?

"I came to check on how things were progressing with Asrail," Sybbyl said. "I gather the trees have already told Synne that we have her grandmother? When can we expect the Hunter to come? I'll have the Coven move here in preparation."

"Asrail is gone," one of the females in the five said.

Sybbyl glanced around to see more and more of the Gira turning her way. "It matters not that she's dead. Her body will be enough to draw out Synne."

"We never said she was dead," another female said.

The lone male replied, "We said she was gone."

Sybbyl struggled to keep her fury in check. "You let her go?"

"We did," a third female answered.

Sybbyl couldn't believe what she was hearing. "Why would you do that? I worked hard to get Asrail, not just for me but for you."

"Now that's a lie," the fourth female said. "You captured Asrail because you couldn't get any of the others. And you gave her to us because you knew you had no other choice."

That wasn't exactly true, but Sybbyl wasn't going to split hairs. "Where is she? I need to capture her again."

"She'll not be harmed," all the Gira said in unison.

A chill raced down Sybbyl's spine. Something had absolutely changed. And it was time to find out what. "What's going on?"

A tall woman walked out of the forest from behind the five. Her long, blond hair hung freely about her. She wore breeches and had two short swords strapped to her back, but it was the sword she carried in her hand that got Sybbyl's attention. The staff in Sybbyl's hand began to vibrate, an indication that the sword held a bone of the First Witch.

It was likely the very sword Avis had stolen.

The woman said nothing as she reached the five, and they moved aside to let her through until she stood facing Sybbyl. "I wondered how long it would take for you to come."

"Where is Avis?"

The woman quirked a brow. "Why would you think we would know where one of your witches is?"

"Because of that," Sybbyl said and jerked her chin to the sword.

The woman merely smiled, not answering.

"Who are you?" Sybbyl demanded, noting the woman's odd accent.

Blue eyes looked her up and down. "Runa."

"You say that as if I'm supposed to know you."

Runa chuckled, but the smile didn't reach her eyes. "You had no cause to know me before, but you will after this."

"And why is that?"

"Because I'm queen of the Gira."

Sybbyl busted out laughing. Until she realized that no one else was joining her. The laughter faded as she held Runa's gaze. "You're serious?"

Runa shrugged. "Ask them if you don't believe me."

Sybbyl looked to the five. "You can't have a queen, especially not one who is human."

"Why?" the male asked. "Is it because you believed you were our queen?"

One of the females smiled. "And Runa is only half-human. Her other half is Gira."

Sybbyl knew of only one other who was half-Gira—Synne.

"That's right. Synne is my sister," Runa said with a knowing grin.

Everything Sybbyl had put into place was crumbling, but it hadn't fallen apart yet. The nymphs had been a benefit she had exploited, but she didn't need them. And she would prove it. She glared at Runa. "What are your plans?"

"What are yours?" the blonde asked in return.

Sybbyl wanted to scream in frustration, but then she reminded herself that all was not lost. There was still a chance that she would vanquish the Varroki and take over the world. "I highly recommend that you don't stand in my way. The only option you have is to join me. If you do nothing, once I win, I'll hunt you down and kill you."

Runa actually smiled and lifted the sword before her face. "I suppose we'll just have to see what happens."

Sybbyl spun around and walked away, seething with fury.

23

This had to work. There was no other way. But so much hinged on so very many factors. Brom stood atop Malene's tower and looked out at the sea, watching the waves whitecap from the winds and the turbulent currents as the sun sank into the horizon. It had been a rough day with many plans discussed, many more thrown out, and all kinds of scenarios put into motion.

"I'm not surprised to find you up here," Armir said as he came to stand beside him.

Brom shrugged, glancing at him. "I needed some air."

"This is a great place to get it. I know it's Malene's favorite spot."

"And yours."

They exchanged a glance, and Armir smiled. "You're right. How did you guess?"

"If everyone saw this view, they would be up here all the time. Be it the sea, the city, the forest, or the land beyond. It's stunning."

"That it is." They stood in silence for a few moments before Armir asked, "How are you holding up?"

Brom shoved his hair out of his face. "I'm no' sure. I'm ready to find Runa, and I know there's a chance she's out of my reach now, that I may never have her beside me again. I'm anxious to get the battle going, but I know there are so many moving parts to our plan that anything could go wrong."

"We've planned for some of those."

Brom slid his gaze to Armir's pale green eyes. "There's no way we can plan for everything."

"Our chances of winning are good. I could not say that before Malene brought you here. I think with you, we can end this before too many die."

Brom didn't want to carry the weight of that, but there was no way he could release the burden now that Malene had said he was the key. He never would have guessed that by setting out to find Runa, he would assert himself into a war that had the potential to change the entire world.

"You love her," Armir said.

Brom nodded. "All it took was one meeting, and I knew we were meant to be together. The one night we had was...wonderful."

"Aye. I can see it every time you speak of her or even say her name."

Brom smiled and looked back at the sea. "I kept telling myself that I couldn't fall in love with someone that quickly, that there needed to be time for us to get to know each other. Now, I know how wrong I was."

Armir made a sound in the back of his throat.

Brom turned his head to look at the commander. Armir was staring off in the distance, but he wasn't looking at the sea. "You should tell her."

"What?" Armir asked with a frown as he looked at Brom.

Brom smiled. "You should tell Malene how you feel."

Armir's lips parted as if he were going to deny that he felt something, then he looked back at the water. "Perhaps. In time."

"You have no idea what tomorrow will bring. I wish I would've told Runa how I felt. I wish I would've done more. I have a second chance now, and nothing will stop me from telling her my feelings."

"What if she doesn't return them?"

Brom shrugged. "If she doesna, then I'll accept that. However, I know how she felt in my arms. I know she feels something for me. Is it love yet? I can no' say, but I'm willing to wait until she's sure."

Armir smiled and slapped him on the back. "You know you're welcome here anytime. You're Varroki."

"Even though one of your warriors broke the code and slept with my mother? He told her he was supposed to remain celibate."

"Everything happens for a reason. Haven't you figured that out yet?" Armir asked with a grin.

Brom laughed. "I'm beginning to."

Their smiles died as the sun finally sank into the horizon.

"It's time," Armir said in a soft voice.

Brom turned on his heel and walked to the stairs. He ascended to the first door and entered Malene's chamber, where everyone waited. Armir was right on his heels and closed the door behind them.

After a day of recovery, as well as food and a short nap, Malene looked hale and hearty once more. She gave him a nod. "Ready?"

"As I'll ever be," Brom said as he made his way to her.

Everyone stood in a circle except for Helena. She sat before the fire, facing them. Jarin called to her, but the witch didn't answer. Everyone then looked over at her. As they watched, she began to slowly rise into the air.

"Her eyes," Lachlan whispered.

Helena's green eyes were now glowing as brightly as an emerald. Jarin rushed to her, but before he could touch her, Malene batted his hands away.

"Don't," the Lady of the Varroki said.

Jarin shot her a dark look. "Something is happening to her."

"She's not in pain," Armir said.

Helena suddenly spoke, but it wasn't her voice that came out. "The time is now. The others have been called to right the balance once more. Where there is poison, there is a cure. You know the way."

The last part was spoken with Helena looking right at Brom. It felt as if he'd been punched in the gut. Helena lowered back to the floor and blinked. Whatever had overtaken her was gone. She looked to Jarin, who wrapped his arms around her. The warrior held her tightly as everyone else looked at Brom.

"Who was that speaking?" Synne asked.

Malene said, "Thea, the First Witch. I've heard her voice in my head many times."

After Jarin had gotten Helena on her feet, she looked at him. "You know what Trea was referring to, don't you?"

"I do," Brom admitted.

Lachlan's frown deepened. "What is it?"

"Runa," he answered.

Synne smiled at him. "You think you can reach Runa through the Gira?"

"I do," Brom told her.

Armir nodded at Malene. "I think we should get going then."

"Wait," Helena said. "Trea showed me something that I

think you all should know. First, you won't be the only ones fighting against the Coven."

Malene looked pleased with the news. "Did she say who would join us?"

"Braith and Leoma and Ravyn and Carac. She's commanded Braith to bring the skull."

Jarin's brows shot up on his forehead. "And here we thought it would be better not to have the other bones here."

"Trea wouldn't lead us wrong," Malene stated.

Helena swung her gaze to Jarin. "There's one more thing. She said if I go, and the power of the heart combines with the other bones, we're all but ensured a victory."

"But?" Jarin said when she paused.

"Trea warned me there is a chance I could lose the baby if I go."

Brom was glad that he wasn't in Jarin's shoes, because he wasn't sure what he'd do. Some might say the couple could have another child in the future, but nothing was ever guaranteed.

Jarin asked, "What do you want to do, my love? It is your body."

"It's our child," she argued.

He grinned and gave her a kiss on the lips. "True, but no one knows more than you how important this battle is. Whatever you decide, I'll stand by your decision."

"I'm going," Helena declared.

The seven of them gathered together in a circle, holding hands. Everyone with magic said the spell Malene had taught them earlier. Brom braced for the pain as the final words fell from his lips, and they were transported from the tower in Blackglade to the forest in the Cairngorm Mountains.

Night blanketed the land when they arrived. Brom turned away to empty his stomach before he collapsed. He spotted

Armir and Malene holding onto each other just as he lost consciousness.

"Brom!"

He was jostled awake by Armir, who slapped him on the face. Brom jerked upright to see that Synne and Lachlan were having just as much trouble.

"I'm good," Brom said.

Armir helped him to his feet. "Do you know where we are? Malene got us as close as she could, which is probably closer than we should be."

"We don't have a lot of time," Malene stated.

Brom turned in a circle to get his bearings. "Which way is the Coven?"

Jarin pointed to the north.

Brom faced in that direction, his thoughts full of Runa. He had to get to her and quickly. "Will the Gira be near the Coven?"

"They're at a loch," Synne said. "It's not too far from the Coven."

Malene gave Brom a nod. "We all know what to do."

"If even one of us fails, it's over," Armir said.

Helena lifted her chin. "We won't fail."

Brom exchanged a look with Armir. "Good luck."

"Same to you," the commander said before he turned to face Malene.

Brom, Synne, and Lachlan set out in the direction of the loch, while the other four headed to the Coven. The rest of the Varroki waited at Blackglade in case there was an attack there.

"Which direction?" Brom asked Synne.

She pointed, and he began jogging through the snow. Time was of the essence, and each moment that passed without Runa was one against them—he knew it in his gut, in his very *soul*.

The three of them ran when they could, walked when they had to, and rested only briefly. Brom knew why Malene had dropped them so far from the Coven, but he wished they could've gotten closer to the loch and the Gira.

"Wait," Synne told him, grabbing his cloak to stop him.

Brom slid to a halt and looked at her. "What?"

"The Gira."

Brom had been so focused on getting to the loch and finding Runa that he hadn't been thinking about the Gira. He looked around. "Are they here?"

"Aye," Synne whispered.

"How many?" Lachlan asked.

Synne moved in front of them without answering. Suddenly, there was movement at one of the trees. A woman's shape took form as she turned to Synne.

"Asrail," Synne cried and rushed to her.

The Gira enfolded Synne in a hug as the two held each other. Finally, Asrail pulled back with a smile. "I knew you'd come."

"We need to get to Runa," Synne told her.

Asrail nodded, a grim expression on her face. "I tried to warn her what the Gira wanted, but it was too late."

"What did they do to her?" Brom demanded.

Synne said, "This is Brom. He's come to help Runa. We all have."

Asrail drew in a breath and released it. "They've made her their queen."

"What?" Brom and Synne asked in unison.

Asrail shot Synne a sad smile. "They wanted her, and if she refused, they would've killed her and come for you to lead them."

"I...I don't understand," Synne said. "They tried to kill us."

"I know, my child. But things change," Asrail replied. "You both have incredible gifts, and you're both unique."

That got Brom's attention. "What is Runa's gift?"

Asrail studied him for a long moment.

He grew anxious and sighed loudly. "I love her. I doona care what blood she has or what she can do, or even that she's the queen of the Gira. All I care about is her."

"We shall see," Asrail said. "Come. I know how to get to Runa."

Brom didn't mention that Asrail hadn't answered him. He figured she had done that on purpose, and that was fine. As long as he got to Runa. And he *would* get to her if it was the last thing he did.

The four of them moved quietly. Asrail took the lead with Brom bringing up the rear. With every step, Brom's unease grew until it festered within him like a giant lead ball. He couldn't pinpoint what caused it, which only made things worse. Asrail halted abruptly. Then she turned and pinned him with a hard look.

"What is it?" he asked.

Asrail pivoted and walked to him. "I know what you have."

"Do you?"

Synne hurried to them. "We don't have time for this now."

"We need to make time," Asrail said without looking away from him.

Brom gave the Gira a nod in agreement. "Aye. We talk now."

"Och," Lachlan murmured, irritation straining his voice. "This isna the time."

Asrail lifted her chin. "It is. Because if Brom comes with us to the Gira, he'll use the bone against Runa."

"I wouldna," he stated.

Asrail's gaze lost some of its intensity as sadness overtook her face. "You won't have a choice."

"What does that mean?" Synne demanded.

Lachlan frowned as he shook his head. "Malene said Brom was the key to us winning."

"And he is," Asrail replied. She blew out a breath. "He'll do it by killing Runa."

Brom couldn't have been more surprised by Asrail's statement. Fury whipped through him and with it a force of magic so deep and forceful that he took a step back. "I wouldna harm Runa."

"Even if it meant ensuring that the rest of the world remained safe?" Asrail asked.

Brom squeezed his eyes closed for a heartbeat. "Where is this coming from?"

"A source I trust."

Synne rolled her eyes. "You're going to have to give us more than that. It was Brom who let us know that Runa was fighting against Sybbyl."

"Are you sure of that?" Asrail asked as her gaze swung to her granddaughter.

Brom answered quickly. "I am."

"Because you knew Runa for one night?" The Gira's gaze slid back to him. "You know nothing of her."

"I know what I feel," he argued. "Whether you think that's right or wrong, I doona care. I'm here to protect Runa."

Asrail's shoulders sagged. "You won't be able to."

"Why do you say that?" Lachlan asked.

The Gira appeared to age before them. "There is more magic on this Earth than witches, warlocks, and nymphs. There is magic much older, much stronger. It showed me... things I didn't want to see, including Runa's death by Brom's hand in order for this war with the Coven to end. Where there's poison—"

"There's a remedy," Brom finished, remembering Malene's words at Blackglade.

Asrail nodded slowly. "All these years, I thought Runa and my dear friend Morea had died. Morea never reached out to me, and I never looked for her. We did it to keep both Synne and Runa safe from the Gira. My granddaughters have finally come into my life, and now I'm going to lose one."

"We'll see about that," Brom said. "Take me to Runa."

24

Runa might know nothing of being queen and ruling, but she knew people. And after her brief talk with Sybbyl, she knew the Coven leader wasn't going to stand by idly and do nothing. Sybbyl was furious that she had the sword. Not to mention, the witch suspected the Gira had done something to Avis—and Sybbyl wouldn't be wrong.

Up until then, Sybbyl had thought the Gira were on her side. No doubt she had second thoughts about that, for good reason. Mainly because the nymphs weren't on the Coven's side any longer. Runa wasn't sure what that meant. Yet.

She waited until Sybbyl was out of sight before turning on her heel and making her way back to the area the Gira had made for her. Runa had been pleasantly surprised at how quickly and inventively the nymphs had constructed a shelter out of broken branches and the many rocks around the area.

While it only had three makeshift walls, it would keep the snow off her. The roaring fire also helped to warm her. Then there was the food. Runa couldn't believe the variety of meats the nymphs had hunted—rabbit, various birds, and a deer.

There was no way she could eat it all, and she wasn't sure the Gira would.

No sooner had Runa sat down before the fire than her thoughts turned to Brom. She tried not to think about him. It did her no good, and only made her wish that things could be different. But there was no changing the path she was on.

Her thoughts went to Asrail. How she wished she knew where her grandmother had gone, but perhaps it was for the best that she didn't know. The other Gira would probably object to Asrail being with them. However, Runa had decreed that no one could touch Asrail. Whether they obeyed that or not was the question. All she could do was hope that the nymphs spoke true when she asked where her grandmother was earlier. If she found out that any of them had harmed Asrail, Runa wouldn't hesitate to take her anger out on them. Asrail was family, after all.

Speaking of family…her thoughts moved to Synne. Runa had no idea what her sister looked like, and she probably never would. That made her sad. But if she could keep Synne from taking the mantle of queen, Runa would do it. It was only fair that someone in their family actually have a good life. Synne had begun it, so Runa should finish it.

Even as Runa thought those words, her heart ached for Brom. How could someone she had known so briefly leave such an impression? But she knew. He was special. More so than any other being she would ever encounter—because he was hers.

And she was his.

A tear slipped down her cheek, and she hastily wiped it away. This was no place for crying. The Gira weren't her friends. They were her enemy, just as the Coven and Sybbyl were. Runa couldn't trust anyone, and she certainly wouldn't allow anyone to see something they could perceive as a weakness.

She thought about sending some nymphs out to look for Brom, but Runa knew that for the folly it was. The Gira might accept her because of the blood in her veins, but they likely wouldn't accede to Brom being with them. And even if Runa demanded it as their queen, there was the question of what Brom would do if he found out who and what she really was —and what she could do.

"It doesn't matter," she told herself.

Brom was gone. She needed to let his memory go, as well. She had made sure that he couldn't follow her. He had managed it the first time, and a small part of her had hoped— expected—that he would the second time. But he hadn't. It was for the best. He didn't belong in this world.

Not because he wasn't Gira but because he was a warlock. His place was with the Varroki.

But what if he accepted you?

Runa squeezed her eyes closed. She couldn't allow herself to ask questions like that or cling to a *maybe one day*. She had accepted her fate the moment she took the sword. There was no turning back now. Nor could she sit and wallow in self-pity. She had to think about what was coming next. Sybbyl might attack the Gira. It would be a foolish move, but the Coven leader was furious at the moment. Which meant there was no telling what Sybbyl might do.

The fire felt wonderful, and it reminded Runa of Brom and their time together, but she couldn't stay here. She climbed to her feet, careful to keep the sword with her. She walked from her shelter and looked around for the five. As if they knew she wanted them, they came from various directions to stand before her.

"Scouts need to be set up in a wide perimeter. Make sure

they're somewhere Sybbyl won't think to look for them," Runa ordered.

One of the females couldn't hide her shocked expression. "You believe Sybbyl will attack us?"

"Surely not," another said. "We're too powerful."

Runa didn't want to listen anymore. "I hope she doesn't, but Sybbyl knows I have the sword. She suspects we tracked down Avis and took it. And now she knows the Gira aren't following her beck and call as you once were."

The male nymph took offense at this. "We weren't at her beck and call."

Runa swung her gaze to him. "Really? So, you had every Gira you could gather follow her...why?" There was no response, not that she needed one. She took a deep breath. "Set up the sentries. Tell them not to attack if anyone gets close. They're our eyes only."

A third female huffed. "Then what is the point in having them?"

"The point is for them to notify the second line of nymphs who will surround this camp. They will be set up far enough away that when the first line spots anyone, the second will attack them as well as notify the main camp. That will give everyone else time to prepare for battle and go wherever we're weakest."

There was a beat of silence before the fourth female gave a nod. "A sound plan. You're proving why we chose you as our queen."

"Then stop questioning me," Runa stated. "I won't explain myself or my actions again. You chose me and made sure I had no other choice but to be your queen. Because of that, you follow everything I say."

The five bowed their heads in silent accord.

One of the females asked, "Where will you be?"

Runa glanced down at the sword in her hand. "I'm going to take care of Sybbyl."

They gasped in unison. But none questioned her. Runa was relieved because she didn't want to explain her actions. Going to Sybbyl might not be the smartest thing to do, but the Coven leader wouldn't expect it. Plus, Runa could get in undetected, giving her yet another advantage. All in all, there was a very good chance she could end everything before a war even began.

"When do you go?" the male asked.

Runa looked at the night sky. "Now."

She had only taken two steps when there was a commotion in the camp. Her head swung to the noise to see Asrail walking through the gathered Gira. Runa's lips began to curl at the sight of her grandmother. The grin froze when she spotted a woman with blond hair behind Asrail, one step after her was a tall man with long, black hair pulled back in a queue. Her heart skipped a beat when she spotted the final person in their group—Brom.

For just a moment, Runa thought to run to him, to throw her arms around him and shower him with kisses. Then she remembered where she was and what she was. Their night together in the cave was slowly becoming a distant memory. It would be one she treasured always, but she couldn't continue on while still holding onto it.

It hurt her more than she wanted to admit when the smile that had filled him at the sight of her started to fade. She wanted to cry, to scream at the world for the unfairness of putting Brom in her life and showing her how it could be with him, only for her to lose him so epically.

Runa didn't know how long they stood there looking at each other before she realized that the Gira were watching her. She knew Asrail had brought the group here for a reason, and she didn't want to have that conversation in front of all the nymphs. Runa motioned for Asrail and the others to follow her back to her shelter.

She turned on her heel and looked at the five. "I don't want to be disturbed. I also better not discover any Gira nearby, trying to overhear anything."

Runa didn't wait to see their response. She continued back to her lodgings and stood at the fire. Asrail led the other three into the accommodation until they stood in a semi-circle, looking at her. It took everything she had not to speak to Brom or even look at him. She had wished so hard for him that she would love to believe that she had somehow brought him here. Even if she knew that wasn't the truth.

"Runa," Brom said.

Her eyes moved to him of their own accord. The hurt she saw in his face was like a knife twisting in her gut. "You shouldn't have come."

"I told you I'd follow you," he said.

She lowered her gaze to the fire. "And I told you that it would only bring you death."

"He's here to help you," the blonde said.

Asrail caught Runa's gaze and smiled. "I didn't get a chance to thank you for saving me."

"I didn't expect you to leave." Runa wasn't sure why Asrail had changed the subject, but she was happy she had.

An odd look flashed in her grandmother's eyes. "There are some things we cannot walk away from, no matter what we might wish."

"Bollocks," the man said. "Everyone has a choice."

Runa shook her head. "Not everyone."

"Sometimes, our paths are chosen for us," Asrail said. She glanced at the blonde. "Runa, this is your older sister, Synne."

A breathless laugh escaped Runa. "Synne? Is it really you?"

Her sister smiled and laughed as she nodded. Synne hurried around the fire, and the two embraced. Runa held onto Synne much tighter than she should have.

"I never knew of you," Synne whispered.

Runa fought against a wash of unshed tears. "And I didn't know of you."

Synne pulled back and wiped at her eyes. "This is Lachlan. He helped me get to the Varroki."

"Nice to meet you," Lachlan said, though his gaze lowered to the sword in her hand.

Runa knew it was his, but she couldn't give it up yet. "Thank you for being there for my sister."

"She saved me," he said and gave Synne a smile so full of love that Runa couldn't help but look at Brom.

Runa licked her lips, unsure what to say or do. It was like someone kept changing the landscape, causing her to trip and fall. She was tired of it. "You should leave." She glanced at the others. "All of you."

"I'm no' going anywhere," Brom stated.

Synne walked to stand between Lachlan and Asrail. "None of us are."

But Runa didn't hear her sister. She felt her heart breaking into a thousand pieces. "There are things you don't know about me."

"You're part Gira." Brom shrugged. "What of it?"

She gaped at him. "You say that as if it means nothing."

"Because it doesna. How many times must I tell you before you believe me?"

"That isn't all."

He lifted one shoulder in a shrug. "You're now queen of the Gira. I know they forced you to take the title, or else they would've gone for Synne."

Runa glanced at Asrail, but she couldn't be sure whether

her grandmother had shared that information or not. "I'm not who you think I am."

"Aye, you're exactly who I know you are. You're kind and generous," Brom said as he started toward her. "You're fair and honorable. You're passionate and loving."

Every word brought him closer until he stood before her. Runa wanted to order him to stop, or at the very least turn away from him to put some distance between them. Didn't he realize how much she needed his touch?

"You're beautiful and gloriously powerful," he said in a soft whisper.

She gazed into his hazel eyes, remembering how it had been to be in his arms. How wonderful his kisses, how soft his caress, how cataclysmic the event when their bodies joined.

"Doona deny what I know is in your heart." He reached up and slowly ran the pad of his fingers down her cheek. "The same thing that's in mine."

There was no stopping the tears. "If I could turn back time, I'd take us to the cave once more, and I'd never leave. We could stay there for all eternity."

"Aye," he said with a sexy grin. "Just the two of us."

"And the wildcat."

He chuckled and pulled her close. "Though it defies logic given the brief time we've been together, I know without a doubt that I love you. I thought to live my life alone, then I saw your face in my dream. I knew you were important to me, but I didna know how much so until I first held you."

She knew it was the wrong thing to do, but she lifted her face to his. Their lips brushed, and all the anxiety, the fear, the burdens she'd been carrying disappeared. It was as if everything in the world righted itself. She leaned into him and sank into the kiss. Runa never wanted to let him go, and she was afraid that she wouldn't be able to now.

Brom slowly ended the kiss and looked down at her. "No matter what comes, I'll stand with you."

"You say that without knowing all of my secrets."

"Because I doona care about them. I care about you, and because of that, I accept all of you, no matter what."

Runa wanted to believe him, but she couldn't. Not yet. "How do you feel about the Gira?"

"I've kept my distance from them, if that's what you want to know."

"Aye, but how do you *feel* about them? Do they disgust you?" She watched him intently, trying to discern his thoughts.

He smiled and gave her another quick kiss. "They are part of you, just as you are part of them. I hold no ill will toward them."

Runa's knees threatened to buckle, the relief was so strong. She held onto Brom and rested her forehead against his chest. Yet despite his assurances, she still didn't tell him her final secret because she was afraid of what he would say.

"I'm sorry to break up this reunion, but there's a war brewing," Synne said.

Runa grudgingly stepped away from Brom as he faced the others. "Things are upending quickly."

"The sword," Asrail said.

"Aye." Runa looked to Synne and Lachlan. "The Gira tracked down Avis and took it from her."

Synne's eyes widened. "How did they do that?"

"You don't want to know," Asrail answered.

Runa released a breath. "Asrail tried to warn me what the Gira wanted, but I wasn't quick enough. They surrounded me in the forest and brought me not only the sword but Avis, as well. They wanted to turn the witch over to the Coven, but I warned them that it would alert Sybbyl that the nymphs had the sword."

"Which we shouldn't," Asrail murmured.

Runa glanced at her grandmother, but Asrail wouldn't meet her gaze. When she looked at Synne, her sister shrugged in confusion. Runa then continued. "The Gira left me no other choice but to become their queen. I also saw an advantage to have a bone of the First Witch. So, I took it."

"What does that mean, exactly?" Lachlan asked hesitantly.

Asrail gracefully lowered herself to the ground, belying the fact that she had been near death not too long ago. "It means the Gira no longer follow Sybbyl. When she finds out, she's not going to be happy."

"She knows," Runa told them. "She was here just before you arrived."

Synne winced and sat beside her grandmother. "There goes our advantage."

"She would've found out anyway," Asrail said. "Especially when all the Gira were suddenly no longer around."

Lachlan sank to the ground. "How angry was she?"

Runa bit back a smile when Brom took her hand and gently tugged her down as he sat, as well. She met his gaze, her heart leaping to know that he was with her, that she didn't have to do this alone. But she worried that things would backfire on her. She pushed that thought aside for the time being to focus on more pressing matters.

"Furious," she told them. "Sybbyl knows I have the sword and that we're responsible for getting it from Avis. I believe she'll attack us, so I've set up two perimeters. The first is the farthest away and are silent sentries. They are not to let anyone know they're there. They will alert the second line, which has surrounded our camp. When the attack comes, they'll defend as well as give the camp notice so they can join in."

Brom raised a brow. "Where will you be?"

She looked to the fire before her gaze found Asrail. "I'm using my advantage and going after Sybbyl."

"Alone?" Synne bit out.

Runa was glad that her sister hadn't shouted it, but it was still loud enough that anyone close could have heard her. "Aye."

"No' going to happen," Brom said.

Lachlan shook his head. "I agree. It would be suicide for you to go alone into the Coven camp. You've no idea how many witches there are."

"It doesn't matter," Runa said.

Brom's hazel eyes narrowed on her. "Why does it no' matter?"

"Sybbyl will never see me coming."

There was shocked silence in all but Asrail. Runa held her grandmother's gaze because she was the only one who knew Runa's secret and why it was an advantage that had to be used.

"I'd like to talk to Runa alone," Asrail said.

There was a beat of silence before Lachlan rose and held out his hand to Synne. They departed silently, walking to the loch. Runa turned her head to Brom. He gave her a nod and a smile before he too left.

Once they were alone, Runa looked at her grandmother. "You don't agree with my plan?"

"I didn't say that. I believe you're right that Sybbyl won't see an attack coming. She'll believe that all Gira have left her. That doesn't mean there won't be traps for you," Asrail cautioned.

Runa nodded solemnly. "Morea taught me well. I'll be careful."

"You know there's a chance you won't come back."

"I know. That's why you need to get Synne away from here. I don't want the Gira turning to her to take my place."

Asrail's shoulders raised as she drew in a breath. "There's nowhere Synne can go where the Gira won't find her."

"Which means, I have to live."

"This is a dangerous path you're on."

Runa briefly looked to the dancing flames. "You warned me of that before. I don't think it matters what I want. Everything that has happened was meant to happen. Sybbyl has a bone. I have a bone."

"So does Brom. The odds will tip in your favor if he stands with you."

"You make it sound like that's the wrong thing to do."

"I'm cautioning you, my child. Things seem very clear to you, but that isn't always the case."

Runa narrowed her gaze on Asrail. "If you know something, please tell me now."

"I'm simply warning as one queen to another."

Runa wasn't buying that for a moment. "Nay. There's something you aren't telling me."

Asrail sighed and turned her head away. "What kind of magic do you think is here on this Earth?"

"Witches, warlocks, and Gira," she replied with a shrug.

Dark eyes met hers. "There's always more. Some are weaker, some are stronger. Sometimes, when the path seems the clearest, it's actually the foggiest."

"You aren't making any sense."

Asrail smiled sadly. "Today, after so very many years, I have both of my granddaughters together. One of whom saved me and took my place as leader of the nymphs. My advice to you, dear Runa, is that sometimes it's difficult to tell the difference between enemies and allies. Trust your heart. In the end, that's all you've got."

Runa watched as her grandmother got up and walked out. She blinked, trying to discern what Asrail had tried to import on her, but she couldn't figure out what she'd meant. Her words, however, ran through Runa's head again and again.

It wasn't until a few moments later that Runa realized it was the perfect time to leave. Synne, Lachlan, and Brom were all occupied at the loch. Runa had no idea where Asrail had gone, but she suspected that her grandmother had left on purpose so she could leave to put her plan into motion.

Runa tightened her hand on the sword and got to her feet. Lachlan hadn't demanded the sword back, which was a good thing because she wouldn't have handed it over. She knew it was the only thing that could gain them victory over Sybbyl and the Coven and end the war.

She hurried outside and found the five. "No one is to harm my friends or my sister. They are my guests. Is that clear?"

The five nodded in unison.

"Are the first and second lines in place?"

One of the females nodded. "Set just as you requested.

Runa released a long breath. "If I fail, Sybbyl will come for you."

"Then she's a fool," another female stated.

The male said, "Why don't we take all the Gira and attack her and the witches? We'll make quick work of them."

"I'm trying to avoid a war," Runa told them. "If we can end Sybbyl's reign, why not do it?"

Another female shrugged. "The same reason we've not ended the Coven at all. We don't want to."

"If you hadn't found another queen, would you have taken the sword to Sybbyl?" Runa asked.

The male answered, "Of course."

A shiver of apprehension raced down Runa's spine. "What is Sybbyl's plan?"

"To have witches rule," another female said. "That anyone with magic can live out in the open instead of hiding."

Runa knew that also included the Gira. "And where do the nymphs fit in?"

"Where we always have, at the top of the food chain," the male stated.

That was the moment Runa began to realize what Asrail had been trying to tell her. While she hadn't necessarily considered the Gira her allies, she also hadn't truly considered them her enemies since she was their queen. That was her first mistake.

She couldn't make another.

Brom wouldn't be fooled a second time. He waited until he knew Runa wasn't looking his way before he walked away from Synne and Lachlan to follow Runa. He hadn't gotten far when a nymph blocked his way.

He stared into Asrail's dark eyes, glancing up to make sure he saw where Runa was headed.

"She doesn't want to be followed."

Brom wasn't in the mood to argue. Nor did he have time. He knew firsthand just how quickly Runa could disappear. "I doona care what she wants. Had I been with her the first time, the Gira might no' have found her."

Asrail made a sound that was half-growl, half-hiss. "Lower your voice," she ordered in a hushed tone.

Brom hastily looked around to see if any of the nymphs had heard him. "I doona want to lose her again."

"If you follow her, you're doing exactly what I said you came to do."

He wouldn't have that discussion again. Nothing and no one could make him harm a hair on Runa's head. "Let me go so I can help her."

"You think she needs help?" Asrail asked, peering at him as if he were an enigma she needed to solve.

"Aye. She might be formidable, no' to mention she has a bone, but she's never fought Sybbyl before."

The Gira snorted. "She's never met Sybbyl, not until this night. My granddaughter is intelligent and cunning. Morea taught her well. But I know Sybbyl."

"Does that mean you want me to help Runa?" he asked.

"It does." Asrail swallowed and glanced at the ground. "Remember, we all have paths. Even when we think we're deviating from them, we're really not."

Brom held Asrail's gaze. "I doona care about paths. I care about saving your granddaughter."

"Then you better go."

He started to walk around her, then paused. "What about Synne and Lachlan? Should they remain here?"

"They won't leave either." Asrail blew out a breath. "I'll do what I can."

Brom gave her a nod. "Good luck."

"You'll need it more than I."

He didn't ask the nymph what she meant by that. Asrail obviously knew something. But if she wouldn't tell him, he wouldn't push her. Besides, he didn't have time. Brom wanted to run out of the Gira camp, but he kept his pace to a walk. No other nymphs stopped him, and he didn't look over his shoulder to see if any noticed him leaving.

It was easy to see Runa's footprints going up the mountain, which he followed farther and farther away from Synne and Lachlan. He felt beneath his shirt, where Trea's bone now rested. He had made a small hole and looped a piece of thin leather through it, which he'd then tied around his neck. That way, the bone was with him all the time. And it was out of sight.

He thought about Malene, Armir, Helena, and Jarin. Brom had no idea where they would be with the Coven. He could only hope that whatever Runa planned wouldn't wreak any havoc with the others. Runa had no idea who they were, nor they she. Which was another reason he had to hurry and catch up with her.

Brom briefly thought about using his magic to locate Runa faster. He was going to fight the Coven anyway. In the end, he thought better of it. Let them discover him, Jarin, and Armir at the last minute. The thought of that brought a smile to his face.

It wasn't long before it vanished. He had reached the top of the mountain and paused as he searched for Runa. The moonless sky made it difficult for him to see. Thankfully, it wasn't long before he picked up her trail again. Brom moved faster now, though he kept quiet. He made his way quickly down the mountain until he caught a glimpse of Runa ahead of him. One minute she was there, and the next, she was gone.

Brom hurried to where he'd seen her. Once more, her tracks just stopped. Like she had vanished. He looked around, his gaze going up to the trees, thinking he might spot Runa there. But no matter how hard he looked, there was no sign of her.

He clenched his teeth, furious that he had been duped again. And he still couldn't figure out how. The one thing he did know was that Runa was going to the Coven camp. Since he could sense a Witch's Grove near, he suspected that was exactly where Sybbyl and the others were. Brom began to lift his leg when he took notice of the trees.

His gaze moved slowly around him. He wasn't sure what made him pause, but something had. Brom set aside his need to find Runa and sought to figure out what had caught his attention. While he couldn't pinpoint exactly what it was, he did suddenly remember that Asrail had made a point of saying that both Synne and Runa had gotten gifts from their nymph blood—and they each had different skills.

Brom knew Synne could converse with trees. He'd had no idea that the Gira could do that, but there was one thing he knew the nymphs could do—blend in with the forest. And just like that, he realized how Runa had been able to make it seem as if she disappeared.

That was why she had asked him so pointedly how he felt about the Gira. If he was repulsed by them. His heart hurt for what he was sure the others must have said to Runa. On the other hand, now he understood why the Gira had wanted Runa to be their queen. She was the sister most like them.

Brom had a choice now. He could continue on, ignoring what he'd figured out and wait for Runa at the Grove. Or he could tell her now.

His head jerked to the side when he heard something. The sound had been muffled, but he knew it wasn't from an animal. Before he could decide what to do, he was yanked back against a tree and turned around. Brom only got a brief look at Runa's blue eyes before she put her finger to her lips and pushed him down into a crouching position.

The tree she had chosen had a portion hollowed out at the base. He tucked himself in there as she stood before him, blocking him from prying eyes. Tense moments passed before he heard the crunch of several footsteps. He wasn't able to see anything to tell how many walked by. Whoever it was didn't speak a word, making it even more difficult. For all he knew, it was Malene and the others.

Another several moments slipped away before silence descended once again, and Runa backed up. Brom saw her skin shift from bark to human in a blink as he straightened. She turned away from him.

"Is that what you didna want me to know?" he asked her in a soft voice.

She shrugged, keeping her back to him. "You don't have to say more."

Brom walked to stand in front of her. "But I want to. I doona care what you look like. While I think you're beautiful in this form, I love your heart, your spirit."

"You wouldn't say that had you seen me in my other form before. You certainly wouldn't have spent the night with me."

He quirked a brow. "You'll never know what I would have done because you didna give me the opportunity."

"I didn't want to be hurt. Not by you."

"Which is why you ran from me."

"And because I didn't want you involved in any of this."

He shrugged, twisting his lips. "And here I am anyway."

"Go back," she urged.

Brom shook his head. "I'm no' going anywhere."

Anger filled her features. "Really? I'm sure I can make you." In a blink, her clothes disappeared, as did her skin, all replaced by the bark-like hide of the nymphs. Runa held out her arms, Lachlan's sword still in her hand. "Is this what you wanted to see?"

"It is." Brom noted that even the double swords she carried were gone. He wasn't sure how clothes and some weapons disappeared, but others didn't. "Where are your swords?"

Confusion caused her brows to draw together. "You don't have to pretend to care. You can leave now. I won't tell anyone what you did."

"Your swords," he pressed.

She sighed loudly. "I didn't need them or my clothes. That's all I have to do, think what I need and what I don't, and it melts away to reveal this."

"That's amazing," Brom said as he looked down her naked

body. He knew the curves well, had held them in his hands and dreamed about them every night since. The only difference was the skin. "What you can do is so unique that I have no words for it. You shouldna hide that. You should embrace it."

"You wouldn't say that if you had walked in my shoes. I belong to two worlds, yet I can't live in either."

Brom quirked a brow. "Seems like you fit quite well in both. You get to decide what you want, lass."

"That was taken from me."

He looked pointedly at the sword in her right hand. "You carry a bone of the First Witch. You can decide any bloody thing you want."

Her lips softened. "I hadn't thought of that."

"I'd love to discuss it more with you. Shall we return to the Gira camp?"

Runa shook her head. "I want so very many things. Mainly, I want to spend the rest of my life with you. I want to watch every sunset and sunrise in your arms, fall asleep next to you each night, and wake up by your side in the morning. I want to laugh with you and argue and everything in between. I want…you."

"We can have that."

"Nay, we can't. I can end Sybbyl. She and the other witches will never see me coming. I can take her out quietly."

Brom grasped Runa's arms, feeling the prick of the bark on his palm. "If you manage to kill Sybbyl, the rest of the witches will slaughter you. You'll never get out of the Grove alive."

"At least Sybbyl will be gone. Maybe I'll get lucky and get the staff. I'll have two bones, and the witches will have to do a lot more to kill me."

"You doona have magic," he told her, worry settling in his bones like stones. "The bones magnify magic."

Runa smiled softly at him. "I'm part Gira, and that means I have magic."

"You can shift from one form to the other, which I admit is rare and spectacular. That doesna mean you can do spells. The sword may help you shift quicker, but it'll do nothing to stop the witches' magic."

Her chin lifted. "I guess I'll find out."

"Let me come with you."

Runa sighed. "We've been over this."

"I'm coming," he told her as he released her arms. "You can knock me out again, but I'll still get up and follow you. The only way you'll stop me is if you take my life. Or…we can do this together. I've lived without you, and I doona like it. I want you in my life, and if I can't have you, then I'm as lost as I was before. If you die, then I'll die right beside you. We can go into the next life together."

She watched him for a long moment before she let the bark fade away, and her human form return. Runa held out her hand. The moment he grasped it, she wrapped her fingers around his. "You don't have to do this."

"We make a good team. You went out on your own, and look where it got you," he said with a teasing grin.

"You do make a good point."

They shared a smile before he pulled her against him for a frantic kiss. He wished he could use the spell he'd learned from Malene to jump them to Blackglade, but Runa would never forgive him. As much as Brom wanted to protect her, he realized that he couldn't. All he could do was respect Runa's decisions and stand by her, no matter what.

He ended the kiss and pressed his forehead to hers. "We have more nights ahead of us. More sunrises and sunsets. Years and years of laughter and arguments. I know that with all my heart."

"I love you," she whispered and put her hand on his cheek.

"And I love you."

"Well, isn't that nice?" a voice said from somewhere around them.

Brom jerked his head around as he searched for the woman.

"Sybbyl," Runa whispered.

Brom spotted what looked like black smoke moving against the snow. More and more smoke gathered, rising until a woman walked from it holding a staff. She wore a black gown that molded to her frame. Her face was beautiful, but the evil inside her overshadowed that. Atop her head of golden hair was a black crown.

Sybbyl wore a self-satisfied smile, like a cat who had gotten into the cream. Her blue eyes moved to Brom. "You're a handsome one."

"This is between you and me," Runa said.

Brom shot Runa an angry look, which caused Sybbyl to laugh. Brom wanted to punch her, but he decided to let the Coven leader believe that he wasn't a threat.

"Protecting your man?" Sybbyl stated with a shake of her head. "Aren't men supposed to protect women? They rarely do, you know. We've always been the ones who did everything."

Runa rolled her eyes. "Do you want to fight or talk?"

"So eager to die, I see." Sybbyl tsked. "Hand me the sword, and I'll allow the two of you to walk away and have the life you so desperately want."

"Do you really believe I'm foolish enough to think you'd allow that?" Runa demanded.

Sybbyl flattened her lips. "I gave you a chance. Don't forget that when you're gasping for breath."

Runa lifted the sword. "I'm queen of the Gira. Do you really think it'll be me who dies?"

"Too bad you're on the wrong side. We could've made a good team. We still can," Sybbyl said.

Brom waited for Runa to tell the witch to shut up. Or attack. Instead, she hesitated as if she were contemplating the witch's words. He stared at Runa, silently urging her to ignore Sybbyl.

"How?" Runa asked.

He blinked, unable to believe that Runa was taking this road. She had wanted to go after Sybbyl herself. As a matter of fact, Runa had been hell-bent on doing just that. Why was she thinking of changing her mind?

Sybbyl's smile returned. "You're smarter than I gave you credit for. You have a bone. I have a bone. The Gira are extremely useful in battle. They make quick work of enemies while having fun as they do it. You join me, and we can use both bones to take over the world and put humans without magic in their place. Witches, Gira, and anyone with magic can move about freely."

"And the others?" Runa asked.

Sybbyl glanced at Brom. "You mean those without magic? They'll live in fear, hiding so those like us won't find them."

"The Gira told me you want the Varroki."

"Oh, I do," Sybbyl said with a nod of her head. "They have warlocks, something we don't have. I know nymphs have males, but the magic we have only goes to women, except for the Varroki. We'll get the Varroki men to ensure that we witches continue on forever."

Runa nodded slowly. "All while making yourselves more powerful. Is that when you'll try to wipe out the Gira?"

"I would never do such a thing. Not if you're an ally. If you and the nymphs decide to stand against me, then I'll dispatch you with the rest."

Brom fisted his hands, fury burning hot through him.

"That is a fair offer," Runa said. "I'd be a fool to toss it aside."

"Runa," Brom said in dismay.

Sybbyl laughed. "And this is why I think only women should rule."

"Then you've never met the right man," Runa stated.

Disappointment filled the witch's face. "So, that's how it is?"

"That's how it is."

Brom barely had time to digest Runa's words before Sybbyl sent out a blast of magic, black tendrils filling the air. Runa lifted the sword and blocked the blow, as well as a second and third volley. Sybbyl moved quicker and quicker. A startled cry shot from Runa when she didn't move fast enough to stop the magic, and it cut through her.

26

The pain was…unbearable. Runa couldn't hold onto the sword. It fell from her numb fingers, landing in the snow. She watched it happen in slow motion, trying with all her might to hold onto the weapon.

Her mind demanded that she move, but her body couldn't respond. Agony exploded inside her again and didn't let up. She heard laughter in the distance that sounded like Sybbyl. Runa tried to look for Brom, but her eyes were growing hazy. Suddenly, the world careened, and she was falling until strong arms she knew well caught her.

"I've got you," Brom whispered.

She smiled, or she tried to, anyway. Runa wasn't sure about anything but the unending torture of pain. If she had listened to Brom, they would be back at the loch with the others. She could've lain in his arms, reveling in the love that had found them so unexpectedly in a land ravaged by magic and power.

Runa had been sure that going after Sybbyl was the right thing to do. Maybe it had been, had she not showed Brom where she was. Perhaps had she let him face the witches she could've found Sybbyl and ended the witch's life.

So very many *maybes*. But she knew only one thing for sure. Runa was going to die. There was no doubt about it in her mind. She didn't know what kind of magic Sybbyl had, but whatever it was, it was powerful. Runa supposed it could be the staff. Though, there was no use even considering that now. What was done was done.

Brom had tried to warn her that she didn't have the magic needed to go up against Sybbyl. She should've listened to him instead of thinking she always knew what was right. Time and again, it had been proven that she should take others' advice, and she had repeatedly ignored that.

Now, she was paying the price.

"Doona die on me," Brom demanded near her ear. "Stay with me, Runa."

She wanted nothing more than to be with him. She wanted that more than anything else in the world. Brom was…everything. He was her present and the future. He was love and acceptance. He was hers.

Runa tried to call his name but only managed to cough. Something trickled from her mouth. She swallowed and tasted blood. She raised her eyes, searching for Brom's face, but all she found was darkness. It surrounded her. That's what was eating her from the inside out—darkness and evil.

Brom wiped the blood from Runa's mouth as fury and fear mingled inside him. It was a potent and compelling mixture. When Runa went limp in his arms, there was only one thing he wanted to do. He gently lay Runa's head upon the snow and got to his feet to face Sybbyl.

She held the staff in one hand and the sword in the other, a confident smile upon her lips. "There's no saving her."

He let the anger and horror at what had happened to Runa grow within him. He embraced it, welcomed it. The last several years of his life had been lived in solitude, something he had accepted would be his path. Then he'd met Runa and got a glimpse of something wonderful within his grasp.

And Sybbyl had taken it from him a blink.

She would pay.

The witch raised a blond brow. "Do you really think you can stand against me? In case you didn't know, I'm a witch. With two bones of the First Witch. That means I can kill you with a thought."

Brom simply stared at her. When he felt his flesh begin to heat, he looked down to see sparks jumping off his clothes. He took a deep breath and let his power rush through him. The bone beneath his tunic amplified his magic and quickly doused the flames.

"Who are you?" Sybbyl demanded, unease contorting her features.

Brom sneered at her. "How does it feel to know that you're no' as powerful as you believe?"

"You're a human without magic."

"Am I?" he asked. "I could be, but should you make such assumptions?"

Her gaze narrowed on him. "You stopped my magic."

"I'm going to do a lot more than that. I'm going to stop you—once and for all."

Blue eyes widened. "You're a Varroki."

"And you just killed the woman I love. I'm going to make you pay for that," he stated.

Sybbyl lifted the sword and the staff. "You'd be a fool to go up against me. I have two of the bones."

"You might have them, but you doona wield them."

"Of course, I do," she replied acerbically. "If I have them, they're under my control."

He snorted, shaking his head at the foolishness of others. "You think because you have them that you control them? That just shows how little you know of the bones and what they're capable of. Have you no' wondered why the Blood Skull made sure no Coven witch ever got to it? The skull decided that, no one else."

"I know I got the staff and the sword." Sybbyl shot him a flat look. "You can't say that."

Brom released a long breath. "Do you know why you're going to fail? Because you assume you know more than you do. You think you're smarter than others. That your magic is more powerful."

"It is."

He shrugged indifferently. "Perhaps, but the fact that you fail at grasping knowledge and basic facts tells me you willna see the dawn."

Sybbyl looked up. "The sky is already beginning to lighten. I think you're only talking because you know your time to die is now."

"Have you heard Trea's voice in your head?"

Sybbyl froze. "What?"

He smiled because he knew the witch had. "Tell me, does she give you encouragement or help guide you?"

"You have no idea what you're talking about."

"I take that to mean she doesna. If she's making your life hell, you should ask yourself why. You may have one of her bones—two now—but she doesna want it in your control. And she's going to do everything she can to ensure it doesna stay there."

Sybbyl gave him a scathing look. "And I suppose you're going to take them from me."

"You're damned right, I am."

The moment the words were out of his mouth, he sent magic at her. Sybbyl deflected it, but he wasted no time sending a second wave that hit its mark. The witch cried out in pain and doubled over. Brom didn't hide his smile when he saw the torn material near her waist and the dark stain of blood on her gown.

"You'll pay for that," Sybbyl stated angrily.

Brom prepared himself for her strike. He dodged three hits of magic, throwing his own out in between. But Sybbyl's fourth strike hit him squarely in the chest and sent him flying backwards through the air, head over heels. He slammed into a tree and was left gasping as the breath was knocked from his lungs.

He tried to hold onto the tree and get his bearings, to figure out how far he was from the ground, but his hands wouldn't work. Air whooshed around his face as he plummeted to the frozen earth. The thick snow did nothing to soften his landing.

Brom knew he had to get on his feet and face his opponent before she struck again, but no matter how many times he demanded that his body work, it refused. It felt like an eternity before he could draw air into his starving lungs. Then he pushed himself onto his hands and knees. Everything hurt. He didn't know what ached worse—where the major injuries were, or whether the worst of it was from Sybbyl's strike, hitting the tree, or falling to the ground. None of it mattered. He had to get to his feet.

Only by using a nearby tree was he able to pull himself to a standing position. His eyes were blurry, so he blinked a few times to clear them. He saw no sign of Sybbyl as his eyes scanned the forest. The hairs on the back of his neck stood on end, alerting him that someone was near.

Brom spun and dropped to his knees an instant before magic slammed into the tree, splintering it. Huge chunks of bark rained down upon Brom, causing him to use magic to protect himself. He glanced at the tree in time to see a large portion of the top coming directly at him from high above. Brom dove out of the way. He rolled, coming to his feet as he sent another blast, but once more, Sybbyl was nowhere to be seen.

He slowly turned, looking for her. When there was no sign of her, Brom rushed to where Runa lay. Before he reached her, he caught movement out of the corner of his eye. Brom dove, twisting and getting off a round of magic directed at Sybbyl. His gaze latched on to the wave of magic coming at him. In slow motion, he saw it aimed for his chest. Brom turned onto his back in midair and saw it skim by his tunic, slicing the top without harming him. He landed hard on his back and immediately jumped to his feet. Pushing aside the pain that radiated from every fiber of his being, Brom sent two more strikes of magic at Sybbyl.

They were both injured. Brom wanted to think the witch was hurt worse than he was, but he didn't think so. She had two bones of the First Witch to amplify her power, he only had the one. He had no idea where Malene and the others were. All he could do was stay on his feet long enough for them to find him so they could end Sybbyl.

But Brom wasn't sure he would be able to. He winced and glanced down at his side where a large cut poured blood. With a hand on it to help stanch the flow, Brom knew his strength was leaving him quickly.

"You're no match for me," Sybbyl said as she eyed him with derision. "You think because you're a warlock that you're better than me?"

He snorted at her, noticing that she was favoring her left side. "I know that I'm fighting on the side of good."

"Good?" she said with a cackle. "I'm the one fighting for the rights of all with magic!"

"You take lives as if you have the right to decide who lives and who dies."

Her lips peeled back in a sneer. "Those without magic have been doing that for centuries. It has to stop."

"Your way isn't the right way," he said as blood poured through his fingers and dripped onto the snow.

She shook her head. "You should be dead. Why aren't you dead?"

"I'm a Varroki."

Her gaze narrowed. "It's more than that." Her face went blank. "You have a bone."

Brom smiled in response.

"All this time, you could've been fighting with me instead of against me. Think of what we could have accomplished."

"You might kill me, but you'll never get the bone."

"Oh, I know I'll have it."

He grinned. "You can certainly try."

His words lost their edge when his knees buckled, and he dropped to the ground. Quickly, he said a healing spell, hoping it would conserve some of his strength. He knew it couldn't help much, but all he needed was more time.

Sybbyl didn't come to him, however. He'd been hoping that she would make her way to him so he could attack her again. Going to her would take the last of his energy. He glanced at the sky to see the first streaks of blue scattered amid the clouds as the night lost its hold.

"And you thought you stood a chance against me." Sybbyl laughed, the sound echoing through the forest. "A warlock with one bone. Once again, I've proven the might of the

Coven. After I kill you and take your bone, I'll wipe the Gira out. Then, I'll go for the Varroki."

"You'll never find them."

"I always find what I'm looking for."

He simply smiled in response.

Her gaze narrowed on him. "Why are you grinning?"

"Look behind you," he told her as Malene, Jarin, Helena, Armir, and two other couples fanned out around Sybbyl.

27

Runa knew she was dying, and there was nothing she could do about it. Nothing but stifling, oppressive inky blackness surrounded and clung to her. She couldn't move to shake it off. While she couldn't see anything, she could sense the darkness piling on her, filling her from the inside.

She wanted to scream and claw her way out of it. Why wasn't anyone helping her? Where was Brom? He couldn't be dead. Her mind simply couldn't imagine that Sybbyl had bested him. But, deep inside, she knew that was probably the case. Brom was strong, or at least that's what she thought.

She understood very little about the magic of witches and warlocks, at least not enough to compare Brom and Sybbyl. All Runa had known going into this was that as long as she had the sword, and Brom had his bone, they had a slim chance of besting Sybbyl. But she had lost the sword. Runa recalled the heavy weapon tipping out of her numb fingers.

Had Brom gotten to it? He had been closest to the weapon. She hoped he had reached it. If not, if the worst had happened, and Sybbyl had three bones. Unless…Brom hadn't let her know he was a warlock or had a bone.

Runa thought about Brom. Determined, stubborn, honest, trustworthy. He never would've stood by and let the witch take the sword without a fight. As much as Runa hoped Brom had let Sybbyl go, she knew that wasn't him. He would've stood up to the witch and shown her that he was a warlock.

For all Runa knew, they were still battling it out. She couldn't see or hear anything. Or feel anything. She pretended as if she were in Brom's arms because that was the only way she could face her death.

"*Runa.*"

The voice was wispy, like the clouds she used to watch as a child. She frowned, wondering where it had come from. She didn't recognize it. Nor could she determine if it was male or female.

"*Runa.*"

This time, it was louder, allowing her to hear the feminine tone, though deeper than most. What she noticed then was that it was soft and soothing. She wanted to answer, but her lips wouldn't move.

"*All will be well. Trust us.*"

Us? Who the hell were these people? And what did they want with her?

Dread pooled within Sybbyl as she stared at the eight people behind her. Her gaze went to Braith, who held the Blood Skull. Trepidation the likes of which Sybbyl hadn't experienced since she was a small child filled her.

All her plans had revolved around her gaining as many of the First Witch's bones as possible and taking out the Varroki before she went after the Blood Skull. And now, the Warden, along with his Hunter wife, Leoma, had come to her with the skull.

Sybbyl used the time to use a healing spell to mend the injury Brom had given her. It had been a lucky shot, one that shouldn't have gotten through, but it had. There was no way she could face the others in her present condition. At least the injuries Helena had given her were mending.

Her gaze landed on Ravyn and Carac. The couple had survived, despite everything she'd done to try and end them. At least she had come out ahead with the Staff of the Eternal. The staff had given her the upper hand and allowed her to take over leading the Coven.

Helena and Jarin were beside the other couple. Sybbyl was pleased that they were here. The witch and the warlock had gotten away from her, but she still intended to take their child and raise it as hers. Along with the other bones. Having the Heart of the First Witch was nearly as powerful as the Blood Skull. Sybbyl would have them all eventually.

And then, she would be unstoppable.

Her gaze swung to the middle of the group, where a petite woman stood next to a tall, imposing—and very handsome—warrior. The woman's flaxen hair had three small braids from her temples to her ears on either side that were then woven into one large plait. The man had golden hair gathered at the back of his head with a leather strip. More leather held the long length every few inches until the end. But, even more curiously, his head was shaved on either side, showing various tattoos.

"Who are you?" she demanded of the male and the female.

The woman lifted her chin. "I'm Malene, Lady of the Varroki."

"Interesting." No doubt, the man beside her was a warlock. Sybbyl couldn't help but inwardly smile at the knowledge that at least three Varroki males were within her grasp. Her witches would be pleased to have some fun with the men. After she chose which one she wanted for herself, of course.

Malene said, "You have one chance. Lay down the sword and staff. Otherwise, we'll strike you down where you stand. You see the Blood Skull. You don't stand a chance against us."

"I disagree," Sybbyl said. "If you believed all you needed was the skull to end me, you all would've done it weeks ago. Not even a village of witches could stop me when I destroyed Edra's abbey and all within. You eight are nothing."

The Varroki beside Malene quirked a brow. She looked at him, wondering what he would be like as a lover. Perhaps she'd keep all three to herself for a while. After all, she deserved to have some fun.

She knew that she had the power, but she couldn't dispel the dread that continued to rise within her like the tide. It had to be the appearance of the skull. Yes, that's what it was. Just the Blood Skull. Sybbyl had faced all but Malene and the Varroki before. Some of them might have gotten in some good strikes, but in the end, she held two of the First Witch's bones. She had taken out the Hunters. She had united the Gira.

Yet, she couldn't help but recall Brom's words from earlier about how the bones would go against her. She wasn't entirely sure if what he'd said was a lie. After all, how long had the voice in her head made her doubt herself and her plans? Brom said that Trea had led him to find the bone. If he had spoken the truth, then maybe he was right. Perhaps the bones didn't want her in control.

Then again, they didn't really have a choice. She had them now, was the one commanding them. If the First Witch really wanted to make certain Sybbyl and the Coven didn't rule, she wouldn't have let any bones fall into Sybbyl's hands. The exact opposite had happened.

And in her eyes, that meant she was exactly where she was supposed to be. The dreams she had aspired to as a young child were within reach. Already, she had claimed so very much. Soon, she would sit on a throne where everyone bowed to her.

She glanced over her shoulder to Brom, who was still on his knees, looking weaker and weaker by the moment.

"Did you come to talk or to fight?" Sybbyl asked the eight.

Leoma said, "We've come to fight you and everyone who stands against us."

"Then you've come to die." Sybbyl shrugged, twisting her lips as she did. "Then again, all of you were destined to die by my hand anyway. I've already faced some of you," she said, looking pointedly at Ravyn and Carac and Helena and Jarin.

Carac issued a loud snort. "You say that as if you won against us."

"I am the one holding the staff," Sybbyl pointed out.

Ravyn lifted one shoulder in a shrug. "That will soon be remedied."

"Now you sound like Brom. Look how he fared against me." Sybbyl smiled.

Jarin jerked his chin to her. "Looks like he drew blood."

"Same as I did," Helena replied.

Malene moved forward a step. "And now it's my turn."

Sybbyl wished she knew more about the Varroki. What little she knew, she'd heard as rumor throughout her life. She wasn't sure what was truth and what wasn't. But the way Malene stood, it spoke of someone who was either extremely powerful or foolish. Sybbyl wished she thought Malene was foolish.

There was something about the way Malene watched her. As if she knew all of Sybbyl's secrets. Or maybe it was that Malene knew the secrets of the universe. Either way, it sent a chill running down Sybbyl's spine. In any other event, Sybbyl would've exited and lived to fight another day. Unfortunately, she had set things in motion for just this moment.

Granted, she had expected to fight those before her, though not how they stood now. Regardless, she had known she would meet extremely commanding and formidable enemies on the field. So what if the Blood Skull was here now? It would've happened eventually.

Once more, Sybbyl became aware of the silence of the voice in her head that had been so prevalent and incessant before. Something was wrong. Very, very wrong. Though she couldn't seem to figure out what it was.

Regardless, she had the Staff of the Eternal and the sword. That would be enough to counter whatever came her way.

"Brom."

The voice in his head startled him. He'd been focused on healing his wound so he could fight Sybbyl. His gaze moved around him, looking for someone but Sybbyl and the others. But there was no one.

"Do not fear us."

"Who are you?" he whispered.

"When the time is right, you'll know what to do."

He frowned, thoroughly confused. "I'll know to do what?"

But there was no answer.

Asrail hurried to Synne and Lachlan. When she reached them, she grabbed their wrists and pulled them back from the edge of the loch.

"What are you doing?" Synne asked.

Asrail cut her a look to silence her words. "Keep your voice low."

Lachlan's brows drew together. "Asrail, what's going on?"

"You need to get far from the loch."

"Why?" Synne asked.

Asrail glanced at the water to see it begin to ripple. "The balance is about to be restored. You need to get as far from here as you can. There isn't time to tell you more."

"Come with us," Lachlan urged.

Asrail smiled sadly before she turned to Synne and enfolded her in an embrace. "I cannot. Know that you and Runa were loved more than either of you will ever know. Your friends are up on the mountain. Hurry," she said and gave Synne a slight push.

Her granddaughter's confused look was like a knife in the heart. Lachlan seemed to realize the urgency to get moving. He took Synne's hand and started walking away. Asrail wanted to go with them more than anything.

Synne looked back at her and held out her hand, silently urging Asrail to go with them. She looked at the water, then back at Synne and Lachlan as they headed out of the camp. For the first time in her life, Asrail had the opportunity to think of herself. It was the first time in so very long, that she wasn't sure what to do.

She took a small step after Synne, whose face split into a smile. Asrail looked at the loch again. The water had gone as still as glass once more. The decision was now out of her hands. All she could hope for was that Lachlan got Synne out before it was too late.

Elin kept putting one foot in front of the other. She couldn't remember when she had stopped running from the Coven, Hunters, and Varroki. One day, she simply turned around and began a trek to…she didn't even know where she was headed. The thought had simply filled her mind to go toward a destination, and she'd been unable to ignore it.

For all she knew, she was going to her death. It's what she deserved after what she had done to Synne, Lachlan, and the Varroki. She wanted to cry for giving in to Avis's promise. Elin could say that she was lonely and wishing for her family, but it was only an excuse. She knew Avis better than anyone, and it had been folly to believe anything her sister said. Especially when her sibling had promised her that they could be a family again.

Avis had always known just what to say to get anyone to do what she wanted. Elin had never fallen for that. Until this last time. She felt used and betrayed. Worse, she had set her sister free to wreak havoc on the Varroki. She didn't even want to think about what Avis had done to Lachlan and Synne.

Elin hated that she'd been too much a coward to stay behind and face the consequences of her actions. But after she'd set Avis free, her sister had embraced her. Elin hadn't foreseen the spell that knocked her unconscious. When she woke, she realized what Avis had done, and she started running.

Elin should've gone to tell Malene and Armir what'd happened. She should've gone to check on Synne and Lachlan. More than anything, she should've seen if Avis was still in the city so she could stop her.

At the very least, Elin should've gone after her sister.

Instead, she'd run from everything and everyone. What a coward she was. She didn't even want to imagine what Asrail would think of her. If the Gira was even still alive. Elin hadn't even tried to find her. What could she do, after all? She was simply a witch the Coven would force to join them or die. It wasn't as if Elin could fight against the Coven. But she should've.

Even if Avis had gotten the sword from Lachlan, Elin should've gone after her. It would've meant Elin's death, but she would've at least chosen a side.

Elin paused beside a tree in the forest and put her hand on the trunk. She was so tired. Tired of running, tired of hiding, tired of…everything. Her weakness had tipped the scales toward evil. All because she missed her sister and the time when they had been a family.

One way or another, Elin would make things right. She wasn't sure how just yet, but she'd find a way. Somehow.

A sound jerked her head up. She couldn't tell which direction it had come from. The sunrise was lighting the forest, though not quickly enough. The deep snow made walking difficult. Her skirts were soaked, and even her boots were damp, making her toes numb.

Elin glanced behind her, then started walking again. She trudged up the mountain, using trees and boulders to aid her when the climbing got rough. When she saw a stream, she stopped beside it and cupped her hands in the icy water for a drink. The frigid temperature hurt going down, but it had been a long time since she'd eaten or had anything to drink.

That made her frown. She couldn't remember the last time she'd had food. Or slept through the night. Yet, she didn't feel hungry at all.

The trickling water shifted until a shape took form. Elin sat back on her heels when she found herself looking into a face made out of water.

28

Malene suddenly realized that she hadn't been chosen as Lady of the Varroki to take her people into a new age. She hadn't been chosen because she had the most to give or the most power. She was Lady because she was supposed to stand against Sybbyl and end the reign of terror the Coven had over the land.

For so many years, Malene had wished to leave Blackglade and venture out into the world. Now, as she stood on the icy mountain, all she wanted was the warmth of her tower and hours of conversation with Armir. She wasn't sure she would get either again. She wouldn't change things even if she could because she knew that, in the end, the balance had to be restored, no matter what. If that meant her sacrifice, then so be it.

She lowered her gaze to the ground before she looked at Armir. Their gazes met, bolstering her spirit. He had trained her tirelessly. He hadn't gone easy on her because he knew she had little time to prepare and a lot to learn. Malene wished she had another month. Even another day. But their time was up.

Everything that'd happened over the last few years had

come down to this moment. She wanted to believe that good would triumph over evil, but evil had managed to win too many times before. It couldn't this time. The stakes were too high.

Malene gazed into Armir's soft green eyes. She wished she were brave enough to tell him how much he meant to her. She had no fear in her regarding standing up and facing Sybbyl or the Coven, but she was terrified of telling Armir her feelings. Mainly because she didn't want to lose him as a friend. And if he didn't return her affections, then she would, in fact, lose him. To her, that was a fate worse than death.

Because Armir had always been there for her in some form or fashion. In her darkest moments, for her greatest accomplishments, and during her loneliest days. He was the anchor in the stormy chaos of her life. If it hadn't been for him, she never would've made it. She understood that now.

How she had hated his stoicism at first. It hadn't been until she saw beneath his apathetic nature that she found the man beneath. There was so much more to Armir than anyone knew. He was loyal, direct, honorable, and sincere. His love of his people and Blackglade was evident in everything he did.

And he didn't get nearly the credit he should.

She shut her mind to Armir and her irrational feelings. Malene closed her eyes and waited until her head was clear before she looked at Sybbyl. Then Malene opened herself up to the magic coursing violently through her. She'd always held it in check, afraid of what might happen if she released it.

The only time she'd come close was when she'd bent the pillars at the top of her tower. She'd held back even then because she wasn't sure what would happen if she released all of her magic. She still wasn't sure, but if there was ever a time to find out, this was it. All she could hope for was that her friends would be safe.

"I can see your fear," Sybbyl said with a smirk.

Malene managed to hold in her retort. Besides, it didn't matter what she said. Sybbyl would think whatever she wanted, and Malene didn't care what the witch thought.

Sybbyl threw back her head and laughed. "The panic the Varroki have instilled in witches has been for nothing. Look at you, standing there, waiting to attack. What kind of witch are you?"

"I'm not a witch," Malene replied.

That took Sybbyl aback. The smile died on her lips. "How can you lead the Varroki if you aren't a witch and have no magic?"

"I never said I didn't have magic." It gave Malene great pleasure to see Sybbyl trying to work out what was going on.

The witch squared her shoulders and shot Malene a dry look. "Trying to get inside my head, are you? It won't work. I'm too smart for that. And it doesn't matter who you brought to fight, none of you can best me."

"Perhaps it's time we learn just who the strongest is."

Sybbyl's sneer was back. "I could've killed each of you by now."

"Then why haven't you?" Helena demanded.

Malene watched Sybbyl closely, noting how the witch's nostrils flared in fury when Helena spoke. For all her bluster, Sybbyl was scared. *That* was why she hadn't attacked them. If Sybbyl truly believed that she would win, she would've struck at them the moment they appeared. Instead, she had regarded them much as they had evaluated her.

Not to mention, it had given Brom time to regain some of his strength. Malene purposefully didn't look his way, but she knew he was using the time wisely and healing himself. It had been pure luck that they had even found Brom and Sybbyl. Malene had no idea how the two had come to battle each other, and it didn't matter. Brom was injured, and it looked as if Runa were dying.

The only way Malene could help Brom and Runa was to pull Sybbyl's attention away and allow Brom to get to Runa. Malene wanted to look back at Armir once more, but she stopped herself. She had spoken to the others privately, informing them that she would go after Sybbyl alone. The rest were to keep Armir from coming after her and ensure that no other witch tried to interfere.

Malene started toward Sybbyl. As she did, she opened herself up to the magic within. The force of it surged through her veins and pooled in her palms before it shot from her hands, bathing the area in blue.

Sybbyl's eyes widened. Malene was prepared when Sybbyl sent the first volley of magic at her.

Armir started to follow Malene when Jarin moved in front of him. Armir cut the warrior a look. "Get out of my way."

"I can't," Jarin replied.

Armir glanced at Malene's back. "She ordered you to stop me."

"She said this was her battle, not ours."

"Then why did the bones call you all together?" he demanded, looking at the others.

Helena pointed. "Because of them."

Armir looked to where she had indicated and saw a mass of witches pouring through the trees. A glance showed they were coming from all around. He hated not being by Malene's side, but he would do whatever it took to protect her. And right now, that meant keeping the Coven from joining Sybbyl.

There were only seven of them against a multitude of

witches. Still, they stood a chance given the force of the Blood Skull, Helena, the Varroki warriors, and the Hunters. It wasn't long before the ground was littered with the dead.

Brom hurried around Sybbyl and Malene to try and get to Runa. He'd nearly reached her when he saw more than a dozen witches surrounding Ravyn and Carac. The witches worked to separate the couple, weakening them. Together, Ravyn and Carac moved as one, picking off each one, witch by witch. Yet the Coven sacrificed the weaker members to get close to the couple.

Brom noticed that the witches had just about managed to split the couple apart. He glanced at Runa, then rushed to help Ravyn and Carac. He hurried to them with magic flying. Four witches went down before any others even noticed that he had arrived. Then, the others split their focus between him and Ravyn and Carac, giving the couple the time they needed to bolster themselves.

Brom remained long enough to pick off more of the witches before he tried to go to Runa again. Once more, he found that he was needed. There were just too many witches and only a handful fighting against them. He couldn't tell if Runa still breathed, though right now, all he could do was hope that she held on long enough for him to get to her. Because if he went to her now, and the others lost, then he would doom them all.

He moved to stand with Braith and Leoma for a time before he joined Jarin and Helena. It wasn't long before he found himself alongside Armir. For every witch that was killed, another took her place. Ash filled the air from the mass of dead witches, the gray bits hanging like snow flurries before they drifted away.

Suddenly, there was a loud boom that shocked everyone into halting. Brom's head swung toward the sound to see Malene and Sybbyl locked in combat. The blue radiance from Malene's hands held back Sybbyl and the two bones.

"Malene," Armir whispered.

Brom grabbed his arm, stopping the commander before he could go to her.

"Let me go," Armir stated furiously.

"What are you going to do?" Brom jerked his head to Malene. "She's in the middle of combat. There's nothing you can do."

"The hell there isn't. I can help."

"She doesna need your help."

Armir leaned close, his gaze daring Brom to interfere. "The hell she doesn't."

"She's strong and powerful. She can handle Sybbyl."

Armir yanked his arm loose. Without another word, he turned and started toward the women. He didn't get two steps before Malene shouted something, and the radiance began to shift and bend, enveloping her and Sybbyl in a massive bubble. Armir ran toward them, but he didn't get there in time. He slammed against the bubble just as it closed. He was thrown backward.

"Malene!" he yelled, but if the Lady of Varroki heard him, she didn't let on.

Brom saw a group of witches coming for Armir. He ran to intercept them, taking a hit of magic that knocked his legs out from under him so that he slammed face-first into the snow. The ice was like tiny daggers cutting into his skin.

Armir shouted his name, alerting him that he was about to be hit with more magic. Brom rolled to the side and jumped to his feet to face his foes. He and Armir stood back-to-back as they blocked shots of magic while sending their own. Brom knocked plenty of hits away, but others got through. He was still weak from his encounter with Sybbyl. Fortunately, he hadn't left her unscathed either. Brom really hoped that gave Malene the upper hand. He wanted to check on her and Sybbyl, but there were too many witches for him to take his eyes off them for even a heartbeat.

A loud cackle split the air a heartbeat after a cry of pain. Brom looked to the bubble and found Malene on the ground, breathing heavily with blood pouring from a wound near her neck. Sybbyl stood over her.

This was it. Brom couldn't believe they were going to lose. He'd never believed that Sybbyl could defeat Malene. And yet, he was seeing it with his own eyes.

"Nay," Armir whispered.

Sybbyl raised the staff and sword over her head, pausing long enough to smile maliciously down at Malene. The weapons plunged toward Malene as Armir cried out her name. Brom couldn't look away. He watched in utter shock as the Lady of the Varroki stopped Sybbyl by blinding her with the blue radiance from her palms. Sybbyl shielded her face and turned her head away as she stumbled backward and fell into the snow.

"The time of the Coven is over!" a woman shouted as she ran through the forest in a tattered cloak and gown.

"It's Elin! Someone get her," shouted a witch.

Synne put her hands over her ears, hoping to stop the Giras' bone-chilling screams. Lachlan tried to keep her from looking back as they climbed higher, but she was having none of it. She wanted to know where Asrail was.

When Synne did look at the loch, she stood in numbed silence as beings rose from the water. Except they couldn't exist because they *looked* like the water itself, simply shaped like a person.

"We need to go," Lachlan insisted, tugging on her arm.

Synne searched the group of Gira for Asrail. "Not without my grandmother."

"She knew what was coming. She wanted you out."

Synne shot him a glare. "She was coming. I saw her start toward us."

Lachlan's nose flared as he turned Synne to the camp. "Those things from the loch are killing the Gira. Asrail was by the water. Lass, I want nothing more than for your grandmother to be here, but I doona think she is. No' anymore."

Synne wanted to argue that he was wrong, but she knew he wasn't. The water creatures were swift and vicious as they cut the Gira down as if they were nothing. A tear escaped, and Synne hastily wiped it away.

"We need to go," Lachlan whispered urgently in her ear.

Synne said nothing as she turned and started racing up the hill. There was still time to find the others and join the battle.

29

B rom stared in shock as the snow began to shift and come alive. One pile near him formed into a person that slowly rose from a squatting position to stand and face him. He swallowed as he stared in awe and wonder. He'd never seen anything like it before, and he wasn't sure if it was friend or foe.

More and more snow beings appeared and started attacking the Coven by wrapping their arms around the witches and essentially smothering them in snow. Within moments, there was nothing but ash left of the witches.

One of the beings stopped near Brom and smiled. Brom looked into its eyes of snow and nodded his head.

"We told you that you would know when it was time."

Brom recalled the conversation in his head. "What are you?"

"Snow nymphs," it said and turned to stop a retreating witch.

Brom's gaze swung to Runa. He didn't know how he knew, but he knew he had to get her out of here. He ran toward Runa, dodging the snow nymphs. Brom tripped on a rock hidden in the snow and tumbled to the ground. He found his gaze on the giant blue bubble that held Malene and Sybbyl.

He rose up on his elbow when Malene got to her feet and stood over Sybbyl, much as the witch had done to her moments before. Sybbyl tried to raise the sword, but Malene knocked it aside with her magic. When Sybbyl attempted to use the staff, Malene waved it away with her hand, leaving Sybbyl with nothing but her magic to use against the Lady of the Varroki. Brom wasn't the only one watching. Even the snow nymphs were enthralled.

Malene threw back her head as her arms went out to her sides, and the blue radiance intensified. Armir shouted her name, beating on the bubble. The frantic fear in his voice caused Brom to frown as he climbed to his feet.

The light grew brighter and brighter until Brom had no choice but to look away. Then, suddenly, it was gone. He hurriedly looked up, but there was no sign of the bubble, Malene, or Sybbyl. Armir dropped to his knees, dismay etched on his face.

Brom shivered, not from the cold but from the eerie silence that filled the forest. He looked around, noting there were no more Coven members. Only the other seven members of his group, Elin, and the snow nymphs remained.

"Where is Malene?" Jarin asked.

Brom swallowed, sorrow filling him because he suspected that Malene had given herself to the magic when she took out Sybbyl, which had killed both of them. Given how Armir sat on his haunches in the snow, he had come to the same conclusion.

Brom glanced at Armir once more as he rushed to Runa's side. He put a finger beneath her nose and felt the soft brush of her breath. It was faint, though, too weak for his liking. He gathered Runa in his arms.

"I've got you," he whispered just before he began the healing spell.

Someone tugged at her. Runa could feel the pulling, but she couldn't tell what it was. The darkness had yet to recede, which made everything even more frightening. She couldn't see or speak. She couldn't hear, either. But she could feel.

"Trust us."

It was the same voice as before, but it spoke in her head. That alone made Runa uncomfortable. She didn't know who the voice belonged to or what they wanted with her, but it didn't matter. She didn't want anything to do with them.

"It's nearly over. Then, you can finally be free."

Runa couldn't help but feel there was a double meaning in that. For her, it meant no longer being queen of the Gira and being able to live the life she wanted with Brom. She was relatively sure the voice had another meaning in mind.

She shouted Brom's name as loudly as she could in her head. Runa hoped that some kind of sound would pass her lips. Maybe it did, though she didn't know since she couldn't hear anything. Whether that was from someone preventing her from hearing or if there was nothing to hear, she wasn't sure.

At least there was very little pain now. Was her wound getting better? Or worse? She wished she had heeded Brom's words before she fought Sybbyl. He should've had the sword, but Runa had been so sure of her victory. She was so used to doing everything on her own that she hadn't learned how to trust anyone. She claimed to trust Brom, but if she had, she would've listened and believed him when he warned her about

Sybbyl. Then she wouldn't have lost the sword and been wounded.

She was better than that. Morea had taught her better than that. Runa refused to believe that her stubbornness had lost the battle. She wasn't going to give up on Brom or the others, because she knew that good would triumph over evil one way or another.

Runa fought to move something, anything on her body. She strained, bellowing her frustration in her head when her limbs didn't obey. It would be so easy to give up. She might find some peace then. She had been fighting for so long, desperate for a place to fit in. She had found that with Brom. But now, she couldn't have him.

She frowned then, wondering where that thought had come from. If there was one thing she was sure about, it was Brom. In this life or the next, they would be together. She'd never stop looking for him, never stop loving him.

And she knew he would do the same for her.

She *would* be with Brom. Runa wasn't going to give up on him.

Her body jerked and moved, but she wasn't the one doing it. She heard laughter as if she were in a deep tunnel and the sound was high above her.

"Runa? Open your eyes, lass," Brom said as he gently shook her.

The spell had begun to heal her body, but quicker than he was used to. Still, it had loosened the band of steel around his chest. He called her name once more. To his delight, her eyes finally fluttered open.

"There you are," he said with a smile.

She blinked at him before her lips curved. "Brom."

"How do you feel?"

"Fine."

He hid his frown. He'd seen the deep wound in her chest. Then again, his magic had healed her. There had been too much going on for him to accept anything so casually. Yet, he had the woman he loved in his arms, and she was smiling at him.

"I'm glad to hear it. I'm sure you'd like to get out of the snow." Brom got to his feet, helping her up as he did.

Runa dusted herself off and looked around. "Where is the Coven?"

"They were decimated," Leoma said with a laugh.

Ravyn blew out a breath and shot Carac a wide smile. "It feels so good to have them gone."

"They've caused a lot of trouble for a long time," Helena said with a nod.

Jarin linked his hand with Helena's. "We won."

"Won?" Runa asked as her gaze scanned the others' faces.

Brom noticed that the snow nymphs kept their distance, preferring to stay near Armir. Brom wanted to ask the nymphs what they wanted, but he was happy they hadn't attacked them.

"Runa!"

Everyone turned to see Synne and Lachlan running toward them. Both were out of breath. Synne enveloped Runa in an embrace.

"What is it?" Braith asked.

Lachlan took a couple of deep breaths. "These beings came out of the loch and killed the Gira."

"All of them," Synne said in a muffled voice as she clung to Runa.

Brom looked at Runa's face, but she didn't seem too upset

to hear this, while Synne was crying. Then again, Synne had spent more time with Asrail, so perhaps their connection was stronger.

"We had some help, as well," Carac said.

Brom nodded to the beings. "They're snow nymphs. I bet those at the loch were water nymphs."

"I've never heard of them," Synne said as she pulled back from Runa and stepped away.

Lachlan shrugged. "Asrail did say there were beings of this world we didna know about."

"That she did." Brom noted that Runa hadn't said much. She was looking at everyone, however. When she noticed him staring, she reached for his hand. He realized that he was looking for something that wasn't there. Runa was alive, but no doubt she had suffered horribly. He needed to give her some time.

Suddenly, Synne stiffened at the sight of Elin. "What is she doing here?"

"She brought the snow nymphs," Leoma said.

Anger contorted Synne's features. "That doesn't matter. She needs to pay for what she did at Blackglade."

"What is Armir doing?" Lachlan asked.

That stopped Synne, causing her to glance at Armir. Then she looked at the others. "Where is Malene?"

"Gone," Ravyn said in a soft voice. "She killed Sybbyl, and the magic consumed them both."

Elin shook her head. "Sybbyl isn't gone. She's right there."

To Brom's astonishment, Elin pointed at Runa.

30

Sybbyl laughed as she looked at the group. It was odd walking around in someone else's body, but at least she was still alive. It had been close. Too close, actually. Had she not struck Runa, and had the Gira queen not held on as tightly as she had to stay alive, Sybbyl would be dead.

But she had felt her magic calling to her from Runa's body. It had taken little effort to inhabit her form and take command of it since Runa was buried under too much darkness to dig herself out. She had begun healing the wound shortly before Brom added his spell, which had only sped up the recovery.

"Did you really think you could get rid of me that easily?" She didn't hide her smile at the shocked and angry expressions on the others' faces. "I told all of you that I was destined for greatness. Perhaps not in the body that was mine, but that doesn't matter. What this proves is that I'll live forever, moving from body to body. You'll never be able to kill me."

She tightened her hands on Brom. "I've even got my pick of three Varroki men to fill my womb with seed."

"I warned you before that you'll never hav⸍ Jarin said.

Brom jerked his hand from hers. "And you w⸍ mine."

"Even if you do get with child, it won't be yours,⸍ stated. "It won't have any of you in it."

Ravyn laughed. "That's right. If you get pregnant⸍ Runa's body, it'll be Runa's child."

"Which means, it won't have your magic," Braith rep⸍ with a smile.

Carac nodded. "Music to my ears."

Sybbyl rolled her eyes. "I'll raise it, which counts for a lot."

"It'll never happen," Synne stated.

Sybbyl threw out her hands. "Who is going to stop me?"

Brom frowned because it felt as if someone were trying to get his attention. He looked around and found his gaze locked on one of the snow nymphs. The being gave a nod as if Brom were supposed to understand. Then it dawned on Brom precisely what he was supposed to do.

The nymphs had told him that he'd know. Asrail had also warned him. He'd been so adamant that he couldn't do it. Now, as he stared at his beloved Runa, her body currently occupied by none other than Sybbyl, he knew he wouldn't hesitate.

"That doesn't even scare me," Sybbyl said as she pointed to the skull Braith held.

Braith quirked a brow at her. "Then you're a fool. We were brought here because of the First Witch."

"So what? She's dead. And while she had great power, she can't kill me. None of you can." Sybbyl threw back her head and laughed.

"Brom!" Armir shouted and threw him Lachlan's sword.

Brom caught it and pulled Sybbyl toward him as he

ınged the blade into her stomach. Her eyes bulged as black
ıoke billowed out of the wound. She clawed at him, trying
ɔ stay on her feet. Brom yanked the sword free, but she had a
ırm grip on his other hand. He tossed the weapon to Lachlan
as Sybbyl's knees buckled and she hit the ground.

No matter how hard the witch fought, there was no stopping her death. The more black smoke filtered from Runa's
body, the weaker Sybbyl became until she was gone. Brom
kneeled beside Runa, more heartsick than he thought possible.
He'd believed he had saved her from the brink of death. Realizing that it had all been a trick was the cruelest kind of
torture.

"What just happened?" Synne asked in a whisper.

Armir came to stand beside them. "Brom had to kill her."

"Just as Asrail foretold," Lachlan said.

Jarin put his hand on Brom's shoulder. "It's for the best.
Runa can finally rest in peace."

"She was alive," Brom said. "Runa fought. That's what
Sybbyl said. She fought to stay alive before Sybbyl took over."

Helena squatted down beside Brom and caught his gaze.
"There's still a chance that she's in there. You fought so hard
for her. Don't give up now."

"I'll help," Elin said. Then she looked at Synne. "And I will
pay for what I did. First, let me help here."

Armir, Jarin, Helena, and Elin gathered around him and
Runa. Finally, Brom nodded to them and placed his hands on
her. Together, they began the healing spell.

Her hearing came back in a rush. It was so loud that Runa
tried to turn away from it. Her body, however, still wouldn't

move. On the heels of the noise was debilitating pain that crashed over her in wave upon wave until she screamed.

She didn't know how long she battled the agony running through her body before she realized that there was light. A pinprick that gradually started to grow. She focused on it to take her mind off the pain. The more light that surrounded her, the easier she could breathe. No longer did it feel as if she were being held down by something.

While she basked in the light, her thoughts drifted to Brom and how he had healed her injured knee when they first met. The rush of magic through her had been heady and amazing, leaving chills prickling her skin and making her desire him even more—if that were even possible.

She smiled because that's what Brom did to her. He accepted all of her without hesitation. If only she had told him everything to begin with, but she had been too much of a coward. That was time wasted. She might have told him of her love, but they'd had no chance to do anything else with Sybbyl's arrival.

Runa's heart hurt because she knew she might have lost Brom forever. She didn't know if she hung between the world of the living and the world of the dead. She wasn't sure if Brom had fought Sybbyl or not. She wasn't sure of anything, and that made things so much worse.

She took a deep breath. Only then did she realize that the pain was almost gone. There was only a small twinge, and even that was ebbing away. It was then that she felt it, Brom's magic. His wasn't the only one, but because she had such a connection to his, she could pick his out amidst the others.

Suddenly, she felt the cold of the snow as it dampened her clothes and chilled her skin. She wanted to move her body, to lift her lids and search for Brom. But a part of her worried that this was all a dream, and she would be left disappointed once more.

But she had already lost so much by being afraid. She couldn't do that again. If she were to have the life she dreamed of, she needed to face this head-on. Runa opened her eyes and blinked against the bright sun and blue skies through the limbs of the trees swaying above her.

Something grabbed her hand. She curled her fingers around it and turned her head to find herself looking into Brom's beautiful hazel irises, more gold than ever. His smile was wide as he hastily blinked his eyes.

"You came back," he said and gathered her in his arms.

Runa wrapped her arms around him tightly. For several moments, they simply held each other. He had been all she could think about, and now, she was in his arms. She squeezed her eyes shut, amazed that she was alive. "I love you," she whispered.

"And I love you," he said and kissed her head. He sniffed, adjusting his arms to tighten his hold.

She blinked open her eyes and saw something on the periphery of her vision. Runa turned her head to find a couple watching her. That's when she pulled away from Brom and looked around.

"There's a lot we need to fill you in on," Brom said.

Runa's gaze returned to him. She cupped his cheek. "You're alive."

"We did more than stay alive. We won," he said. Sadness filled his gaze. "Well, we lost one."

Synne knelt beside her and wrapped her arms around Runa's neck. "I thought we had lost you, too. Thank you for hanging on."

"I'm not entirely sure I had a choice." Runa pulled back and shared a smile with her sister. There were tear tracks down Synne's face that made Runa's gut clench. "What is it?"

Fresh tears fell from Synne's eyes. "Asrail."

"It might be better if we start from the beginning," Brom said. "First, let's get out of here."

Runa got to her feet with Brom's help and noticed that her tunic and vest were not only cut but also covered in blood in two spots. One was from Sybbyl's attack. She wasn't sure what the second was from, but she would find out.

Instead of returning to the loch, the group walked in another direction. There were so many questions running through her mind, but Runa managed to keep from voicing them. Their group walked for another half-hour down the mountain until they reached a small cottage with smoke billowing from the chimney.

A woman bent with old age smiled at them. Her hair was stark white, and there were many lines upon her face, but her eyes were sharp and clear. No one said anything to the old woman as they walked past her and entered the domicile. Runa immediately went to the fire and stuck out her hands in an effort to warm them. It felt as if she would never get warm again.

The silence was uncomfortable. Thankfully, Brom came to stand beside her. His nearness offered more warmth that she eagerly accepted. Runa watched as two of the other women in her group tried to help the old woman, but she shooed the young ones away.

It wasn't long before the old woman motioned everyone to the table. Once they were all seated, the food was passed around, and everyone's plates were filled. The old woman took a seat at the head of the group and sighed loudly before her gaze met the man's at the other end of the table.

Runa was curious about him since he had a shaved head

and tattoos. She suspected that he was a Varroki warrior just because of the way he held himself. Although, he looked very sad.

"I wondered who it would be coming off the mountain," the old woman said. Then her blue eyes met Runa's. "This one has a lot of questions. I think it's time she learns what happened."

Brom lowered the piece of bread he had been eating and nodded. "It is time."

Runa put down her spoon and listened. By the time she had been properly introduced to everyone, learned of Asrail's fate, Malene's battle with Sybbyl, the snow and water nymphs, and the fact that Sybbyl had briefly taken over her body, everyone had finished their food, and the table was cleared.

"I missed a lot," Runa said.

Helena smiled at her from across the table. "You were fighting your own battle, though you didn't know it."

"I'm not sure many others could have withstood it," Leoma said as she nodded to Runa. "It proves how formidable you are."

Ravyn grinned. "And why the Gira wanted you as their queen."

Runa shifted in her seat, unsure if everyone knew of her ancestry. Then she realized it didn't matter. The only one she cared about was Brom. "Thank you," she told Leoma and Ravyn.

"What now?" Jarin asked.

Runa's gaze landed on Armir. Discovering what happened to Malene, the Lady of the Varroki, helped her to understand Armir's despondency. Armir hadn't said a word since she had woken, and Runa had a feeling that he wouldn't. His grief was too new, too raw.

Helena put her hand atop Jarin's as she glanced at Armir. "We return to Blackglade."

"And what of her?" Synne asked as she gazed pointedly at Elin.

Runa frowned as she looked between her sister and the brunette witch. "What did Elin do?"

"I was the one who released my sister, Avis," Elin said before Synne could. The witch moved her gaze first to Lachlan and then to Synne. "I'll never be able to apologize enough. I believed Avis when she said that she wanted to be a family again. I was tired of being alone, and I made the mistake of trusting her."

"It wasna a mistake," Lachlan said.

Synne shot him an angry look. "You nearly died."

"I didna," he told Synne calmly. "Elin didna do anything to harm us."

Synne rolled her eyes. "I disagree."

"Look at her," Armir said as he lifted his eyes to Elin. "Take a long hard look at her, Synne. If you think Elin hasn't suffered, then you haven't looked closely enough. I believe her when she says she was tricked."

Jarin nodded. "Besides, if Elin was guilty, she wouldn't have helped us against the Coven."

"I agree," Helena said softly.

Elin swiped at her cheek and cleared her throat as she got to her feet. "I'm prepared to return to Blackglade and face whatever punishment you deem I deserve."

"The Varroki won't be punishing you," Armir said and dropped his chin to his chest.

Synne blew out a breath. "If Lachlan can forgive you, then so can I."

Elin bowed her head and turned to walk to the door.

"Where are you going?" Carac asked.

The witch paused at the door and looked over her shoulder at them. "I don't know."

"Wait," Runa said as she rose and walked to Elin. "You should know that Avis is dead."

Elin nodded and glanced at the sword strapped to Lachlan's back. "I assumed so but thank you for telling me."

Runa watched the witch walk from the cottage. After the door had closed, she faced the table. "Do we know if all the Gira are gone?"

"Based on what we saw, all the tree nymphs at the loch were killed," Lachlan said.

Her eyes slid to Brom. "I need to see."

"Then you shall," he told her.

Armir got to his feet and bowed his head to the old woman. "Thank you for opening your home to us."

"You all need to rest. Stay the night," she said.

Braith shook his head. "We've imposed enough already."

"I said you need to rest." The old woman held his gaze until Braith relented. Then she rose and walked away.

Brom took Runa's hand and led her to the fire. He sat and pulled her down before him so she leaned back against his chest. They twined their fingers and simply sat together for a time as everyone paired off. Some went outside, some remained at the table, and others moved to corners to talk privately.

"Are you all right?" Brom asked.

She leaned her head back against his shoulder and shrugged. "I'm...fine. I'm just trying to reconcile the fact that last night I had planned to take out Sybbyl on my own, yet I ended up not being a part of the battle at all."

"That isna true. If you hadna been so strong mentally, you wouldna have been able to survive what Sybbyl put you through. You do see that, right?"

She rolled her head to him and smiled as he looked down at her. "I do."

"What was it like?" he asked.

Runa swallowed and looked at the fire. "Blackness. That's what took me first. Oddly, there was very little pain. However, I couldn't see, hear, talk, or move. I didn't know if you were battling her or if you had gotten away."

"I wouldna have left you."

She glanced down at his bloodied shirt. "You were hurt."

"She got in a lucky hit. I hurt her as well."

That made Runa smile. "I was so idiotic to think I could take out Sybbyl myself. Nine of you were involved."

"Actually, it was mainly Malene. I saw her face. I think she knew exactly what was going to happen. That's why she put up the bubble so Armir and the others couldna stop her. He's in love with her."

Her gaze slid to Armir, who still sat at the table, lost in his own thoughts. "I could tell he cared, but I thought maybe it was just because she ruled the Varroki."

"It's much deeper than that."

"You like the Varroki."

There was a smile in his voice when he said, "Their city is beautiful."

"Do you want to return there with the others?"

Brom looked down at her and waited until she met his gaze before he said, "I want to go wherever you do. It doesna matter to me as long as we're together."

"Do you think the Varroki would allow me inside the city?" she asked hesitantly.

He shot her a lopsided grin. "Without a doubt."

31

B rom didn't close his eyes once that night. He couldn't stop looking at Runa as she slept in his arms. It wasn't until dawn approached and Armir quietly walked outside that Brom gently laid Runa down and hurried to follow the commander.

The Varroki warrior stood outside, watching the sky. "I had a feeling you wished to talk."

"I did," Brom said as he came to stand beside him.

"Then talk."

Brom glanced at the snow. "What happens now that Malene is…?"

"You can say it," Armir said. "She's gone. Malene is gone. What happens now is that the magic finds another to take her place. I'll be shown the girl, and I'll set out to find her and bring her back to Blackglade to start the process all over."

Brom watched Armir closely. There was irritation in his voice and fury in the way he held his body. "You're angry at Malene."

"I am," Armir said and glanced at him. "Malene should've allowed us to fight. We could've taken out Sybbyl together."

"Maybe. Maybe no'. You trusted Malene to lead you, and she did what she saw fit."

Armir snorted, causing his breath to billow around him in a pale cloud. "I thought she would be around for a lot longer."

"She made quite a few changes that will continue to have a good impact on the Varroki."

"Perhaps."

Brom kicked at the snow and crossed his arms over his chest. "I'm beginning to think it isna Malene you're upset with but yourself. You had a chance to tell her your feelings and you didna."

"You got your woman. You're lucky."

"I know," Brom said with a nod.

Armir faced him. "What are your plans? Will you be returning to Blackglade with us?"

"Runa is worried she willna be welcome."

"She'll be welcome. You both will."

Brom blew out a breath. "I'd like to come."

"Let me know. We'll be heading out later this morning."

Armir walked away, leaving Brom alone. After a moment, Brom returned to the cottage to find everyone awake. Helena had used magic to mend and clean Runa's clothes. Brom decided to do the same with his tunic. The old woman was nowhere in sight. A large loaf of bread rested on the table that everyone ate from. Then, they went outside.

"We're going to return home," Braith told the group.

Carac nodded. "Ravyn and I are, as well."

"Shall we travel together, then?" Leoma asked.

Ravyn smiled. "It would give us some time to catch up."

"Then it's settled," Braith said. "What of the rest of you?"

Lachlan looked down at Synne and smiled. "We're returning to my clan now that things have been solved with the Coven."

"I'll be training Hunters," Synne told Leoma and Ravyn.

Leoma nodded in approval. "Because there will always be evil witches."

"With all three of you training others, there should be more Hunters than ever," Carac said.

Braith's gaze swung to Brom and Runa. "What of you two?"

"We're going to Blackglade," Runa said as she looked at Brom.

Brom smiled, lacing his fingers with hers. "Aye. Blackglade."

"It's good you're returning with us," Jarin said. "There's a lot more to learn."

Ravyn said, "Then this is where we part ways."

Everyone said their good-byes. Once the six of them had set out, Brom faced Runa. "Do you still wish to see the loch?"

"I do," she replied.

Armir drew in a deep breath. "We'll go with you."

"What of the old woman?" Runa asked.

Jarin glanced at the cottage. "I've not seen her since last night."

"Who is she?" Helena asked.

Armir shrugged. "I've no idea, but she had a place and offered us shelter."

"Interesting," Brom said.

The five of them set out. The trek up the mountain was without incident. When they reached the place of the battle, there was no sign of the snow nymphs, though Brom had a feeling they were always around, watching. They didn't stop, though Armir's gaze lingered on the last place he had seen Malene.

It wasn't until they were on the other side of the mountain and descending that they saw the first signs that there had been a battle. They moved around the body of a dead Gira. The farther down they went, the more nymphs they found. When they reached the loch, the sight was tough to take in.

"Water nymphs did this?" Helena asked in shock.

Brom had to agree. The Gira were ripped to shreds. He was thankful that Runa hadn't been here with this happened, because he knew she would've probably been attacked, as well. That made him look warily at the water. "Should we be here?"

"We mean no harm," Armir said.

Runa quirked a brow. "Perhaps, but I do have Gira blood."

"I'm not sure this was about the Gira exactly," Jarin said. "The water nymphs have had plenty of opportunities to take out the tree nymphs if they wished. Instead, they waited until now."

Helena twisted her lips. "When the Coven was trying to take over."

"But the Gira were no longer aligned with them," Runa said. "And if it was about a bone, I'm the one who had the sword."

Brom saw the still water begin to move as if something just below the surface came toward them. He wasn't the only one who noticed. Soon, they all stood facing the water. But it wasn't a water nymph who came out. It was Asrail.

She smiled when she saw Runa. "You survived."

"I did," Runa said and walked to her grandmother to embrace her.

Brom waited until they had stepped back before he asked, "What happened? Lachlan and Synne said the Gira were attacked."

"They were," Asrail said. "When my kind put me in the water to torture me, the nymphs spoke to me. They kept me alive. And they told me what they had planned. I wasn't sure where I fit in, but I knew I had to get those I cared about out of the camp in case the water nymphs couldn't tell who was friend or foe."

Armir's face was lined with concern. "But why the Gira?"

"Because the balance had been tipped. It needed to be set right again. And, unfortunately, that involved the cleansing of my kind."

Runa shook her head. "You're lucky to be alive. Synne thought you were coming with her and Lachlan."

"I was, but I realized that my place was here. I fought alongside the water nymphs, and they offered me a place with them," Asrail explained.

"But you're a Gira," Runa argued. "You should take over as queen again."

Asrail smiled and shook her head. "I've had a long life. I've been queen and then lived many more years in solitude, hiding. Now, I just want to enjoy what time I have left. I don't know how long I'll remain with the water nymphs."

"You deserve to be happy," Brom said.

The Gira's dark eyes slid to him.

"You were right," he told her. "I did have to kill Runa, but it saved her."

Asrail bowed her head to him. "Good luck to all of you. And, Runa, this won't be the last time you see me."

They watched as Asrail returned to the water and slipped beneath the surface. Brom faced Runa and waited until she met his gaze before asking, "Do you feel better now?"

"Much. I wish Synne had been here."

"You can still tell her."

Runa glanced at the water one last time. "I guess it's time to go."

The five joined hands. Brom kept his gaze on Runa as the four of them began the spell. He gave Runa's hand a squeeze. In the next breath, they were in Malene's room in the tower.

Brom caught Runa before she fainted. He barely lowered himself to the floor before he too passed out.

When he came to, he remained still, waiting for his stomach to settle. He gradually sat up, and once he was sure he wouldn't be sick, he lifted Runa into his arms and carried her to the bed. Then he put a bucket near her for when she woke.

Brom stood as the door opened. He turned as Armir walked in, looking grimmer than usual. And that's when it hit him. Armir had held out a thin shred of hope that Malene had returned to Blackglade. Now that hope was gone, and Armir had no choice but to face the fact that Malene wasn't returning.

"Where are Helena and Jarin?" Brom asked.

Armir walked to the hearth and stroked the fire. "Jarin is worried about Helena losing the baby. They need some time alone to recoup."

"Do you think she'll lose the bairn?"

Armir shrugged and rose to face him. "I think using magic as we did to get to Sybbyl and then back here will take a toll on the babe. I also believe Helena is strong, as is her child. But only time will tell."

"And what of you?" Brom asked.

Armir blew out a breath and walked to the table. He closed one of the many books Malene usually had out and sank onto the bench. "I think I lost out on the best thing that ever happened to me. You were right. I am angry at myself for not telling Malene how I felt. There isn't anyone out there who can take her place. I've never hesitated to carry out my duties, but I don't think I can do this anymore."

"I think we all need some time to recover. Sybbyl is gone, and a great many Coven witches are dead. We have several bones of the First Witch, and we stopped Sybbyl. That's a win to me."

"We lost a great many along the way, too," Armir said as he briefly looked up to meet Brom's gaze. "But you're right. We did win. The balance has been restored once more. There are rooms for you and Runa in the tower."

Brom started to speak when he heard Runa behind him. He spun and hurried to her side, helping her through the horrible side effects of magical travel. When he glanced up, Armir was gone.

"I'm not sure I ever want to do that again," Runa said as she reclined against him on the bed, hours later after she had rested and eaten.

Brom chuckled. "It gets easier the more you do it."

"I'd rather not find out."

"Armir said there are chambers for us here."

Runa lifted her head to look at him. "That's good, right?"

"Aye. I'd love to see more of the city as well as learn more about being a Varroki."

"We can stay here for as long as you want."

He grinned. "Are you sure?"

"You told me you didn't care where we were as long as we were together. I feel the same. I don't have a home, but you do. You know where your people are, and you haven't had the option to be here before. There's nothing pulling us anywhere else. So, we stay."

"Have I told you how much I love you?" he asked as he kissed her neck.

She laughed and wrapped her arms around him. "Actually, you haven't. At least, not recently."

"I'll make up for it," he said as he claimed her mouth.

EPILOGUE

Six months later...

Runa still couldn't believe that she had now been Brom's wife for over four months. She smiled at the sunlight coming through the window in the tower as she rolled on top of him, kissing him awake. He grabbed her hips and ground against her.

"Now that's how a man likes to be woken," he said with a smile as he looked at her.

She grinned. "We've been married for four months now."

"Aye. Are you happy?"

"Deliriously so." She tossed back her blond locks. "And you?"

He eyed her before grinding his arousal against her. "I think that answers your question."

Runa's smile dipped. "You didn't wake me when you came to bed last night."

"Nay." Brom pulled her down so that her head was next to his. "Jarin and I still have no' found Armir."

"He may never return."

"We've come to realize that."

Runa sighed. "I hope he finds peace out there."

"Jarin willna be leaving the city anytime soon with Helena so close to giving birth."

"Maybe it's better that you let Armir go. If he wanted to stay, he would have."

Brom kissed her temple. "He's needed here, though. I hope he finds his way back."

"Well, as much as Armir is needed, I'm glad you and Jarin aren't going out anymore."

"Why?" Brom asked.

Runa rose up on her hands and looked down at him. She'd tried to stay awake last night to tell him, but she had been so tired. She rolled off him onto her back. Then she took his hand and placed it over her stomach. He frowned at her for a moment, then his eyes lit up.

She laughed and nodded. "Aye, my love. We're going to have a bairn."

He pulled her against him and held her. "I couldna be happier. We should celebrate."

"First, this." She pushed him onto his back and straddled him as she kissed him.

Armir wasn't sure what exactly he looked for, but he couldn't remain at Blackglade. He had lost many Ladies, but none of them had affected him like Malene. She had been different. Because he had fallen in love with her.

And now she was gone.

Somewhere out in the world, he'd find some peace. He had to. Otherwise, what was the point? He'd lost the only thing he'd ever loved, the only person who had opened his heart. Every time he thought of her, he wanted to bellow his rage. Because she was gone.

He kept putting one foot in front of the other.

———

Elin took in a deep breath as she stared out over the wild sea. The isle suited her. No longer did she have to hide. If any Coven members wanted to find her, then she welcomed them. She wasn't going to live in fear anymore. Too much had happened for her to do that.

She had betrayed those at Blackglade because she wanted a family again. Because she was tired of being alone. Asrail had been good company, but she hadn't always been around. Now, Elin was truly alone, and she was coming to terms with that. She wasn't exactly at peace yet, but she was getting there.

———

"It all worked out," Asa said to her pet owl, Frida, as they stood on the west coast of Scotland. "Somehow, everything fell into place."

Frida turned her head to Asa and blinked her big, yellow eyes.

Asa chuckled. "Aye, my beauty, we were lucky. Very lucky." She drew in a deep breath and slowly released it. "What's in store for us next? We could go to Blackglade. We could also visit Leoma, Ravyn, or Synne."

Frida looked away.

"I don't want to go home. I left Norway for a reason." But Asa knew she had no other choice. She had to go back. There were things left undone.

ABOUT THE AUTHOR

New York Times and *USA Today* bestselling author Donna Grant has been praised for her "totally addictive" and "unique and sensual" stories. She's written more than one hundred novels spanning multiple genres of romance including the *New York Times* bestselling *Dark Kings* series featuring immortal Highlander shape shifting dragons who are daring, untamed, and seductive. She lives with her dog in Texas.

Connect with Donna online:
www.donnagrant.com
www.MotherofDragonsBooks.com

facebook.com/AuthorDonnaGrant

instagram.com/dgauthor

bookbub.com/authors/donna-grant

goodreads.com/donna_grant

pinterest.com/donnagrant1

CPSIA information can be obtained
at www.ICGtesting.com
Printed in the USA
LVHW011216141220
674126LV00003B/623